Jean,

my buddy, pal, friend,
best in the world.

May you enjoy the adventure...

Susan Elizabeth G. P. A. L. Richards

Below The Glow

Susann Elizabeth Richards

This book is dedicated to my special friend Pat Bounds

whose joyful spirt delighted all who knew her.

She is dearly missed.

CHAPTER ONE

Bill Adams arrived at his Long Island Sound home early on Friday afternoon. It was out of character for him, as he was a workaholic, often working late into the night. The house was empty but knowing Shirley liked to dabble in her garden, he went outside to find her. She was on her knees pulling weeds in the garden.

"There you are," he said.

His voice startled her and her eyes widened, "Bill, what are you doing home so early? Is something wrong?"

"Nope," he said, avoiding her questioning gaze. "I just thought I'd surprise you and take you on a week's vacation around the Sound."

"But why are you here now?"

In jest Bill said, "Am I interrupting something; perhaps you made plans with our neighbor?" Bill gestured toward Richard who was crouched over a bed of flowers. His back was facing them.

"Of course not. It's just that you never get home at this hour."

"Well, I'm home now, so what do you say, let's pack the boat and go. It'll be fun, just the two of us."

"Are you sure?" she asked from where she still kneeled on the ground.

"Of course, I'm sure. Now let's put some provisions on the boat. Use what you have in the kitchen. That'll be enough to get us started."

"But, but—we need our clothes, too."

"Yeah, that's true. You can throw some things together, while I prepare the boat, then I'll pack my own gear. Is it a deal?"

"I was just about to water my plants," she said, pointing to the hose.

"No excuses, Shirley, let's get ready. I'd like to get to Block Island before dark."

She stood up and dusted dirt off her pants. "All right, I'll do the best I can with such little notice."

"I'm sorry, honey, I know you like to plan in detail, that's the teacher in you. But just once let's do something spontaneous."

1

"I'm on my way." Shirley turned toward the house.

The sailboat was in its slip at the dock behind their house, making it convenient for Bill to inspect the mechanical aspects of the boat while Shirley loaded the food and supplies to get them on their way. If they needed anything else, they could easily find provisions at any port in the area.

Bill finished his inspection and helped Shirley carry the last articles onto the boat. "All done. It doesn't take us long when we work together."

Shirley's smile was more of a grimace. "I guess. We're ready then."

The wind was just right for a trip to Block Island, and within four hours they were at the mouth of the new harbor. They passed the red buoy marking the entrance. Pointing at the other boats in the harbor. "Looks like we're in luck, we have our choice of anchorages. Where would like to go?"

Shirley sat on the starboard bench seat near Bill. "Let's go closer to shore, then the dinghy ride in will be short."

"Yeah, but it gets so congested over there."

Shirley sighed, and her eyes narrowed. "Bill, just go where you want to; don't bother to ask my advice; you don't listen to me anyway. Just do what you want to."

"Sorry, I didn't do that on purpose, but you'll be happier away from all the noise later. You'll see."

"Whatever!"

Bill found his ideal spot and dropped the anchor. He didn't ask Shirley for help as he didn't want another confrontation. Once the boat was secured he gingerly approached her. "What'll you say? Should we go into town. I'll buy you a nice meal and we can relax."

Shirley remained quiet, her lower lip sticking out like a stubborn child's.

"Come on," Bill coaxed. "It'll be fun; we can get a drink first and chill."

She was quiet for another long moment, then relaxed her shoulders. "Sure, but let me throw on something warmer."

The town of New Shoreham was the hub of Block island's activity. The island itself was a pretty one with many bluffs that overlooked the ocean, a lighthouse that flashed its bright beam over the sea, and an array of lovely beaches. In the summer months, thousands of visitors clamored there to enjoy the relaxed way of life.

Bill and Shirley spent the evening dining at a local restaurant. Everything was quiet until two men opened the entrance door and threw the contents of a suitcase onto the floor. Small bells spilled all over the floor. At first everyone was amazed; then one by one the customers began to gather the bells for themselves. Shirley scooted out of her seat and picked up two bells.

"Look, one for you and one for me," she exclaimed, holding up her prizes so Bill could see.

After their meal, they left the restaurant and strolled around the town. The crowd was in a party mode, and they began to shout at one another.

Bill and Shirley walked hand in hand, stepping between people along the crowded streets. The darkness was barely visible beneath the lights from the restaurants and pubs.

"Let's get out of here and relax on the boat before it gets too late and crazy," Bill said.

The next morning they enjoyed a leisurely breakfast. Shirley prepared eggs over easy, toast, and piping hot coffee that she served in the cockpit of their sailboat. Shirley sipped her second cup of coffee and smiled. "I saved the bells I picked up. It was a fun night especially listening to all the tinkling of the bells. I felt like a kid. Someone said those men come here once a year with suitcases full of bells to throw at the people. Apparently, they all live in some small town in central Connecticut. I heard them call it Bell Town, but I don't think that's really the name of the town."

Bill looked out over the harbor, seeing a forest of sailboat masts that lined the interior, while he dabbed the last bite of toast in the left-over egg yolk. He only half listened to Shirley as he was preoccupied with his own thoughts. How was he going to tell her, how can a man put his thoughts into words that got caught in his throat every time he started to broach such a serious announcement. He would have to wait until tomorrow, but she had to know soon.

Bill returned his gaze toward Shirley, happy to talk about something as mundane as sleigh bells. "Some guy in the restaurant said the town has been making bells since the 1800s, and at one time produced more than 90% of all the sleigh bells in the world. When the economy went into the toilet, so did the bell production. He thinks there is only one factory left that still make bells."

Shirley took another sip of her coffee as she watched the gulls fly aimlessly above them. She knew enough not to temp the birds with a handout, as they were known to become noisy and aggressive and multiply their ranks within moments. Nonetheless, they were entertaining to watch. The sound of the tiny motors on nearby dinghies filled the air with a sweet hum. Her attention shifted to the small boats loaded with jolly people, busily buzzing to and fro in the harbor.

Bill was anxious to get underway and changed the subject. "I'd like to head toward Montauk Point today; the weather is perfect for sailing. We should be able to maintain a reach for most of the trip. From there we could go to Sag Harbor, and then on to Greenport. Then it will be an easy sail across the sound to home. How does that sound?"

Shirley could not hide her irritation. "There you go again, you always have to be doing something. I don't want to leave yet. It's so nice here in the harbor, and finally we have a chance to spend some quality time together, which is something that's been missing from our marriage for a long time. Can't you just relax enough to enjoy the moment, or me?"

Bill turned away from her and stared out at the blue expanse of water.

"Okay, Okay, I'll get the breakfast dishes cleared so we can get underway!" She banged her half full cup of coffee down on the tray, then clanked the dishes on top of each other and stomped down the galley stairs.

Bill shrugged and rubbed his forehead. "I can't seem to do anything right. Bad karma I guess." He engaged the windless to raise the anchor; then secured it to its station on the bow pulpit. He started the boat's small diesel engine and expertly weaved the sailboat between the multitudes of boats anchored in the harbor. Upon clearing the red buoy at the entrance, he set his course toward the tip of Long Island and raised the sails using the roller furling.

The wind was steady at 15 knots, easily filling the sails to a point just on the verge of a luff. Superb, by the standards of any weathered sailing buff. He enjoyed feeling the wind tickle his ears and the smell of the salt air. They sailed on the edge of Long Island Sound where it flows into the Atlantic Ocean.

After she finished cleaning the dishes Shirley changed into her bathing suit, taking a book with her as she returned to the cockpit and silently rested on a cushion that covered the bench on the port side. The boat was heeled toward port which lowered that side of the sailboat and made it closer to the water. Shirley relaxed as she felt the rhythm of the waves. She became content and soon set her book aside, turned onto her stomach to sun bathe and fell asleep.

Bill had smeared sunblock lotion all over his exposed skin, and his muscles glistened in the sunlight. Standing behind the helm, his six-foot body was tanned and toned. His wavy blond hair tossed about in the breeze and at times it covered his face. Dark aviator sunglasses covered his mesmerizing blue eyes, and his strong jaw held a perpetual grin.

He watched Shirley's body rise and fall with each breath she took. Her body rested about a foot above the waterline. She was a pretty woman with a radiant smile and straight blonde hair that touched her shoulders. She was charming, petite and refined by nature. She always greeted others with the warmth of her inner soul, but over the years she had lost that glow toward Bill.

When they were first married, he looked forward to hearing her tell delightful stories of the naïve students who were anxious to learn. She taught the fourth grade and adored the children as much as the children and their parents adored her.

Lately, he would arrive home late from work and quickly eat his meal, then prop himself in front of the television until he fell asleep. Shirley still had many pleasant stories to tell, but now she only shared them with her girlfriends or her mother. Bill felt increasingly like an outsider. He continued to gaze at her, wondering what kind of thoughts filled her mind, as she had become distant. Was she hiding something from him?

He hoped that getting away on the sailboat would give him time to think, as nothing helped him relax better than the serene silence of sailing. He inhaled the smell of the sea as the breeze peppered his skin with a salt water spray.

Bill had worked long hours at his job as a projects engineer, but the pay was great and they lived a lifestyle accordingly. They had a home on the water, two newer model cars, and a class act sailboat. Life had been good until Friday when he received the news which shattered his dreams. His job had been eliminated due to cost constraints and the stagnant economy. Over the last several months his budget had been reduced, restricting his use of resources. Retrospectively he should have seen it coming, knowing now that he had really screwed things up.

The sailing conditions on Long Island Sound couldn't be better. It was a gorgeous day made for daydreamers, lovers, and sailors. The bright red sun shone brightly in the azure blue sky. Small puff clouds drifted lazily above, slowly changing their shapes. Sea gulls darted about, squawking nosily as they chased one another looking for a morsel of food. A steady 15-knot warm sea breeze remained constant, and the sailboat maintained a perfect reach. The water splashed its hull as it sliced through the deep blue waves like a saber.

There was a subtle change in the weather which was not evident at first, but slowly the sailing conditions became variable, and the wind just about died, causing the sailboat to lose momentum. It happened at such a leisurely pace it gave Bill ample time to adjust the sails as he saw fit. He thought by bringing the sails in tighter there would be a better chance for a more efficient sail and he wouldn't have to start his engine. While he liked to sail, he didn't relish being in irons. His eyes swept the water for the signs of cat's paws. He knew that the small ripples with rounded, glassy crests were an indicator that the wind was going to pick up soon.

Standing behind the helm, he scanned the horizon, when out of the corner of his eye he noticed movement alongside the port side where Shirley was sleeping. At first it appeared to be a torpedo, but as Bill became more focused he saw the dorsal fin. The monster was three quarters the length of the boat and was keeping pace with the movement of the craft. He instinctively knew it was a great white; they were known to inhabit the waters between Massachusetts and Long Island. The fact that great white sharks are the largest predatory fish on earth and can grow up to 20 feet and weigh close to 5 tons was real cause for concern.

He immediately wanted to warn Shirley and have her move over to the starboard side, but he didn't want to startle her. Leaving his position behind the helm he moved quickly and quietly to her side. Just as he was about to reach down to awaken her, a massive gust of air came out of nowhere to rock the boat ferociously. The wind came directly from the starboard side, causing the sailboat to heel even more to the port, so much so that the rails were awash.

Black clouds converged overhead and suddenly poured rain over them like a waterfall. The sky was ablaze with zig-zag streaks of fire followed by booming rumbles that bowled across the water. The sailboat was on the verge of a knockdown; Bill needed to act quickly to release the lines holding the sails tight. He fought the wind and scrambled to release the lines controlling the main sail and the jib. He was just close enough to grab them both, but as he did, he slipped on the wet deck and fell to his knees as the sailboat was blown off course. Luckily his action loosened the lines, and the wind spilled from the sails, but it caused them to flap erratically. The boat rocked violently. Without a helmsman in control, the boom swung wildly, banging from side to side.

Bill tried to stand but the deck was awash with water; he braced himself on the port-side bench, bent his knees and finally stood. Suddenly he noticed that Shirley was nowhere in sight. His mind did an instant replay. Where did she go? Had she gone below? Another possibility came to him in a flash of horror! Oh no!

"Shirley!" he yelled. She couldn't have been swept overboard. Bill knew he had get himself back behind the helm and regain control of the boat. Then he heard Shirley's scream. The shrill sound drifted over the crashing waves. "Help me, Bill! Please, Bill, quickly! Oh my God! It's a shark! Bill!"

He turned toward the sound and saw her flailing in the water. The waves pushed her farther and farther from the boat. Instinct made him grab the floatation cushion by the hatch, hurling it with all his might in Shirley's direction. Now her blood curdling screams were deafening, and terror gripped him. He had to get the boat under control at all cost. He must rescue Shirley.

The next step he took was his last as the boom hit his head broadside, and he was knocked unconscious.

CHAPTER TWO

A violent squall line suddenly moved through the eastern edge of Long Island Sound. Bill hadn't see it coming, and it hadn't been part of the updated weather forecast report. The weather change was abrupt and deadly.

The day following the awful accident that incapacitated Bill, his sailboat was found floating aimlessly in a northerly direction. A private pilot in his four-place Comanche airplane flying to Nantucket Island, was preparing to make his final approach toward the landing strip on the south side of the island, when he noticed a sailboat adrift at sea. He flew his plane back around to get a better view of the boat.

The sails were loose and flapping. There was no one behind the helm. Taking his plane even lower the pilot saw a body lying flat on the deck. He was unable to detect any movement. Radioing the flight tower at Nantucket Memorial Airport, he reported his findings and the coordinates of the sailboat's location. The Coast Guard Station at Brent Point was notified immediately that a rescue team was needed to investigate the unusual situation aboard the sailboat.

The distress call was relayed, and the Coast Guard deployed a forty-seven-foot rescue boat which quickly located the lone sailboat on its northerly journey.

As the Coast Guard Rescue boat began closing in on the sailboat, the female skipper Marcy Conway picked up her bull horn, bellowing, "This is the Coast Guard; we will be boarding your vessel." She did not detect movement as the rescue boat pulled alongside the sailboat.

After the crew secured the lines, three of the four crew members boarded the sailboat to find Bill lying on the deck. They began assessing his vital signs. He was breathing, but his breaths were shallow, and his pulse was weak. The deck was streaked with blood coming from under Bill's body. Following closer scrutiny they discovered a large wound on the side of Bill's head.

9

"This guy must have been hit hard by the boom. A wound of this magnitude needs a specialist's attention," the skipper said. "We better line up a trauma team. They'll be equipped to treat wounds like this."

Back on board her craft, Marcy called the Emergency Department at the Nantucket Cottage Hospital. Identifying herself, Marcy explained, "We have an unconscious male with a severe head wound aboard his sailboat. Have an ambulance meet us at our docks, and notify the neurosurgeon on call, he'll be needed in the E.D. From the looks of it, this is a case which will require a medivac transfer to Mass General's trauma unit. We are on our way with an ETA of less than fifteen minutes." The skipper hung up, turning her attention to the injured man. "Place a neck brace on him, but be extra careful when you move him on the back board. We don't want to cause him any more harm; he's in enough trouble." The crew worked in synchrony, securing Bill onto a backboard, then transferring him onto their rescue craft. When Bill was safely aboard, they swiftly headed back to the docks on Nantucket.

Marcy Conway made another call to the Coast Guard Station on Martha's Vineyard. Bill's sailboat was a navigational hazard, and she was the one responsible to see it was taken to a safe harbor. The shoals and buoys close to Nantucket were unnavigable for most sailboat's deep keels. The waters around the vineyard were deeper and easily accessible. Speaking with the crew leader there, she relayed the boat's identity and location.

The trip to the dock was quick. The ambulance was waiting for their arrival. An I.V. of normal saline was started on Bill by the rescue crew although Bill remained unconscious. The neurosurgeon in the E.D. assessed Bill's condition as critical, initiating the transfer to Massachusetts General Hospital's Trauma Center .

Upon his arrival there, the trauma team was waiting for him and immediately transferred him to a special surgical suite, where the doctors performed surgery to release the pressure on his brain caused by the impact delivered by the uncontrolled boom. Following surgery Bill was transferred to the Intensive Care Unit, placed on mechanical ventilation, and given multiple medications. Bill's recovery was remarkable, and within a week he was transferred to a surgical wing. His condition was improving to the point that plans for follow-up care were needed.

A Case Manager, Wendy Mullins, was assigned to Bill's case. She was about twenty five, energetic, and skilled at her work. Her hair was dark brown, her blue eyes sparkled, and a beautiful smile covered her face. All this was wrapped up in a white lab coat. Wendy's initial interview left her with many puzzling, unanswered questions. She knew that patients with head trauma didn't always remember the events that led up to and through the event, but Bill was so adamant about the occurrence, she couldn't ignore his credibility. Plus, she had been unable to contact his wife Shirley.

"Wendy, I'm telling the God's honest truth, you've got to believe me. Shirley was swept overboard when the wind came up. The boat almost capsized. She was in the ocean crying out with all her might for help! Help that never came! Because of me—I was too stupid to see the boom coming. If only I had, I could have saved her."

"Oh, excuse me, I just felt some goose bumps there, sorry." Wendy refocused on Bill's story. "Mr. Adams, the Coast Guard rescued you at sea. Would you mind if I contact them? They might be able to offer some insight."

"Sure, my God! Yes! I want them to start to search for Shirley! I never got the chance to tell them she was washed overboard. She was screaming, and the shark…! Oh, I can still hear her. She knew that shark was going to get her." Tears rolled down his face, he began to tremble, losing all his self-control and began sobbing.

Wendy pushed the nurse's call button immediately, "I need a nurse in here stat! Come quick! Mr. Adams needs attention right now."

When help came, Wendy left the room with the intention of returning later in the day to continue the interview. She was under pressure to arrange a discharge plan for Bill. Patients who suffer severe head trauma had to be discharged into a safe environment, and ignoring this protocol- could lead the hospital to face liability problems. Precautions needed to be in place to protect Bill from harm, and the buck stopped with her.

Returning to her office Wendy's curiosity got the best of her, and she ended up calling the Coast Guard Station on Nantucket. Like the hospital, the Coast Guard had accepted behaviors to be followed. Identifying herself, Wendy requested to speak with the person in charge. She waited as her call was transferred to Marcy Conway.

Wendy explained that she was working on a case that involved a rescued patient with a severe head wound.

"I assumed you are referring to Mr. Adams," Marcy replied.

"Yes, my patient's name is Bill Adams, and he has given me his permission to speak with you."

"How may I help you?"

"Mr. Adams insists that his wife had been aboard the sailboat, and that she was swept overboard. Did you find any evidence of her being onboard, or find any indication that she may have been in the water near the boat? He also said that they were headed for Montauk Point. How could that be when his boat was found off Nantucket?

"When he speaks of the incident he sounds rational, but what he tells me seems totally irrational. Is there anything that you are aware of that could be helpful to me? I have not been able to contact his wife and may have to discharge him to a Mental Health facility."

"Mr. Adams' sailboat was floating on the edge of the Gulf Stream when it was discovered. All indications led us to believe that it was afloat for maybe a day or two. To answer your question, I'd say yes, it may be feasible that he was heading toward Montauk. Severe weather was reported in that area earlier in the week. His sailboat could have easily drifted into our area. It could have been pushed eastward by the storm, entering the outer edge of the Gulf Stream, which is like a river within the ocean. It carries a greater volume of water than all the rivers in the world combined. As the water warms, it rises and flows toward the lower levels of the oceans. This movement can move at speeds of three to five knots."

Wendy sighed—she wasn't interested in a geography lesson, she wanted answers. She interrupted Marcy. "So, you're saying that Mr. Adams is telling me the truth."

"Could be. When we found Mr. Adams, the gulf stream was running a little over four knots. However, this is the first I've heard about his missing wife, although some of her personal belongings, including a wallet containing her driver's license, was discovered on the sailboat."

"Wow! Didn't you start a search for her?"

"No, we didn't. There was no distress call, and the lapse of time was unclear."

"Then she *could* have fallen into the water and drowned."

"Yes, that's possible, but we have not received any reports of a body washing up anywhere."

"What about sharks? Would it be possible that she was attacked by a shark?"

"Well, yes, that's always a possibility in these waters. There are many of those monster's out there."

"What's your opinion, do you think that he could be telling the truth?"

"Based on what he told you and what we observed after arriving on his boat, it has some credence. I'll contact the Coast Guard Station at Montauk Point to see if they have any information that would pertain to this case."

"I would appreciate that. This man really needs help and support. I think besides all his troubles, he is suffering from post-traumatic stress disorder."

"I'll contact you if I receive any new information related to this case," Marcy said.

After the talk with the skipper, Wendy sat quietly at her desk. She knew professional ethics forbade personal involvement of any kind with patients. However, Bill was different. She knew his survival depended on her ability to keep him safe, and something about his case touched her heart. Unconsciously she wiped a tear that trickled down her cheek.

CHAPTER THREE

"Where's your buddy? It's not like Bill to be late."

"No, it's not," Mike said, looking at his watch and then back at the waiter. Bill was a half hour late, and that was not like him. Best friends, they had known one another since grade school. The two met every week for beers, peanuts, and to share news. He knew Bill's job sometimes delayed his arrival, but he always called Mike to let him know he'd be late. Not hearing from Bill, he called his friend's cell phone. There was no answer, so he left a message. Then he called Bill's home. Shirley should know what was keeping Bill, but there was no answer at their home.

It was out of character for Bill not to call him, so Mike called Bill's work phone, only to find it was disconnected. Then he called Bill's secretary, and she informed him Bill no longer worked there.

"What the hell's going on?" he said outload to the empty table.

Mike paid his tab and drove to Bill's house which was closed up tight. He walked down the path to the back yard to discover that the new Hunter sailboat was missing from the dock. That explained a lot, but a gnawing pain in his stomach told him that something had happened to Bill. He sat quietly on the dock and gazed into the water, reflecting on his recent discoveries.

Behind him he heard someone coughing. Standing up, Mike saw the next-door neighbor working in his garden. He walked to the fence of hedges dividing Bill's property from the next yard.

"Hi, I'm a friend of your neighbor Bill. I haven't seen him in a while; do know where he might be?"

The man acknowledged Mike with a frown as he looked up from his task. He was in his mid-forties and still physically fit, indicating that he did more than gardening. He had dark hair and eyes, and his face was clean shaven but he had garden soil across one cheek and sweat on his brow. "What's your business here? I don't know you."

"I'm a good friend of Bill's, and I haven't heard from him this week. We usually meet on Tuesdays to catch up with each other, and he didn't show today. I was wondering, since you're his neighbor, maybe you might know where he went."

"Nope, don't know. Bill's not a friendly guy. He seems to be working all the time. He leaves his wife Shirley alone, and she has to manage the best she can. He should be ashamed of himself. A nice girl like that should be treated better." He continued pulling weeds from an already neat bed of herbs.

"Okay, thanks. Sorry to bother you."

"Yes, mister, you are bothering me. Now if you asked about Shirley, I could give you some information." He wiped his hands on overalls that had seen better days, then pulled a sparkling white handkerchief from a pocket and wiped sweat and soil from his face.

"What are you, some kind of clown? What's the difference; Bill and Shirley are a married couple."

"Bingo, that's what I'm trying to tell you. Bill only cares about Bill, and if you're his friend, I'd bet you're no better."

Mike's irritation with this guy was increasing with each sentence he uttered, but he needed the information he was withholding. He suppressed the urge to throttle him. "For God sakes man, what do you know about Bill and Shirley?"

"Well, last I heard they were in Block Island heading for Montauk. I was here in my garden when they made plans to go sailing. They seemed excited. Shirley mentioned how she loved sailing along the Long Island coastline, and as they pulled away from their dock Bill yelled out to Shirley, "Block Island here we come! Sorry but I didn't catch when they would be back."

Mike felt the heat of anger rise up his neck and into his face. "Thanks, mister, was there anything else you'd care to tell me?"

"Nope!"

As Mike walked back to his car, he realized something was wrong; he felt it in his bones. For one thing, he was sure the guy knew more than he was letting on. And why hadn't Bill called him? He had just lost the job of his dreams, and he hadn't called to let him know! It was so out of character for Bill.

Mike got back in his car and drove toward Groton, wondering who he should call? Bill's parents had died together in a bus crash years ago.

The only other person Mike could think of was Shirley's mother, and he knew she spent the summers in Vermont with her oldest daughter. Back at his apartment, Mike called Bill's cell phone again, but this time there was no ring at all. The phone must be dead. His next phone call was to the U.S. Coast Guard.

***

Richard watched Mike walk away and soon heard a car drive off. His shoulders slumped as he too was worried about where Bill and Shirley were. Not Bill. He didn't care about the jerk, but he cared about Shirley. Their friendly gardening friendship had started with casual conversations over the hedges as Shirley pruned her Hydrangea bushes. The blooms were big balls of color, blue, white, and her favorite, purple. Richard had been in his garden trimming his rose bushes, and one comment led to another. Every day they learned more about one another and were soon sharing their personal histories. Richard sensed that there was something in his character that was attractive and alluring to her.

Richard enjoyed hearing about her teaching days, and he could almost hear her voice. "I love having the summer off, but I really miss my students. I can remember from my earliest childhood days wanting to be a teacher when I grew up." She knew he was a history professor at the local community college. "Tell me, Richard, how did you become interested in teaching?"

"Well, it wasn't so easy for me. My father was a construction worker. His personality was as hard as nails. He spent more time drinking with his friends than with my mom and me. My mom was a gentle soul, and he treated her with little to no respect. One day when I was away at school in the first year of college, he took her on a fishing trip, but she never returned. My mom couldn't swim. I think he threw her over board. The next day her body was found in the lake.

"There was no evidence of foul play, but there were no witnesses either. My father claimed his innocence by telling the investigator he wasn't home when she disappeared. He said after they returned from fishing, he went to the store, leaving my mom perfectly content at home."

"Oh, my God, Richard, how awful! What made you think he could do that?"

"Because he never showed any remorse over her death. And he quickly started dating sexy women who hung around the local bars. Even bragged about being single, even to me. One night I had it and confronted him in front of his friends. He called me a momma's boy and hit me hard with his fist. From then on, all I wanted to do was get away."

Shirley had put her arms around Richard, giving him a hug, "Oh, you poor soul. I'm sure that was hard on you."

Richard had enjoyed the embrace but remained agitated "Back at school, I changed my major from liberal arts to teaching, with hopes of changing the world for others who may have shitheads for fathers. After I graduated, I left home and severed all contact with him."

Shirley hadn't moved from their embrace. "Well you did the right thing. I'm sure you're a great teacher." She kissed him tenderly on his check.

Richard remembered being confused by her behavior, but he loved the softness of her body next to his, loved the flowery scent of her perfume. "What about your husband; he doesn't spend much time with you? Doesn't that bother you?"

Shirley still hadn't moved. Richard remembered her touch on his back and how she'd gazed into his eyes. "Oh, Bill is a hard worker and has a demanding job, that's all. He's not mean."

"But look at you, Shirley, I can tell you're lonely." Richard remembered stepping away from her. He had taken taking the pruning shears to cut a yellow rose from a bush nearby and now placed it behind her ear and took her hand. "Why don't you come with me; let's talk some more." He had led her to his back porch where they settled into his old fashioned swing.

Richard closed his eyes and allowed his memories of Shirley to take him away from the mundane days of his life.

CHAPTER FOUR

Wendy Mullins entered Bill's hospital room accompanied by a tall, distinguished gentleman. The man was stately with impeccably groomed white hair. His white coat outlined his torso like a frame around a portrait. Above the breast pocket of his coat a name was embroidered: Phillip Lord, M.D.

The hospital ward outside the door was busy with traffic. Wheelchairs banged down the hall, call bells begged for nurses assistance, and the overhead PA system continued to summon doctors.

Bill lay in his hospital bed watching T.V. His eyes widened as he tracked their approach.

Wendy spoke first. "Mr. Adams I'd like you to meet Dr. Lord; remember we spoke briefly about his visit yesterday."

Dr. Lord's blue eyes seemed effervescent, and his blue shirt and tie exacerbated their intensity. His smile was comforting, lighting up his face. With professional dignity, he greeted Bill. "Mister Adams, I understand you have been through quite an ordeal recently, and I am here to discuss your transition from the hospital." Bill eyed the man with suspicion, listening with a shadow of doubt.

"Have you given any thought to your follow-up care?"

"Sure, I'll be going back to my home in Connecticut. I also have to pick up my sailboat; it's being stored somewhere on Martha's Vineyard at the Coast Guard Station. My friend Mike and I will sail it back home. I keep it at a dock behind my place."

"Have you spoken to your friend recently?"

"No, not yet, I can't find my cell phone. I think it's still on my boat."

"Mister Adams, may I call you Bill?"

"Sure, what's the deal?"

"The treatment team here has some concerns about your safety after your discharge. Due to the severity of your recent trauma, we feel it best for you to spend a few weeks in a Behavioral Health Facility before returning to your home."

Bill's anger was evident as his eyes shot daggers at the doctor, and he sat straight up in bed. "Wait a minute; you're not going to put me in a nut hut with a bunch of crazies and a staff that are kooks themselves.

"Bill, that's an interesting perception of mental health professionals. I assure you that the staff members who work at those facilities are well qualified, compassionate individuals who devote their lives to helping people such as you in dealing with unfortunate experiences that disrupt their lives."

"Why don't you just give me some happy pills, and send me on my way, or are you afraid I'd O.D., and then your ass will be grass!"

"Bill, settle down, I'm here to help you make important decisions. You have been through life shattering events. You have a severe head injury along with the loss of your wife and your job. Most people would have difficulty with only one of these situations. You are an intelligent man, so, let's discuss the facts together."

Bill squirmed in his bed. The discussion was becoming overwhelming and disturbing. "Look, I know I need help. I still hear Shirley's screams, but I'm not going to a funny farm, and that's it!"

"Good, we're making progress. After unusual events such as you have had, some people find it difficult to stop thinking about what happened. You must realize that your mind and your body are in shock. In order for you to move on it is important to get in touch with your memories and emotions. That is why I am recommending the guidance and support of experienced therapists. If you will agree, I'd like to discuss your circumstances with your friend Mike."

"Yeah, call him; he'll be there for me. I know he will."

"He will have to understand how your unexpected, uncontrollable, and inescapable events are a severe threat to your life and personal safety. If he will agree to provide you with safe surroundings and effectively manage your compliance to outpatient counseling, and the involvement of a support group, I'll consider discharging you home. Remember, your recovery will be a gradual ongoing process, and healing will not happen overnight. Nor will the memories disappear completely. Support from others is vital to your recovery." The doctor paused, looking toward Wendy, then continued. "Wendy will finalize your discharge plans. Good luck. I'd like to hear from you in a month."

"Thanks, doc, I'll do that." Bill was emotionally numb. He wasn't the type who was used to feeling weak, but he was smart enough to know he must overcome the resistance to seek help and learn to accept it. Looking back at Wendy, he said, "That was intense."

"Yes, Dr. Lord is one of the very best. He is admired by all who know him. Now, if you will give me the number where I can reach your friend, I'll make the call from here." Wendy dialed Mike's apartment but there was no answer. Placing a the call to his office, she was greeted by a voice saying, "Electric Boat, Engineering Department, how may I direct your call?"

"May I speak with a Mr. Michael Murphy?"

"What is the nature of your call?"

Wendy gave a short explanation and said to Bill, "I'm on hold, and they're playing elevator music."

To Wendy's surprise, an anxious voice bellowed into the phone, "Bill, where the hell are you?".

"Is this Mr. Murphy?" Wendy asked. After he said yes, she explained who she was and that she wanted to speak to him about Bill's condition.

"Sure, sure, but what's all this formality about?"

Wendy spent the best part of the next half hour explaining Bill's situation to Mike. Before handing the phone to Bill she told Mike that Dr. Lord would be calling him to discuss Bill's discharge plans, and he would be providing Mike with vital details on how to cope with Bill's symptoms, plus how Mike's involvement will help Bill in his recovery process. Finally excusing herself, she gave the phone to Bill.

"Bill, how you doing? Things sound severe. Tell me what the hell happened."

"Well, I'm not dead, almost lost it though, but the worst is, Shirley's gone." Choking up, he added, "Hey Mike, can you come here? It'll be easier if I can see you. I can't go over it on the phone. Can you come right now? If you are here, I might get out sooner—before they lock me up."

"Hey, don't worry, I'm on my way."

"Thanks, I knew I could count on you." Hanging up the phone, Bill pulled the covers over his shoulders and rolled up in a ball.

CHAPTER FIVE

Bill's discharge from Massachusetts General Hospital went smoothly. Mike met with Wendy and Doctor Lord to finalize the discharge plans, and to assure both that he understood the responsibility of providing support to Bill. Mike arranged to take a month off from work to assist Bill during his recovery from his head trauma, the disappearance of his wife Shirley at sea, and the unexpected elimination of his job with the Navy. After finding the sailboat at the Coast Guard station on Martha's Vineyard, Bill and Mike set sail back to Mystic.

Sailing his boat on a near perfect day was a welcome contrast to the bleak, sterile hospital environment. The bright sunlight, clear blue sky, and glistening sea water spattered with white frothy suds couldn't be more inviting.

The trip back was without incidents. Arriving in Mystic, they prepared to dock it in the slip behind Bill's house. Mike stood on the bow.

"You know the routine," Bill shouted. "Just grab the line around the piling and tie it to the cleat on the deck. I'll do the same with the stern line."

The boat sailed gracefully into its slot, while the men secured it with ease. "Nice maneuver, Captain," Mike said.

Together they washed the boat down before removing the few articles that Bill and Shirley had brought with them on their fateful trip. Plugging the cell phones into electricity was a priority, as both had lost their charge.

Bill managed to handle his emotions well during the trip with the help of his prescribed medications.

As they made their way off the boat, Bill was disturbed by the sight of his overgrown lawn. He was annoyed that his yard looked unkempt and neglected. The two men shuffled through rich green grass which was above their ankles. Bill shook his head in disgust. "This place is a mess! I didn't plan to be gone so long. If I'd only known, I would have hired a lawn service."

"Bill, cool it! We'll take care of it in due time. Let's get inside, clean ourselves up, and relax."

They proceeded through the backyard toward the enclosed pool area. The closer they got to the screen door, the louder the sound of a weed-whacker became. Mike was the first to see the neighbor he had met earlier in the week. Turning to Bill he growled, "That guy is a real jerk! When I was over here looking for you, we had a talk. The guy wouldn't even tell me his name."

"That's Richard for you."

"He doesn't like you very much."

"Huh?" A surprised look crossed Bill's brow. "I hardly know the guy. I seldom see him, and he's never tried to be the least bit friendly. I think he's some kind of professor at the community college."

"What about Shirley? Do you know if she was a friend of his?"

"I don't know, maybe they have a casual acquaintance. She's home all summer, and she enjoys working in the garden, but she never mentioned anything about him to me."

"Well, Bill, that guy knew that you and Shirley were on your way to Block Island."

"Really? That's weird."

Mike realized too late that he should never had brought up the subject due to Bill's unstable condition. "Let's get into your house, you need to rest."

From the corner of his eyes Bill saw Richard approaching. He looked tired, his clothes were soiled and dripping wet with perspiration.

"Hey, where's Shirley? I thought that she went sailing with you?"

Mike took the lead and stepped between Richard and Bill. "Buddy, Shirley's whereabouts is no concern of yours. Now move your sorry ass off this property. You are trespassing."

"I'm not leaving until you tell me where she is!"

Losing control, Mike grabbed Richard's tattered shirt under his chin, bringing it up to his face. They were inches apart. "I told you to leave, now get out of here, or someone's gonna get hurt, and it's not gonna be me!" Mike pushed Richard so hard that he fell to the ground.

Getting up quickly Richard rushed toward Bill with a closed fist. Mike intercepted Richard and pushed him away from Bill. "I told you to get out; this ain't a joke. Don't make me hurt you!"

"What did you do, Bill, after she told you?" Richard screamed. "Did you hit her? Is that why she's not with you? Where is she? I want to know? Is she with her mother? Or did you throw her in the sea to let her drown?" Richard's eyes narrowed as he stared with hatred at Bill. "That's it, you murdered her! You low-down bastard!"

Mike charged Richard and hit him square in the jaw. Richard fell to the ground.

Mike kicked him in the kidney. "Now get the hell out of here!"

Richard stared up at Mike. "I'll get you for that!"

"Try it, you prick. It's your word against mine, and I don't see any witnesses." Bill was staring into space.

Richard got to his feet and practically ran away. Mike recognized the lost expression on Bill's face.

"What's going on?" Bill asked when they got into the house.

"Nothing I can't handle, buddy," Mike said.

The inside of the house felt eerie in the quiet darkness. The curtains and blinds were drawn, and the little light trickling in through the windows threw hazy shadows. Everything was in its place, neat and tidy as it had been left.

Guiding Bill through the kitchen, Mike said. "Look, you need to rest. Take a shower first, and you'll feel better. I'll get you a Zoloft, then you can lie down." Watching his best friend grieve was agonizing.

"You're right." Bill headed toward his bedroom.

Shaking his head in disbelief, Mike knew the disclosure of Shirley's secret and betrayal was lost on Bill. But it was evident to Mike that Shirley had been having an affair with Richard, although what she saw in the guy was beyond him. Mike needed evidence. Her cell phone might be the key.

While Bill was in the shower, Mike looked for the phone that Bill had taken off the boat. Seeing Bill's smart phone plugged into the charger on the bureau, Mike searched for Shirley's phone. He found it on her bedside table next to the charger. Taking both the phone and the charger, Mike went into the spare bedroom where he plugged the phone into the charger, then began to unpack.

CHAPTER SIX

On a spit of land bordering the north shore of Montauk facing Long Island Sound sat a weather-beaten saltbox house built in the 1800s. It was in the middle of two and a half acres of prime real estate, which many of the local money hungry realtors were chomping at the bit to acquire. To their misfortune the land belonged to the original owner's kin, Butch Clark. The property was deeded with the stipulation it was to remain in the family until the last heir dies or is willing to sell the property.

At the age of 38, Butch was a recluse and a confirmed bachelor with no desire to give up the family farm. Butch was an avid fisherman. His prized fishing dory was moored at his private dock. He enjoyed being out on the water every day, weather permitting, and could be found fishing along the coast or out to sea within a 50-mile radius of his home. When he wasn't fishing, he tended his garden.

Butch's muscular build and torso would make a prize fighter envious. He always appeared unkempt, wearing bib-overalls and faded plaid shirts, which looked like they should have been discarded weeks prior. His hair was the color of straw; long, and shaggy, it fell over his blue eyes, which were hidden under a soiled wide-brimmed hat. His handsome face was covered with a scruffy beard, which hid his warm smile. He could easily be mistaken for a member of the Duck Dynasty clan.

A few days earlier Butch was out in his dory trolling when black clouds began rolling in, bringing a storm his way. Not wanting to get caught in a squall, he returned to his home to wait it out. The severe squall tore up the sea pretty bad. After it passed, Butch decided to continue fishing and headed back out to sea; his bait bucket was nearly full so he baited all his lines and began trolling in circles, with high hopes of bringing home some fine blue fish for his supper.

As he circled about in his dory, he noticed a white object floating on top of the waves. It would appear then disappear, bobbing up and down on the unsettled sea. He was curious, and he made a habit of always inspecting the debris washing about in the ocean. He proudly displayed his collection of artifacts by hanging them from a tree in his yard.

Approaching the object, Butch recognized a floatation cushion. Then he spotted someone's arms wrapped under the straps. Quickly he hauled in all the fishing lines, slowly moving toward the person clinging to the float. He could see it was a young woman.

"Lady!" he yelled but heard no response. He grabbed his bull horn and repeated himself. "Lady!" This time he saw a reaction.

The woman opened her eyes which appeared terrorized. "Help!! Please help me!" she screamed. She acted as though she was about to release the floatation pillow.

Butch cried out, "Don't let go, I'll be right there." He knew she would drown if she loosened her grasp. He couldn't position his boat alongside her, impossible as the rocking movement of the waves made the rescue treacherous.

He placed the boat's motor in idle, reached for his longest gaff, and tried hard to bring the float close enough to tie it to his boat, so he could pull her up.

As the woman caught sight of Butch lifting the gaff, she wailed, "What are you going to do with that? Hack me up?"

Butch wasn't used to hysterical females and was annoyed. "Lady, just hold on. I'm not going to stick you. For Pete's sake, I just want to hook it around your damn float. If you can grab hold of the gaff, I'll do the rest."

The woman looked up at the gaff but couldn't release her hold on the float. "Come on lady, just use one hand, you can do it."

With great trepidation the woman reached for the gaff and once she caught hold of it with one hand, she froze.

"Lady, you got to put it around the freaking float. Can you do that?"

"I can't move!" she screeched.

"All right, just hold on." He managed to attach the gaff beneath the strap on the float and started to pull it toward his boat. She was almost close enough for Butch to grab when the gaff slipped out.

"Ahh, why'd it do that?" He threw the gaff into the dory, then said. "Now listen to me. Kick your feet hard and head for me. Are you ready? On the count of three, kick. One, two, three, kick!"

To his surprise, she began kicking her feet so hard she wacked herself into the dory. Leaning over the side of the boat, Butch hauled the woman and the float into his dory. She was shivering uncontrollably. "Don't you dare move, just sit still. I'll get a towel."

He knew she was in shock, probably suffering from hypothermia and needing medical attention, but right now she needed to dry off and get wrapped in something warm. Inside the dory's cabin, he got two towels and a flannel shirt. He handed the towel to the woman, but she just stared back at him.

"Lady, ya gotta dry off. So I'm gonna help ya. Don't worry, I ain't gonna hurt ya." Butch started to towel her off. "What happened to you out there? Are there others?"

"I don't know." Her voice quivered.

"Well, what's your name?" Butch persisted.

"I don't know."

"You don't know who you are, or how you got out here in the middle of the freaking ocean? Did you fall off a boat?"

"I don't know. Please stop, I just don't know."

Butch stopped his questioning but continued to dry the woman off before helping her into the flannel shirt. He then found a wool blanket and wrapped her securely in it. "Now you just sit there in the sun. You gotta warm up."

"Warm up," she said. "Warm up."

As Butch turned the dory toward the coast, she fell silent.

CHAPTER SEVEN

The following morning as Bill prepared for his appointment at the local Mental Health Clinic, the doorbell rang. Mike was in the kitchen having a cup of coffee and stepped to the front door. He opened it and saw a uniformed police woman standing in front of him.

"Good morning, I am Sergeant Carlson from the Mystic Police Department. I'm here to investigate a report filed by one of your neighbors."

"Oh, really?" Mike said sarcastically.

"Are you Mister William Adams?"

"No, ma'am, I'm not, but I am his caregiver."

A confused look crossed the sergeant's face. "Is Mister Adams here?"

"Yes, ma'am, but he has a very pressing medical appointment. Is there some way I can help you? I have been authorized by a psychiatrist and a case manager at Mass. General to prevent Mister Adams from exposure to stress related situations. If you wish, I can give you their contact numbers, and I'm sure they will be glad to help you answer the questions you have about the neighbor's report."

Puffing out her well-endowed chest, the sergeant said, "Fine, I'll take those from you." She pause then added. "Is Mrs. Adams available?"

"No, ma'am, she isn't." Mike wanted to get rid of the snoopy cop as soon as possible. "Just a minute. I'll get those numbers for you, wait right here."

The business cards from Wendy and Dr. Lord were on the kitchen counter. Snatching them, he returned to the front door and handed them to the officer. He thought there was something suspicious about the policewoman. Her visit seemed out of place. He knew he was the one she should confront. Whatever it was, made the inquisition questionable. He gave her a cold glare. "I'm sure these folks will answer your concerns. Good day."

Before Mike could shut the door in her face, she threatened. "I may be back," she said before walking away.

Mike was certain the call had been instigated by the guy next door, and he reminded himself to listen to Shirley's cell phone messages. He returned to the cup of coffee he'd left on the counter. It was cold, so he put it in the microwave to reheat it.

Mike took a sip of coffee just as Bill appeared. He was clean shaven and neatly dressed in jeans and a blue polo shirt. Propped on his head was a Boston Red Sox baseball cap. "I guess I'm ready to face the shrinks as they probe into all my mental problems."

"Look, Bill, they are professionals who want to help you manage your situation. Just think positive. You don't need a pity party; we've talked about that. So, buckle up, and deal with the cards you've been dealt, and move forward."

"You're right. Let's get going. Was I hearing things or did someone ring the doorbell. It sounded like you were you talking to someone?"

"Yeah, it was some girl wanting to sell you something. I told her we were on our way out, and she left."

"Kinda early for that nonsense, isn't it?' Leaving the house, Bill reluctantly shuffled to Mike's shiny red Camaro parked in his driveway. Settling into the front passenger seat. The traffic was light, and they soon found the clinic nestled among a slew of other outpatient service buildings. Mike stayed while Bill completed the registration process. "Gotta go; call when you need a ride."

Mike's mind was set on Shirley's cell phone. Speeding back to Bill's house he tried to remain calm. Once there, he turned on Shirley's cell phone.

It was just as he suspected; Richard and Shirley were having an affair. The boat trip was a total surprise, catching Shirley off guard. She texted Richard telling him they were on their way to Block Island. Her intention was to tell Bill she was leaving him for Richard. Then she would take the ferry boat back to New London. When that didn't happen, she sent a second text message as they headed for Montauk. "Bill is a self-centered louse. I'm telling him today," she wrote.

"That's my girl! I love you with all my heart. Rich."

Mike wandered back into the kitchen, wondering what to do with the new information. All he wanted to do was to pulverize Richard, but he knew better. What was wrong with Shirley? How could she leave Bill for that idiot? He paced around the kitchen for a while before deciding to call Wendy.

Mike told her about the policewoman showing up at Bill's doorstep. Then he told her about Shirley's affair with her neighbor. He conveniently failed to mention his altercation with Richard.

Wendy was eager to know more about the saga and waited for Sergeant Coleman to phone her. By late afternoon she couldn't stand the suspense. She placed a call to the Mystic, Connecticut police department and asked to speak to Sergeant Coleman.

"Sorry, miss, but the Sergeant is not at work today. Her next scheduled shift is in two days. Would you like to be connected to her voice mail?"

"No, thanks, I'll call back." Wendy hung up the phone, whispering to herself. "What's happening?"

***

Three months had passed since Bill began his therapy. Dr. Lord and Wendy frequently conversed with Dr. Laura Green, the chief psychologist at the clinic and Bill's primary therapist.

Bill recovery was progressing well; his head wounds had healed nicely, and he had made some major changes as he moved forward with his life. The shocking betrayal of Shirley hadn't bothered him as much as his own guilt did. He was still having flashbacks of Shirley's screams for help, but they were becoming less and less.

After a month Mike returned to work. As a lark, Bill placed a "For Sale by Owner" sign on his front lawn. To his surprise he had a buyer within a week, and his house was currently under contract to be sold. He moved his sailboat to a marina in New London, then moved into Mike's apartment.

Dr. Green met with Bill weekly; today they discussed Bill's current stress level. Covering the walls of her office was a coat of light green paint. The pictures hanging on the walls were all done in soft water colors, depicting flower gardens and open meadows. The room was designed to give comfort to the patients during their sessions. Bill loved looking at the pictures of the meadows. They reminded him of the open fields he had loved roaming in as a child and the special day he lay in a field of dandelions, watching the fluffy white seeds float aimlessly above him. They sat in plush arm chairs facing each other. Bill couldn't relax, and was noticeably tense.

"Look, Dr. Green, the guy Richard who lives next to me won't give up. He's constantly barraging me about drowning Shirley."

Looking at Bill with comforting eyes, Dr. Green said, "Bill, I think it would be best for you to distance yourself from the man. Have you thought of selling your house, and finding something smaller?"

"I guess I should tell you. I placed a for sale sign out last week and got a bid right away. I've moved in with Mike while waiting for a closing date. You're right, I really don't need such a big place. I also sold Shirley's BMW. There's no need to have two cars."

"That's a good start. You've had a busy couple of weeks. What else is on your mind?"

"I feel like I just want to get away from everything."

Pausing briefly before answering him, she said. "Bill there is an organization you might be interested in which helps veterans suffering from PTSD; as you know, this is part of your problem. It's called the Sierra Club. You may benefit from getting involved with them. Why don't you look them up on the web and see what they are all about. Do you have any other concerns this week?"

Bill's inner turmoil continued to disturb him. "Besides wanting to get away, I'm also feeling that maybe it would be best for me to go back to work. What do you think, should I start to look for a job? I'm in a constant conflict on what I should do. You know, I could get a position as an engineer somewhere, but I'd never be satisfied with just any job. My life's dream was to develop the small submarine that I designed. That's my passion, and screw those that want to stop me."

"Well, let me do some research and see what I can find for you. That should keep me busy until our next visit. You too should look into different options for yourself. I'll see you again in a week."

"Thanks, doc." With that Bill left the office.

Secretly he was becoming wanderlust, wanting to get away from it all seemed better than having a job with responsibilities. It seemed like a miracle when Dr. Green told him about the Sierra Club, how the organization helps veterans suffering from post-traumatic stress disorder. It energized Bill, and he planned on stopping at the local library to do more research on his own.

Returning to Mike's man cave, he was full of boundless energy. He was in the small kitchen filled with colonial ambiance, when the granite counters and maple wood cabinets seemed to close in on him. Sunlight penetrated through the large bay window, warming the enclosed area. An antique maple table sat in front of the window. The décor was charming, with calico curtains framing the windows. Pictures of red barns and covered bridges were on the walls. All of this was overlooking the patio and a dense wooded area beyond.

Bill couldn't wait to tell Mike about his plans. To celebrate he purchased a couple of steaks and a six pack of beer. Bill made a salad and was giving it the finishing touches as Mike arrived home

Mike looked distinguished in his shirt and tie, a sharp contrast to Bill's cut off shorts and navy sweat shirt covered with a chef's apron.

"Hey, what's happening here?"

Bill had a smile like a Cheshire cat. "Good news, I think."

"Does that mean that the Red Sox won today, or are you taking Wendy and me to this week-end's game at Fenway Park?"

Bill continued to smile. "The latter may work, but tonight I want to discuss my plans. I know that I can depend on you to keep me sane. Let me finish with this, and then we can talk."

Mike got two beers from the refrigerator and headed to the patio. "I'll be out here; I'm oozing with anticipation."

Appearing outside within minutes, Bill picked up a can of beer and slugged down the first gulp.

Looking back at his friend with skepticism, Mike inquired. "Oh, great chef, what's your news"?

"Today Dr. Green told me about this organization, The Sierra Club which offers wilderness expeditions for veterans returning from combat. Their philosophy is that vets are better able to cope with their symptoms if they get involved with outdoor activities such as hiking, mountain biking, white water rafting, or any other strenuous activity. Anyone with this post stress situation like I have can benefit from relaxation, seclusion, and peace that results from being in the natural world. It helps challenge the nervous system to move away from the traumatic event."

Mike didn't like it. "What's this got to do with you? Now you want to go away by yourself. Then you'll get lonely and depressed, ending up desperate or dead. It's not a good idea. End of story. Let's eat."

"Mike, you don't get it. I'm going sailing into the tropics where I can have peace and tranquility far away from this maddening world of Richards and job responsibilities."

"Speaking of jobs, what are you going to do without an income?"

"I don't need one. I'll get by with the money I get by selling everything."

Looking Bill in his eyes, Mike said. "Get a grip. It's a pipe dream. How are you getting to the tropics? It's a long trip for a lone sailor. No therapist in their right mind would let you do that. You're suffering from multiple tragedies. Talk about stress; you're pushing the envelope."

Lighting the grill, Bill got the steaks. "I can tell you don't like my plan."

"What was your first clue?"

"Look, I'll do more research. I'm telling you, I can do this. I have coping skills that will get me through tough times. I'm up for the challenge, and I am taking positive action."

***

Bill wasn't discouraged by Mike's response to his plans. He was ready for his next meeting with Dr. Green, having practiced his pitch to her. Approaching her office, he was animated and excited. The beginning of his session went well with a brief discussion on Bill's feelings. The conversation then focused on his plans for the future. Bill was ready for it, and outlined his proposal. "Doctor Green, I think I'm ready to be on my own, and I want to just get away. I'm thinking of sailing around the Virgin Islands. You know— like the people you told me about in the Sierra Club. Just get away and be one with nature." Watching the doctor's face, Bill waited for her reaction to his plan.

Listening intently to Bill's proposal, Dr. Green was encouraged by his progress, but knew it was not the right time for him to set out on an adventure on his own. Leaning forward, she chose her words cautiously. "Bill, your plan is sound and well thought out. I'm impressed that you used the information about The Sierra Club to fulfill a need you are searching to accomplish. I don't believe that now is the right time for such an endeavor. You need to be with people who will offer you support. I'm sure that you've heard this before, it's a vital part of your recovery."

Remaining quiet, Bill was disappointed, and he hadn't expected her answer, but could see the sincerity in her eyes, and he trusted her. Straightening his composure and contemplating his options, he spoke. "Look, I know you mean well, but I'm not sure that you, or anyone else, will really know when the right time will be for me to move on. All I know is that I want to achieve the peace that comes with being in the natural world."

Smiling, Dr. Green said, "Bill, together we will come up with a challenging endeavor that will benefit your needs. I'm still working on a project for you."

CHAPTER EIGHT

With Bill in mind, Dr. Green's personal investigation led to an arrangement with the Woods Hole Oceanographic Institution located on Cape Cod. During the following week's meeting, she shared her findings. "I'm sorry, Bill ,but you are just not prepared to go off on your own. You are still too fragile. This option seems the best choice for you." Bill's sullen face and tight body showed his disappointment. "I'm not saying you'll never be ready to go off on a sailing adventure, and it is worth trying at some time in the future. Right now, give this some thought."

Bill was thinking. "Well, I must admit it would be challenging. If you think it's best, I'll give it my all."

"Good."

Dr. Green arranged for Bill to be admitted to an internship program aboard the submersible called Alvin. A detailed pre-employment physical was required, because the job's duties required a significant amount of strenuous exercises. The position was mentally and physically demanding, requiring him to spend at least six months as a member of the operations crew. Completing the program, Bill would be able to become a qualified Alvin pilot.

With both Dr. Lord's and Dr. Green's blessings, Bill set out on an at-sea adventure aboard a submersible much larger than the one he had designed for the Navy. His previous experiences helped him fit easily into the duties of maintenance, condition, and computer analysis, as well as the preparation of scientific equipment. As a certified scuba diver, he would be participating in all phases of vehicle launch and recovery.

Returning to his land base at Woods Hole, he realized the experience had forced him to work with others. Being part of a cohesive team, he was constantly receiving support and was never isolated or alone. Best of all he benefited from the seclusion and peace that came with being under the sea in a world of wonder. He was well liked by the crew, and his superiors offered him a full-time position. They gave him a few weeks to decide. The position was tempting, but Bill's own plans kept beckoning him.

***

Sitting at a high-top table on the outside deck of Cap'n Kidd's bar and grill, sipping on a cold glass of beer, Bill awaited the arrival of Mike and Wendy. It was late April, and there still was a chill in the air. The April showers had decided to take a day off, allowing the sun's rays to warm him. The breeze was soft as it floated by, bringing with it a soothing salt spray.

The droning of a car's motor ceased and was followed by the slamming of two doors, startling Bill from his daydream. Looking toward the parking lot, he smiled, watching his best friend and Wendy walk away from the red Camaro. Seeing them together made him happy. It was Wendy's diligent discharge planning that had brought the two of them together. Striving to ensure that Bill's safety was a priority led her to Mike. It was a good groove, and best of all, they both were concerned about him. They were the best friends he could ever ask for.

Watching them approach him, Bill took another sip of beer, thinking how he missed the warmth of having his own soul mate, knowing he'd have to deal with these feeling for a while yet. Shirley was gone, and either way, she probably wouldn't be with him now. It was time for him to move on.

Wendy greeted him with hugs and kisses, while Mike's warm welcome was more refined. Bill's voice sang, "God, it's so good to see you both." Grasping Mike's hand firmly, he remarked. "You look great; life must be treating you well."

"Not only life but Wendy is a gem." Grinning, Mike exhibited a spontaneous cheerfulness. "So, tell us about your Jules Verne adventure. We want to know what life's like under the sea."

A waitress in a pirate suite distracted them by asking if they wanted anything to drink. They ordered, and she disappeared back into the building.

Explaining his saga, he said. "Well the first time we actually submerged, I had an overwhelming feeling of claustrophobia, but with the crew's help, I quickly learned a technique involving breathing control. It was amazing how the worried look covering my face, alerted them. They were at my side instantly, helping to me to overcome my anxiety and regain my composure. I guess they're trained to keep their eyes on the novices. After that episode, I never had the problem again. I'm so glad I was able to do all of it. Now if I ever get a chance to build my own sub I'll be able to pilot it too."

"Do you still want to do that?"

"Sure thing, if I ever get the chance."

Mike knew that the submarine could be a reality for Bill, and it pleased him to see the changes in Bill. "Tell us more!"

"Leaving here we headed toward Central America. The scientists collected samples of water and sea creatures, and we spent time exploring the waters in the Caribbean. Moving back up the Atlantic coast we ended up visiting a sister oceanographic facility in Ft. Pierce Florida. That's where I met this fabulous woman doctor. She's a remarkable person. She and another scientist from Australia invented a special red light which is invisible to sea creatures. Adhering it to the sub enables the scientists to illuminate and film them. A highly sensitive camera records images, and an optical lure mimics a bioluminescent jellyfish.

"She told me the light works like someone screaming for help, and it can be seen from a long way off, causing the attacking predators to assault whatever is charging the fake jellyfish. She was in a Triton mini sub at 3000 feet deep when she got the picture of the giant squid."

Wendy's eyes appeared as big as cannon balls. "Wow, how exciting! That huge squid was on a mission to destroy the small submarine. Unbelievable!"

Wishing to share more of his adventures with his friends, Bill suggested they move inside before ordering their meals. They continued to talk for hours, until it was time for Mike and Wendy to leave. Before the good-byes were said, Mike asked, "So are you going to make this your new career?"

"I've been toying with the idea, but I don't think so. I need to see Dr. Green next week, and I'm hoping that she will release me from her practice. After that, I'll put my sailboat back in the water."

Mike acted surprised. "What are you going to do? You have it made here. This life is suited for you. You could work alongside the scientists, using your engineering back ground; together you could develop new inventions just like that woman you met. It seems crazy to me that you are willing to give all this up."

"Mike, I know, but it's just not what I want to do right now... maybe later."

Mike knew that Bill should make his own choices. And besides, Bill's progress pleased Mike. Trusting that Bill was ready to move on to a new phase in his life, they left each other on a friendly note.

Bill was anxious to finalize his plans, and getting his boat ready for its journey south was a priority. The prospect of his impending adventure consumed his thoughts.

***

Butch Clark took the woman he found floating in the sea back to his place with the intent of bringing her to the hospital and notifying the Coast Guard of his discovery. By the time he reached the dock by his house he had altered his plans. The young woman was attractive and sexually arousing to him. While drying her off, her bathing suit kept falling off exposing her breasts and the rest of her body. She didn't know who she was, or where she came from, and he thought it wouldn't hurt to keep her around. After all, someone should make sure she was safe. And she probably knew how to cook and clean. She could help him with his plants, clean fish, and perform other womanly functions a man requires.

During the following weeks, he spent his time studying the news reports for a missing person alert; he asked the clerks working at the local grocery store if there was any local gossip circulating about a missing person. None of these inquiries gave him any insight on the woman's origin, which pleased him. He assumed she had experienced some extremely frightful trauma resulting in her amnesia. Justifying his behavior was simple because he saved her life, and if at some time in the future she regained her memory, he would assist her in contacting her family and friends. Meanwhile life was good.

The woman idolized Butch. At first it was difficult for her to work, and function at a level Butch expected of her. All that changed as she became more comfortable with her surroundings. Soon she was quick to give Butch anything he asked of her.

"You're such a lovie-dovie little woman. Whatever I ask you to do, you do without hesitation, and you always do it with a smile. Because I don't know what your name is I'm going to call you Lovie."

For the first time in a while, he bathed regularly and wore clean clothes. Being a recluse, the town folk mainly disregarded his behavior. They gossiped about him as some weird dude living in the old Clark house, so when he showed up at the thrift store looking for women's clothing no one paid any attention to his purchases. Even as he withdrew books on amnesia from the local library no one noticed. After reading the books he realized his Lovie may slowly regain part of her memory.

"Lovie's" physical capacity improved faster than her mental ability. One spring day she and Butch were in the garden hoeing the soil for new crops. The newly planted rows were orderly, with seed envelopes posted at the beginning of each row. The blue sky was crystal clear, and the soft sound of the surf could be heard beyond the garden. Lovie sighed as she finished covering the last bunch of seeds with dirt. Looking tenderly at Butch, she said. "I love working out here. I have a feeling I've done this before, and even though it can be dirty work at times, it's great watching things grow. Don't you agree?"

"Yes, it's nice to have a good crop to rely on, and I like that a lot. You've been a great help, thanks."

Lovie's continual questioning made Butch uneasy. On another day she asked him if he knew of a place called Mystic Seaport. His surprise was evident; clearing his throat, he asked, "What brought that to your mind? It's some sea museum located in Connecticut."

In the past that would have satisfied her, but she persisted with her questions. " How long would it take us to get there?"

"Well, that depends, if you go by boat, maybe a day. A fast boat may get you their sooner. If you drive a car it'll take longer cause you gotta go through the city, then head east on route 95 toward Rhode Island."

***

Following that episode Butch started locking Lovey inside the house when he went to town. With her new-found strength, and her love for the freedom of the outdoors, he was afraid she might wander off. While locked in the house Lovey kept getting a compelling notion to call a phone number that haunted her. Picking up the phone attached to the kitchen wall, she dialed the number. When the party answered, she asked, "Did you want me to call you?" There was silence on the other end. She repeated herself, "Hello, this is Lovie, who am I calling?"

She heard a male voice exclaim, "Oh my God! Shirley, is this you?"

"I don't know any Shirley," she said. "My name is Lovie."

Richard almost soiled his pants, "Is this some joke? Is Bill behind this? What's going on? This isn't funny."

"Do I have the wrong number?"

Richard regained his senses. "No, Lovie, I've been waiting for your call. Where are you? I'll come and get you."

"I don't know where I am. I just thought I should call this number."

Richard took a deep breath. "Well, I'm glad you did, now tell me where you are?"

"I don't know exactly," she said, her gaze going to the landscape out the window. "It's on the ocean somewhere. We go fishing a lot."

"WE?" Richard exclaimed. "Who are we?"

"You must know, Butch and me. He's my man, and he treats me nice."

Shock hit Richard and it took a moment for him to control his reeling senses; he didn't want her to hang up on him. "Lovie, tell me, are there any letters or some recent mail around there that may have Butch's name and address on them?"

She had just neatly stacked the mail on the counter close by. "Yes, I can see the mail from here."

Richard was careful now. "Lovie, could you please read me the name and address. I'd like to come see you."

"Do I know you?" she asked.

"Sure you do," he said in a carefully controlled voice. "We are good friends. Now please get me his name." The sound of the phone hitting the wall echoed in Richard's ear, as "Lovie" went to get the mail. He waited anxiously for her to return to the phone.

"Hello," she said, "I'm back. Who'd you say you were, and why don't you know where I am?"

Richard counted to ten. "Lovie, we are friends remember?"

"Oh, that's right. "

"Lovie, tell me what the address is on the letter."

"Yes, the letter says, Butch Clark, RR#4, Montauk, New York, 11954."

"Is that it? No address?"

"That is the address."

Richard knew he wasn't going to get any further helpful information from Shirley. "I have your number now, so I'll be in touch. Thanks for calling ... Lovie. Bye now."

Lovie was confused after the phone conversation, but she soon forgot the episode and went about folding the laundry.

CHAPTER NINE

"Everything happens for a reason...
Sometimes good things fall apart so better things can come
together."

Marilyn Monroe

Dr. Green agreed to discharge Bill from her practice. He showed great improvement in his coping skills and self-esteem. His internship with Woods Hole Oceanographic Institute was a positive move. The only disturbing issue left was the lack of complete closure regarding Shirley's disappearance. To this day there was no trace of her body or the floatation cushion Bill had thrown in her direction. Bill and Shirley's mother chose not to have any service to celebrate her life. They wanted to leave the door open for a miracle.

Dr. Green struck a bargain with Bill by granting him permission to complete his craving to enjoy the peace of nature aboard his sailboat in the tropics. During their last scheduled meeting, she clarified her decision. "I am giving you a free pass to go sailing in the Virgin Islands, but I will not allow you to be alone on your boat all the way to the Caribbean."

Bill was taken aback. "So how am I to get there?"

"Bill, you are a smart man, I'm sure there is a way for you to get there, do some research, check around, perhaps hire a licensed captain. Until you have a safe plan in place, I can't release you from my practice."

Bill turned testy. "Have it your way. Trust me, I'll find a way."

Dr. Green smiled at Bill. "I know you will, and good luck. I expect you back next week with your plan."

Plunging into an extensive research project, Bill discovered a boat transfer company which owned four 556-foot semi-submersible ships used to transport recreational cruising and racing boats to Freeport

Bahamas and St. Thomas in the United States Virgin Islands. One of the ships was scheduled to leave from Newport Rhode Island in early in May.

A unique feature of the large vessels was they were equipped with float-on/float-off provisions. The ships partially submerge, allowing boats to load and unload under their own power, rather than be lifted by cranes. The operation was a calculated maneuver where draftsmen determine the placement of each vessel based on its volume and weight distribution relative to the other boats aboard the ship. The large ship sinks to the level where the boats can be loaded and guided into their bays with temporary support by scuba divers. The ship rises, and as the deck dries, the crew begins welding supports in place, making the boats ready for their trip.

During their next meeting, Bill shared his plan with Dr. Green. She was impressed with the extent of Bill's fact-finding, and gave him her blessing.

Bill started immediately to prepare his boat with the supplies necessary for his journey.

***

On Tuesday afternoon. Bill was sitting on his favorite stool in the Ground Round, eating peanuts and sipping on a brew while waiting for Mike. The place was slowly filling up with the familiar afternoon crowd, mostly those folks who had just completed their workday, all greeting each other with friendly gestures, going about their own business.

Mike arrived at his usual time. "Hey, man, how's it going?"

Feeling the friendly slap on his back, Bill turned to see his smiling friend. "Just fine. The boat is packed with supplies for the next six months, ready for the trip south. Plan on meeting me at the marina early Saturday morning. We'll set sail toward Newport."

Taking his seat next to Bill, Mike waited while the bartender slid a cold mug full of his favorite beer in front of him.

"Great, Wendy will meet us in Newport. What time should I tell her to be there?"

Bill gave Mike a scowl. "You know that our arrival time depends on the weather. Rain, fog, or fickle winds, we are at their mercy. We'll call her when we get close. Tell her to book two rooms at a motel. If we arrive early enough, we can take in the sights. Or maybe you could buy her one of those fancy Newport mansions." He then grinned, unable to hide his excitement of the upcoming adventure. "We'll be able to dock in Newport Harbor on Saturday. Sunday they will load my boat inside the large ship. Once it's secured we can return here." He took another sip of beer before continuing. "I've purchased three plane tickets to St. Thomas. Two round trip tickets for you and Wendy, and a one way for me. The ship is scheduled to arrive there on the 21st. We'll sail my boat off the big ship, then you and Wendy will be free to do whatever you desire. I'll set a course to explore the magnificent islands and coral reefs I've been longing to visit."

"You're taking me and Wendy with you?"

Bill beamed. "It's just for the Bon Voyage. It wouldn't be complete without you there, brother. I know you've used up most of your vacation time taking care of me. Next year you'll have to come and spend some time with me; I'll have my bearings by then."

Mike shook his head. "I guess what goes around, comes around. Thanks."

The two friends got up to leave, shuffling through the hordes of peanut shells on the floor. They vowed to see each other again early Saturday morning.

***

The Saturday morning sail began shortly after daybreak. The sky was covered with a dense fog. By midmorning, the sun's rays shone through the heavy dew, and the fog dissipated, making it an ideal day for sailing. A light but constant wind held the sails up, keeping the jib on the verge of a luff. The-sun warmed Bill and Mike as the sea lapped against the sailboat's hull. Sailing into Newport Harbor they saw Wendy waiting for them on the dock.

After the dock crew secured the sailboat, Bill found the transport officer of the big vessel and questioned him about the instructions on loading his boat onto the large ship.

Meanwhile, Mike and Wendy walked about the docks, admiring the mega yachts of the rich and famous. The splendid shining white hulls of the huge vessels glistened like mirrors reflecting off the sea water beneath them, delighting the couple as ships of this size were rarely seen in their area of Long Island Sound.

Bill completed the last-minute paper work and received his final directions. Leaving the office he searched for his friends and found them wandering on an adjacent dock.

Bill could hardly control his joy. "Wow, what an operation. They have fifty boats in all. Ten of them are heading to Freeport Bahamas, and the rest are going to St. Thomas. What do you say we see the sights around town. I'll tell you all about the operation on the way."

Wendy piped up. "How about a tour of Watch Hill?"

Smiling, Bill took her hand. "Lead the way, missy."

***

Richard wasted no time researching Butch Clark. Within a week his profile on Butch was complete.

Richard set off to find Butch Clark's place and hopefully Shirley. It was a bright sunny day, and the trip along the coast made the long journey bearable.

His perseverance was rewarded when he saw a sign at the end of a dirt driveway that read The Clark Place. He drove his car up to the gray planked saltbox house. After parking his car, he hurried up to the large white front door and started banging on it.

"I know she's here," Richard yelled. "Where are you keeping her? Do you have her locked up like some sex slave?"

Butch jerked the door open. Shirley hovered in the background to investigate the noise. When Richard saw Shirley he pushed Butch out of the way and ran to her.

"My god, it's really you, Shirley!" His heart throbbed with relief. Her hair was longer, and her clothes didn't fit well, but she was neat and clean.

Wiping a tear from his eye, he embraced her and exclaimed, "I've missed you so! Are you all right, baby?"

Shirley smiled up at him. "I know you, don't I?"

"How'd you find her?" Butch demanded.

Richard turned toward Butch but did not release Shirley from his embrace. "She called me, that's how. I have a good mind to have you arrested!" Richard sputtered in Butch's face.

"Look, mister, I don't want any trouble. I found the woman floating in the ocean. She was confused-and needed help. Would it have been better to let her drown? I don't think so. I took her in. Now you've found her, and she seems to know you. Just take her and reunite her with her loved ones, and for God's sake, man, get her the help she needs."

Richard was shocked at the man's words. "God, her no good husband tried to kill her! I know he pushed her off his sail boat." He pointed out the window to the water. "He was hoping she would drown somewhere out there."

"Well, that don't make no sense to me," Butch responded, scratching his head. "If somebody is out to drown someone, they ain't gonna leave them with a floatation cushion, now would they? But then I don't know the fella."

Richard was rendered speechless by Butch's revelation.

"Well, then, Lovie—uh, Shirley, is it? I guess this is goodbye. You can take one of the grocery bags and get your clothes, your toothbrush, and, well—have a good life. I got some fishin' to do." Butch headed out the door and in moments was pointing his dory out to sea.

"Come on, Shirley, let's get your stuff and head home." In less than ten minutes, he settled Shirley in the front seat of his car, placing the meager bag of her "belongings" in the trunk.

As he drove back toward Mystic, Shirley was quiet but docile. She didn't really understand why they were leaving Butch, but she recognized Richard as someone special, which made her more than willing to join him.

On their way to Mystic, Richard tried to explain to Shirley what had happened to her. "Bill was trying to kill you when he pushed you off the sailboat. So, we're going to see to it that he regrets what he did. He hoped there would be no evidence of foul play. I know the type— Bill is just like my no-good father. He only thinks about himself. So, naturally, you could be discarded. He was using you for shark bait."

Shirley panicked when she heard Richard's off handed description of the incident. Terror gripped her as a vivid memory shot through her head. "Oh no!" Her hands went to her mouth. "That shark was going to eat me! It was so big and ugly." Shirley seemed to freeze, her body going rigid, her gaze fixed straight ahead, as if the shark was coming at her then and there.

Richard slowed the car, pulling over to the side of the road. "Shirley, honey, it's okay, it's okay, the shark is gone and you're safe with me now." He tried to pull her into his arms, but she remained rigid.

He knew he had made a grave mistake by revealing too much at a time. He believed that Bill had tried to kill her, but telling her that too soon was most likely too much for her to bear in her fragile state.

He had put his desire for revenge ahead of Shirley's well-being. And if he were honest, his preconceived perception of the tragic occurrence on the sailboat might be completely distorted. Yes, he was out for revenge—he still wanted Bill go pay for what had happened to Shirley—but as he looked at the woman in his arms, the woman he loved with all his heart, he realized his zealousness had caused Shirley's amnesia to return two-fold, almost to a state of catatonia.

CHAPTER TEN

The Jet Blue flight from Bradley International Airport was non-stop to San Juan. From there the threesome took a propeller driven DE Havilland Otter to St. Thomas. Waiting to disembark, Wendy exclaimed, "For a minute there I thought we were going straight into that cliff at the end of the runway."

Bill smiled. "I have to admit it was a bit unnerving, but these pilots have flown into this airport any times."

Mike shook his head. "Well, by the looks of the grounds out there, there have been a few mishaps."

"We're here, we are safe and sound, but you're right, that rock comes up mighty quick." Bill was anxious to move along. "Let's get a taxi, and get to my boat."

This was Wendy's first trip away from New England, and she was eager to see the sights. "Did you see the color of the water? It's unbelievable, it's so clear, and beautiful. I bet I could see clear to the bottom of the ocean. Oh my gosh, did you guys see all those sharks? They frightened me to death." Looking at Bill her face flushed. "Oops, I'm sorry, Bill." She reached out to him. "I didn't mean to blurt it out like that."

Bill pretense was to cover up his feelings, but inside he felt like he might fall apart. Then his ego kicked in. "Wendy, please don't feel as if you have to walk on egg shells around me. Sharks swim in every ocean on this planet. Now let's get a cab."

Carrying their own luggage, they descended the stairs hugging the small plane sitting on the tarmac. The warm air greeted them as they headed toward the terminal building. Passing though it they arrived at the busy taxi area where a parade of cabs lined the street. Multiple taxi cab drivers greeted them the moment they reached the street thronged with visitors eager to get to their various destinations. As they paused on the curb to get their bearings, a cab driver approached them. "How many are you?" he asked.

"There are three of us," Bill said.

"Where are you going?"

"To St. Thomas Harbor in Charlotte Amalie."

"Then get over here now, and bring your bags, let's go, follow me!" The driver rushed them to his cab where he opened the doors. "Get in, it's $10.00 a person." He stowed their bags in the trunk.

Bill didn't have time to contemplate; he took $30.00 out of his wallet and handed it to the man. The three of them got in the shabby older car sporting multiple dents. The cabbie plunged his vehicle out into the mainstream of bumper to bumper traffic.

"Yikes!" Wendy yelled from the back seat. "You're driving like a crazy man! You're on the wrong side of the road, and you're going to hit someone. " Covering her eyes with her hands, she snuggled up to Mike.

Mike patted her on the shoulder. "Just calm down, we'll be all right"

The cabby looked back at his passengers. "In this country, we all drive on the left side of the road, and don't worry, the speed limit is 10 miles an hour. Sometimes we go faster, or we would never get anywhere." He accelerated his cab until it was tailgating the cab in front of them.

The roads were narrow, twisting, and turning down the hillside. The landscape was a perfusion of the most beautifully colored flowers, but the homes were very old and poorly maintained. The road descended into a sprawling harbor where cruise ships of all sizes lined the docks along the waterfront. Thousands of people came to St. Thomas aboard the cruise liners and milled through the shops on the streets looking for duty free bargains.

"Where's your sailboat?" Mike asked Bill.

Fascinated by all the activity, Bill lost his focus. "Oh yeah; it's at the Crown Bay Marina."

The cabby scowled, "That marina is back that way. I'm going to have to turn around, and it will cost you another $10.00 each."

"Whatever floats your boat man, just get us there," Bill said.

When there was a break in traffic, the cabby's taxi shot out in front of a driver coming the other way. The squealing of tires and sounds of horns blowing reverberated in the air. It seemed unbelievable but true—they arrived at the Crown Bay Marina without a mishap.

Bill gave the cab driver another $30.00. The three of them jumped out of the cab, grabbed their luggage, and smiling at each other, they watched the driver speed away.

They located the transport ship at the far end of the main dock and hustled toward it. When they reached it they all were huffing and puffing.

"That was a workout," Mike panted.

"It'll be smooth sailing from here on," Bill said with a smile. "You two wait here while I check on the procedure and the time for launching my boat. That'll give you time to catch your breath."

Watching Bill rush off, Wendy looked at Mike, shaking her head in disbelief. "This place is really weird. The sea environment is so beautiful, but most of the houses look to be in need of some serious work. Yet, the shops are loaded with more wealth then you could possibly buy. From the looks of it they seem to offer anything your heart could desire, if you're a rich tourist. Nothing seems to fit right."

Giving Wendy a big hug, Mike explained. "My dear Miss Case Manager, you are no longer in the good ole U.S.A. and we can't change the world. Enjoy the moment and learn from the experience. We will see the sights, and I'll buy you some trinkets. It'll be fun."

Wendy smiled, hugging him back.

They released their embraces when they heard the sound of footsteps on the dock. Turning they saw Bill grinning ear to ear. "We're good to go. Just follow me; we'll stow our gear on the boat. Once it's floating, the scuba divers will guide us off, and we'll sail away. Most of the other boat captains were here when the ship docked; we're one of the few remaining boats."

The procedure was easy, and soon they floated free. The threesome sat in the cockpit of the sailboat. Adjusting the main sail, Bill asked. "Where to?"

"Let's head back to the main harbor," Mike suggested. "I saw a bunch of sailboats on moorings west of the cruise liners. It looked like it was a protected bay, and there was a dingy dock close by. I'd like to take Wendy to see the sights, while you get yourself settled. Later we could go to dinner at one of the seaside places."

Bill's demeanor slumped slightly. "I thought we could go for a sail first, but if you want to see the sights, that'll work. I'll have plenty of time to go sailing, and you two will be leaving tomorrow. We'll just motor sail over there and grab a mooring."

The trip seemed quicker by water than by cab. Bill slowly guided his sailboat into the bay; he waited while Mike hooked a mooring line and secured it to a forward cleat. Once the boat was tightly anchored, Mike lowered the dinghy into the water. He wasn't wasting any time—his mind was set on taking Wendy ashore. Within minutes they were aboard the small craft. They waved to Bill, as the dinghy moved forward. "See ya later." Pointing the dingy toward the dock Mike gave it the gas. The motion caused the warm water to slap against the boat, and a light spray spitted on them.

Watching them, Bill felt another pang of envy, but he dismissed it. He needed to inspect the boat's engine, making sure everything aboard worked properly before he headed into parts of the unknown. Descending the stairway into the salon, he went to work. Satisfied with his inventory, a half hour later he was back in the cockpit. It was time to relax, and watch the activity on shore. Bill reflected on his accomplishment; his plan had finally become a reality.

The boat swayed with the tide like a cradle slowly rocking. The turquoise sea was full of an assortment of hues which gradually interlocked with the light blue sky.

His tranquility was interrupted when the hair on the back of his neck rose. An intense sensation that someone was staring at him swept over him, sending quivers through his body.

Sitting up straight, he searched the shoreline encircling the bay, looking for some clue. Then he noticed a couple looking in his direction, the man was pointing his finger toward the sailboat.

Bill froze and strained to see if he recognized the man and woman invading his space.

His body shuttered. The man looked like his previous neighbor Richard. And the woman—God help him—she looked like Shirley!

What's happening to me? he asked himself. The detection of the couple's identity frightened him. It couldn't be! He stared, his gaze probing their figures.

That's Richard, and Shirley is by his side.

He watched them for another long moment, thinking no, no, this can't be right.

He wanted to rush to shore, but with his dingy gone, getting to land was not an option. Instead, he ran down into the salon, grabbed his binoculars from the table, then flew back up the hatch. By the time he focused the sights, the couple had moved away, mixed into the throng of people.

Bill's hands shook as he lowered the binoculars, closed his eyes and concentrated, playing back the incident in his mind. He fought off a surge of panic and sorrow. *What had they really looked like?*

He must be mistaken, it couldn't have been them! But someone had been out there, looking and pointing at him.

He let out a shuddering sigh. Maybe it was nothing more than a discussion about the make of the sailboat. He fought to control his emotions.

This is downright crazy. Shirley is gone. I know I've been through some hard times, but I saw their faces. Bill started to sweat, and he felt his heart race. He told himself that he had to ignore this. It was nothing more than a fantasy, and it's over. Bill inhaled deeply a few times, then sat back down on the bench seat in the cockpit.

He knew he needed to take baby steps one inch at a time and think pleasant thoughts. Dr. Green said to expect flashbacks once and a while. He vowed to himself not to mention the incident to anyone.

Once again, the swaying motion of the boat captured him and let him relax a bit so he could enjoy the tranquility of the moment. As he relaxed he daydreamed about his impending journey. From the cockpit, he could see Water Island across the bay. His mind wandered, and he thought of the pirate haven that St. Thomas had been in the 1700's. The pirates were nothing more than thugs who turned the islands of the Caribbean into a world of crime on the sea. The notorious Blackbeard, the most ruthless one of them all, was supposed to have built a fortress on St. Thomas with a watchtower that was manned daily to protect the cutthroats from being attacked.

***

On the shore, not far from the harbor in the mist of the throngs of tourists, Richard turned to Shirley. "You did a good job, baby. I know he saw us. Did you see his face? He looked astounded, like he couldn't believe his eyes. That's good, he's nothing but a no-good bastard. We will make him pay. He'll lose his mind, and end up in a funny farm. That'll serve him right, and once he's committed, all the other innocent people will be protected from harm." With a sinister grin, he put his arm around her.

Shirley had no idea what she was doing in St. Thomas, but she was content to be in Richard's company, smiling at him she followed him into the busy courtyard.

***

The splashing of waves against the sailboat's hull, and the sound of a small boat's engine aroused Bill from the inner thoughts. He rose from the seat to help his company out of the dinghy. Passing their packages up to Bill first, they then climbed aboard the sailboat.

"Did you two have a good time?"

Wendy beamed with joy. "Immensely, I got a few things for my family and friends. And Mike bought me a ring."

Bill's eye brows rose with wonder. "Well, show it to me."

Wendy held up her right hand and proudly displayed a sterling silver Celtic ring with a green stone surrounded by two trinity knots.

"Oh, it be a great day for ye Irish," he smiled and turned toward Mike. "I thought it would be a diamond."

"We're not ready for that yet, Bill, maybe next year. There are some awesome bargains out there." Mike looked at Wendy. "What do you say, let's put these bags away and sit in the cockpit with Bill?" Together they disappeared through the hatch.

It was late afternoon with twilight rapidly approaching. Mike was the first to reappear from the hatch. He held up a bottle of Champagne. "No bon voyage party would be complete without some of this stuff." He pointed the bottle at an angle facing the stern of the boat and released the cork, which made a loud popping sound. Some of the foaming liquid spilled over the side of the bottle. "This is to celebrate the start of your new life."

Wendy appeared holding three glasses she'd found in the galley. Handing one to Bill, she held on to the others. After pouring the bubbling liquid into the glasses, Mike set the bottle down on the deck.

The three friends raised their glasses. Wendy said, "Cheers to us!"

Looking into Wendy's eyes, Bill said. "Thank you for being my guardian angel, and how lucky for my best friend to have found you." They all sat in the cockpit until dusk. One by one like the stars in the sky materialized, then lights of the homes on the hills above the city started to appear. Soon the whole hillside was a twinkling sensation.

"Somewhere up there is Blackbeard's castle," Bill said. "I hear it's has a beautiful view of the harbor, and there is a restaurant right inside the castle. Let's go there. It's time we had a bite to eat."

Wendy shouted, "Oh no, not another taxi ride!"

Embracing her, Mike said, "What did ya do with your big girl panties? Let's go." That being said they all piled into the dinghy and headed for the shore.

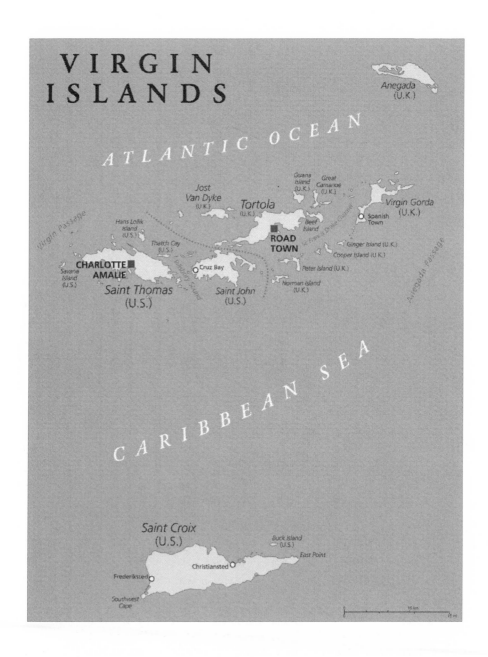

CHAPTER ELEVEN

The next morning Bill sat alone in the cockpit of his sailboat. Mike and Wendy had departed earlier. Their leaving was bittersweet. They were his only contacts to the world he knew. Now he was on his own. No parents, no siblings, no friends, and no wife.

Watching the continuous flow of traffic and the hordes of people from the cruise ships milling around the shops and restaurants was mindboggling. The harbor was one of the most congested anchorages in the Virgin Islands, and it was not what he'd had in mind for his quest to be one with nature. Reviewing his charts, he decided to move along to the south coast of St. Thomas.

Releasing the mooring line from the front cleat, his boat flowed free. He started the engine and followed the channel markers out of the harbor. His destination was Cowpet Bay. He'd read it was a safe anchorage. It also was home to the St. Thomas Yacht Club, and although Bill didn't belong to that elite crowd, he knew that the members would be knowledgeable of the area, and it seemed to be a good place to start his journey.

It took him a few hours to reach Cowpet Bay. Arriving, he pointed the boat's bow toward the north side. When he was close enough to shore, he anchored his boat in good deep sand. Before leaving he decided to swing the dinghy above the anchor line to check if the anchor was holding. Satisfied that it was secure, he took off toward the yacht club's dock.

Guiding over the water gave Bill a feeling of freedom. All his dreams were coming true. The beach at the head of the bay was home to a condominium development, and the bay was alive with many small boats, sailing briskly around.

Bill ran his dinghy up on the beach next to the yacht club dock, then set out to look for the yacht club steward. He found the office where two men standing in front of a window turned toward Bill's entrance.

Bill introduced himself to the men who were courteous, but not overly friendly. "I'm just passing through the area, and I was hoping you'd give me local advice about what I'm going to encounter on my way to the British Virgin Islands."

"Sure, we can do that," said the man closest to Bill.

After giving him local information, they cautioned him. "If you plan on anchoring overnight in our bay you need to be aware there's a current running through the cut, and it might cause you an uncomfortable night. Make sure your anchor is holding good before night fall, or you could end up dragging it."

Thanking the men, Bill returned to his dinghy. Before he got in the small boat, he plummeted himself into the warm clear water. Swimming and splashing around in the surf was fun, smiling to himself, thinking, *this is delightful*. He remained in the water, floating on his back, looking skyward to watch the clouds drift by. Once the pleasure of being in the warm water was over, he got out, dried off, and returned to his sailboat, driving around the bow of the boat again to double check the anchor line. Satisfied it was set, he settled in for the night.

Bill's night was restless. The current was running strong, moving his boat back and forth, causing him to dose off and on. He woke up in a sweat after hearing the sound of Shirley's screams. It kept happening over and over, and he was so disturbed that he went up to sit in the cockpit for a while. The moon's reflection on the water and the stars brightly lighting the sky soothed him.

He couldn't believe his flash backs were happening again, but then realized it must be related to seeing that couple in St. Thomas. *Somehow they really got to me. This is pure nonsense. I've got to get rid of these thoughts. I know there is an ideal place for me. I just need to find it so I can heal.*

Remaining in the darkness, he felt the gentle breeze, and inhaled the salty sea air, which helped rid himself of the pent up feelings. Relaxing in the cockpit he soon fell asleep.

The first rays of sun brought with it the sounds of the day. Roosters crowed, song birds tweeted, and larger birds splashed into the water chasing bait fish for their breakfast. Awaking from his slumber, he went into the salon and prepared his breakfast. Programing his auto pilot with the waypoints recommended by the men at the yacht club, he was ready to leave.

Hauling the anchor, he adjusted the sails and set his course for Current Cut. The sailboat glided through the cut and sliced through the sea on another perfect reach. Bill felt exhilarated. The boat performed flawlessly. He sailed into Muller Bay, a recommended layover before entering the British Virgin Islands, known as the B.V.I.'s to the locals.

He went shopping in the Marina Market, finding enough fresh produce and meat to last him a couple of weeks. After filling his refrigerator, he returned to shore, looking for a local hang out. He found Tickles Dockside Pub. Entering it he sat at the bar, hoping to meet a few local's and talk to them about the port of entry to the BVI on Jost Van Dyke Island. To his right sat a guy named Fred, a marine mechanic. Fred was a big burly guy with dark curly hair and bottomless brown eyes. On his left side sat Jim, who worked at the market where Bill had purchased his provisions. Jim was a slight man with auburn hair and hazel eye. Both men lived and worked in Red Hook. They had extensive knowledge of the area, as did the many others locals sitting around the bar. Everyone there was more than willing to make Bill feel welcome, and they bent his ears for hours, telling their stories of the perils and joys found in the surrounding islands.

Returning to his boat after drinking more beer then he was accustomed to, Bill slipped off to sleep without being awakened by interruptions from his subconscious. At daybreak he was ready for his departure, and he set sail for Tortola, the largest island in the BVI chain. Approaching Great Thatch Island he adjusted his course, sailing directly into Great Harbour on Jost Van Dyke. The break in the reef he'd been warned about was easy to see, and he sailed through the opening unscathed. Once inside the reef he set the anchor. Taking the necessary paper work needed to clear customs, he jumped into his dinghy.

Reaching the dock, he saw the red roofed building housing the Customs Office. Bill went into the small building, spying the agent sitting alone behind his desk. Official looking documents hung on the walls surrounding him.

"Can I help you?" the agent asked.

"Yes, I just arrived from St. Thomas and need to clear customs with you. Here are my papers."

The man looked like an ole salt and grinned at Bill he took his papers. "Your first time here?"

"Yes sir."

The formalities were quick and easy in the most pleasant setting Bill had ever encountered.

The friendly agent with a relaxed demeanor handed Bill his papers back along with a custom's declaration. "Enjoy your stay."

"Thanks, I'm sure I will." After leaving the office, Bill looked around for a place called Foxy's. Fred, Jim, and the other men at the pub last night recommended he stop for a brew. It was an open air restaurant with a dirt floor just as his late-night companions had described.

Foxy was a seventh-generation Jost native. His family ran the bar/restaurant, and he entertained the crowd by playing his guitar and singing. The place was a gold mine and was a legendary yachtsmen's hangout. The specialty drink was made with Foxy's Fire Water. Bill ordered one and sat down on a wooden bench, his eyes scanning the crowd, smiling to himself at the lively activity.

Sipping on his drink he was drawn to the action of a cute red-headed girl who appeared as if she was an activities director. Judging her to be in her early to mid-twenties, she reminded him of Little Orphan Annie. She had bright eyes and an infectious laugh; she seemed to know everyone there.

Before long she made her way over to Bill. "Hi, I'm Molly Tynin; are you new to the area?" Looking at the girl, Bill could see her face was covered with freckles, and there didn't appear to be any space for one more. She was slender and wore a white t-shirt and khaki shorts. "Yep, I just sailed in. After clearing customs, I thought I'd try one of the special drinks."

"Are you alone?"

"Quite."

"Then would you mind if I joined you for a while?"

"Not at all, I'd like that. Who are you? You must oversee the welcoming committee? You seem to know everyone."

"Gosh no," she gushed. "I do know a lot of the people here and on the other BVI's. I'm a charter boat captain, and I take all kinds of people around to the different islands for a week or two at a time. When they're gone there's, another group waiting to take their place. You might think I'd get bored, but I don't. I love to sail, and there is no more ideal place in the world to sail than right here. Don't you agree?" She didn't wait for a comment from Bill but continued with her conversation, "Some time I get a bunch of fuddy-duddies or worse, like drunken kids, but I do the best I can. After all, I'm getting paid, and soon they're history."

Looking at Bill, her blue eyes sparkled, and her smile glistened. He was smitten with her.

Still curious she asked, "So are you here in the islands all by yourself?"

He smiled. "Up until now."

"Well, what's up with that? Are you running away from something? Maybe you're a felon or a woman raper." She laughed.

"No, I'm just a guy wanting to get away from it all and have a chance to enjoy nature." Her spontaneous cheerfulness continued to intrigue Bill.

"Sounds reasonable; you want to take a walk with me? I'll show you some nature."

Bill hesitated. "What do you have in mind? You're pretty bold."

Stopping short, Molly's face reddened. "Oh boy, I guess that didn't come out right. There's a path over there." Looking in the direction of an area Molly was pointing, Bill could see a line of dense trees at the bottom of a steep hill.

"It takes you over the hill, and from the top you can see a beach on the other side. It's really a nice view from up there, you'll see."

Enjoying the redhead's personality, Bill said, "All right, I'm in, let's get going."

"Don't move!" Molly said, standing up. "I'll be right back. I need to make sure my charter people aren't in a hurry to leave."

Bill liked her enthusiasm and cheeriness.

Molly returned with both hands full. She had a playful skip in her walk. "Here take this," she said, handing Bill another drink made with Foxy's Fire Water. "It's a demanding climb up that hill for a city slicker. You'll need some fortification." Sipping the beer from her glass, Molly tried to stop the foam from overflowing. "It's a Guinness, do you want a sip?"

"No, thanks, and what did you mean city slicker?"

Looking at him with a perpetual smile, she said. "You've got the look, that's all. Now don't get suspicious on me. Come on, tell me your story, I'm a good listener."

Bill chuckled. "Could have fooled me, and thanks for the drink." The two headed for a break in the tree line, which hid the path. By the time they reached the opening, Bill felt as if he was in a tunnel. The trees left just enough space for a path of packed sand. Off the path was an impenetrable jungle.

Feeling the effects of the rum, Bill began telling Molly about his work background, how he lost his job, and the boating accident. He felt completely at ease with her and chatted non-stop.

"Your wife was eaten by a shark?" Molly exclaimed. "Are you for real? Things like that only happen in the movies."

"I'm not making it up, trust me, I was there. I watched her struggling in the water, and the monster shark was right next to her. Then I was knocked out cold. The strangest thing about the whole event was that there was never a trace of her body or the flotation cushion I threw to her."

Molly nodded her head, "You're right, that's strange, too strange. I still think that you're making the whole thing up."

Not wanting to discuss it anymore, Bill said. "Believe what you want! That's it."

They weaved their way up the path for a half hour. "We're close to the top," she said, "and you're mighty fit for a city boy."

Bill was glad to be off the subject of Shirley. "Well, I've been very busy lately." He didn't want to get in a discussion about his post traumatic disease, or his six-month stint with the team on Alvin. He had already said too much.

Flashing her smile, Molly said. "It shows." She reached out and took Bill's empty glass, placing the two glasses on the ground, before taking his hands in hers. "Now put your hands over your eyes and don't peek." Bill did as he was told. "I'll guide you the rest of the way." Molly positioned herself behind Bill. "Just move forward until I say stop. I'll keep you on the path."

Enjoying her game, Bill said, "Don't you dare use me as bait for a dragon lizard."

"Don't be silly, it won't be long now," she said with a laugh. Bill felt Molly stop guiding him. "Okay open your eyes."

Opening his eyes he gazed at an amazing sea of turquoise which went to the horizon. Below them was an isolated bay surrounded by a beautiful white sandy beach that extended the entire length of the bay. In the center of the bay Bill saw two very distinct reefs. As he glanced back at Molly, he saw her beaming. "This is spectacular. Thank you for taking me up here. Let's go down to the beach now?"

Molly was reluctant to speak. "Bill, I'm sorry I can't do that. I must get back to my charter group. I told them that I'd only be gone for an hour."

Bill became quiet and put on a long face. "Hey, that's not fair, you feed me more rum and take me to one of the most beautiful places I've ever been, then leave me on my own, never to see you again."

Molly tried to make light of the situation. "I just wanted you to be aware of this beach, but don't take your sailboat over there; it's not safe. The reefs take up most of the anchoring room, and the ground swells can cause unsettled sea conditions. For that reason, people just walk over the hill, and spend their day swimming and snorkeling over the reefs. It will be different experience for you, and believe me, you'll enjoy the day."

"But I wanted to spend more time with you. Now I've changed my mind, you're nothing but a big tease."

Molly was sincere. "I'm sorry, I didn't mean to lead you on; I didn't realize how lonely you are." Reaching up she put her hands around his neck, encouraging him to lower his head. She quickly planted a gentle kiss on his lips.

Bill slipped his arms around her and drew her into an embrace as he returned her kiss with surprising passion. Realizing how good she felt in his arms, he pleaded, "Please don't go. I'd like to see you again. Would that be all right?"

"Bill, I'm not being a big flirt with you. You don't appear to be the kind of guy that's just out for a good time. For the short time I've spent with you I've come to believe you're a man of substance and character, who has experienced a string of bad luck." She stepped out of his embrace and took his hands in hers. "Tell you what, my current assignment will end in a week. This group booked their cruise for ten days. After that, I'll have a few days on my own until my next group comes aboard."

Bill's emotions soared with her capitulation. She was charming, energetic, and enthusiastic. Spending more time with her lifted his spirits. "So could you return here between your assignments?"

"Sure, but you'll have to wait for a week."

Bill hadn't been attracted to anyone like her before; she was captivating. "It's a date! Now don't stand me up." He smiled down at her.

Molly laughed. "Don't worry about me. There's lots to do in these islands. Who knows, you may become enchanted by another young beauty—there are a lot of us around the islands. Now, Bill, I really have to go. And to pass the week, I want you to take a few sails and enjoy the activities in harbors. Don't miss Cane Garden Bay, The Baths, and Norman's Island."

Bill was impressed by her sincerity. "Sounds like fun, but it would be more fun with you."

They were still at the top of the hill holding hands. "Well, if you'd rather, you could stay right here at Great Harbor. You can relax, maybe even go to the beach by yourself, and I'll be back next week." She let go of his hands, pointing to the bay below. "I'll bring my snorkel gear, and we can spend the day together down there. How's that?"

This appeased Bill and he beamed with happiness. "Sounds great! How will you get back?"

"If the ferry from Tortola is running, I'll hitch a ride. If not, I'll get one of my friends to run me over here. Don't worry, I won't stand you up."

They briefly kissed again. Molly said, "That's enough; there'll be plenty time for this later, but damn it, Bill, I've got to get going. If I don't get them to the next harbor soon, we'll never get a mooring"

Gathering up their empty glasses, they began their decent back down the hill toward Foxy's, holding hands for much of the trek. Reaching the restaurant, they parted, and Bill watched Molly scamper off to gather the two couples on her charter boat. They laughed as they walked with swaying footsteps as they followed Molly to her dinghy.

She gently but firmly helped the inebriated party into the small boat, then headed back to a sleek Beneteau sailboat.

Following suit, Bill got in his dinghy and returned to his sailboat where he found his binoculars and watched Molly sail away.

What the hell am I doing? he wondered as a big smile spread across his face. He hadn't felt so hopeful in a long, long time.

CHAPTER TWELVE

Bill sat in the cockpit of his sailboat, staring into the water. He was trying to figure out what was happening to him. Molly was a fun companion; he had enjoyed every minute they spent together, but what now? He really didn't want to get involved with anyone. He was here to get away and be one with nature.

The small harbor was becoming extremely busy for this late in the day. Sailing yachts came from every direction. As soon as the boats were anchored or attached to a mooring line, the occupants aboard the boats jumped into their dinghies, heading to shore. The sound of live music filled the air, and Bill's nose crinkled as he inhaled smoke from a local barbeque pit. Watching the activities, he knew the crowd gathering around him had all the makings of some heavy-duty partying.

Bill knew he could join the party but was content to enjoy his evening alone. As darkness fell, he devoted his time to star gazing. Trying to identify as many constellations he could, considering the longitude and latitude changes were completely different from those he was accustomed to was the real challenge. His private game allowed him to loosen up and unwind. He was so involved he barely noticed the revelry taking place on shore. Eventually he found his way to the forward stateroom and settled in for the night.

Remaining in the comfort of the forward cabin as the early morning light peeked through the curtains suited him just fine. There was no need for him to haul the anchor yet. By the time he rolled out of bed, it was mid-morning.

Making a pot of coffee, he relocated to the cockpit, and was set to greet the day. To his surprise the harbor was empty. Everyone had sailed off to new destinations. Taking his time; Bill thought about his options; one was to returned to the top of the hill and explore the white sandy beach on the other side. Deciding that could wait, he took Molly's advice and set sail for Cane Garden Bay.

He was under sail by noon. As if by magic the sea breeze was perfect for holding a flawless reach. Bill felt alive and enjoyed the cruise. By mid-afternoon he sailed into Cane Garden Bay. Mooring buoys bobbing like water lilies on a bed of turquoise filled the harbor. Bill chose a mooring at the far end of the bay, far enough away from the shore to avoid the evening crowd's fun time, as he was sure this bay would be populated by the charter boat enthusiasts by nightfall. Launching his dinghy Bill ventured ashore. Beaching his dinghy on the sand, he walked along the shore. His feet were bathed in the warmth of the soft powdery dunes. Finding an open air shack selling food and drinks he decided to stop for a snake. Walking up the wobbly stairs, he sat on a bar stool overlooking the water.

"How about a beer and a burger?" Bill asked the bartender.

"What flavor beer?"

"Anything on draft will do."

Pouring the beer in a glass, he introduced himself as Hank.

"Bill," he said, accepting the drink.

Hank was a weathered looking chap with deep wrinkles etched into his darkly tanned skin, evidence of years of sun exposure. His gray hair receded beyond his forehead.

"How would you like your burger cooked?"

"Medium will do."

Bill was his only customer. "Mister, you have the look of a first time visitor."

"How'd you know?" Bill nodded. "I'm just cruising around the area, getting my bearings so to say."

"You alone?"

Bill smiled. "What's this, 20 questions?"

"You got that look, man."

"Oh, is that a bad thing?" Not waiting for an answer from Hank, Bill continued. "Looks like this beach must be a busy place at night. Seems a lot more like Coney Island or Wildwood than an island in the tropics."

"I suppose you're right. This place was different about thirty years back. Stanley's was the only entertainment around. At that time, we were lucky to have ten sailboats in the harbor. They call it progress and tell me I can never go back. So here I am. I stuck it out, and I'm surviving, this is my home. The charter boats will all arrive soon. Everyone jumps into their dinghies, and like hungry spiders, they converge on the beach. There will be a lot of noise, with music blaring from every cranny. Most of them are young, and they get drunk. Then in the morning they move on to another spot, and do it all over. I can't say I blame them. They're here for a good time before they return to their jobs and families back in some dirty, congested, city far away from here. At least Stanley's is still open. If you like steel drum music you should head over there tonight."

Bill laughed and said. "You don't know what you got until its gone. Seems they paved paradise and put in a parking lot."

"Hey, that's a clever line from a song. I'll have to remember it. A parking lot full of moorings, to boot."

Hank placed the burger in front of Bill. The smell of grilled beef was inviting. Biting into the succulent meat, the juice began dripping down his chin. Quickly he grabbed his napkin to wipe the juice from his face. "Now this is some sandwich."

"Glad you like it, enjoy."

Bill's thoughts returned to their conversation, pointing at the boats in the harbor. "Sad as it is, like you said, they're happy to be here, and you can't blame them. This place is a paradise. Warm water, perfect sailing conditions, and lots of party places. Plus, you're making a living while they take over your beach."

"You're right. If this crowd is not your bag, take a sail over to St. John. It's much quieter there. Over half of the island belongs to the U.S. Park System which has all kinds of hiking trails and campsites. The bays are spectacular, and you'll have all the privacy you desire."

"Thanks, I'll remember that."

"Can I get you another drink?"

Pushing his empty plate and glass away, Bill stood up. "No, I'll take a stroll back down the beach while it's fairly quiet." He paid his tab and bid Hank a good evening. He spent the rest of the day entertained by the crowd who made their way into the bay by late afternoon.

The morning sun rose revealing many empty white balls dancing on the water. Reading his yachtsman's guide, he hoped to find a more serene spot. Deciding to head for Virgin Gorda, Bill delighted in another beautiful sailing day. If only the enjoyment of sailing could last into the night.

Virgin Gorda was more isolated then Cane Garden Bay and didn't have a busy shoreline. There were a few mooring lines in the harbor and a quaint town beyond. Bill's evening was nice and quiet for a change.

Rising early to a captivating sunrise renewed his energy, and he couldn't wait to explore the area. 'The Baths' was a formation of granite boulders piled together by Mother Nature on the water's edge. A place like none other, located just south of his anchorage. Grabbing his snorkel gear and jumping into his dinghy, Bill arrived at the baths early in the day, a plus, as there wasn't another soul around. Placing his mask and fins on, he plunged into the water, floating between boulders above colorful fish and coral formations. It was so relaxing, just floating aimlessly in the warm water, losing himself in pleasant thoughts.

Suddenly there was a disturbance and a multitude of splashes. He heard people yelling and laughing. Within moments he was surrounded by bodies pushing, and shoving him. Someone kicked him, and he surfaced.

"What the hell are you animals doing?" he yelled.

No one paid him any attention. Irritated, he looked around for the culprits. Cruise ship tenders were dropping off throngs of passengers. Anger washed over him. The ungrateful visitors were infecting the beautiful sea like a blight. There was nothing left to do but leave his destroyed tranquility.

Reaching his boat, Bill's mood turned foul. He'd come here to get in touch with nature, and what does he get but a bunch of ninnies who only want to raise hell. He decided to hang around a few more days, but from what he'd experienced, this place was not for him. Bill sulked for the remainder of the afternoon as he watched the cruise ship tenders ferry more passengers to the town dock.

By early evening things were quiet, so he ventured into town. The main thoroughfare was a dirt road. The locals, and a few charter boat occupants milled around the shops where modest houses had been converted into businesses. A few restaurants with neon "open" signs flashing invited customers to enter.

Bill's hunger lured him into a pizza parlor. The smell of the garlic, and fresh pizza made him realize he hadn't eaten anything since early morning, and everything smelled good to him. After ordering a supreme pizza and a soda, he asked the waiter, "How was your day? I watched those tenders drop off loads of cruise ship passengers onto this island."

The young man with spiked purple hair appeared to be in his late teens. "Not bad, but we were slammed at lunch, and they kept us hopping. The nice thing about the tourists is they tip us well."

"Tell me, how often do the cruise ships come around?"

"Depends on the week," the waiter said, "we get as many as five ships here in a week. They bring lots of money to these islands. Don't think there are any scheduled to arrive tomorrow. That'll give me a break to get in some fishing."

The thought of a more peaceful atmosphere pleased Bill and he decided it might be worth his while to spend another day here. His pizza arrived hot out of the oven. It was covered with cheese, pepperoni, hamburger, sausage, and an array of vegetables. He left with a full stomach and a new outlook for the next day.

In the morning Bill walked through the town looking for the hiking trail leading to the top of Gorda Mountain. The guidebook said the summit peaked at 1359 feet with views of the ocean a thousand feet below. Finding the trail was easy, and after taking a slug of water from his water bottle of water he meandering up the incline. He stopped from time to time to explore the cacti and to watch the many lizards darting along the path. Climbing upward he enjoyed the sight of birds flying overhead and the yellow and white butterflies floating in the air along the trail.

Reaching the summit, he marveled at the view of the sea from the pinnacle. He sat down on the soft sweet smelling grass and gazed over the amazing, unlimited views.

If only Molly were here to enjoy the view with him. A bevy of white sails danced atop the contrasting shades of turquoise beneath the surface of the calm waters. Hundreds of sailboats amid an influx of cruisers was an awesome sight, and Bill took a seat on a rock to enjoy the private show. Soon he was reflecting on the contrast between the serenity of the day and the drama of the past year.

Eventually the memory of seeing the Shirley look-alike broke the spell, prompting him to head back to his sailboat.

Staying busy was the best medicine to keep sad thoughts at bay, so the next morning, he pointed his boat toward another location Molly had mentioned, Norman's Island. He'd read about its caves hugging the water's edge, allowing snorkelers to swim into them.

Arriving inside the deep-water harbor by midafternoon, Bill saw how well protected the harbor was by the surrounding hills. Many of the moorings were still empty, so Bill took one close by a schooner named "William Thornton," known locally as the "Willy-T," a floating bar and restaurant.

But first, he wanted to take a look at the caves on the south west part of the island where smaller blue moorings were designated for tying up dinghies. Taking a quick swim into one of the caves was all he wanted, just to say he did it. After a refreshing swim, he returned to his dingy and the quick ride back to his sailboat.

Sitting on a bench seat in the cockpit of his boat, sipping on a cold beer, he adjusted himself to the noise, from the "Willy T" and watched the revelry. A wet t-shirt contest caught his attention. At the bow of the ship, young girls wearing tight white t-shirts jumped into the water only to climb back onto the "Willy-T" to proudly strut around, providing entrainment for tourists enjoying another day in paradise.

***

Early the next day Bill set sail from Norman's island to return to Jost Van Dyke where he planned to hang out until Molly showed up.

Once there, he ventured out on his own, following the path that led to the bay Molly had showed him. Following the path leading to the beach he spent time looking for shells and sea glass. Eventually he discovered the Soggy Dollar Bar where dollar bills were pinned to a clothesline. A waiter with long blonde hair and a scruffy beard headed his way.

"I'm Jeff. Can I get you a cold one?"

"Sure, give me something you have on draft," Bill replied. "Do you serve food?"

"That we do; I'll get you a menu. What kind of beer would you like?"

Bill thought about Molly's choice, "How about a Guinness?"

"Coming right up."

Waiting for his order, Bill contemplated the clothes line with money pinned to it, a good advertisement for the bar's logo. Further down the beach he noticed a few hammocks attached to palm trees with green lacy branches gently swaying in the breeze. A great spot for a nap.

The waiter returned, handing Bill an ice-cold mug full of beer. "Here's our list of sandwiches. We have fresh fish special, if you're interested."

"A fish sandwich sounds good to me. What's with all the bills hanging on the line?"

"I just put them there to dry. The water taxi from Tortola just brought a bunch of tourist over here. After their swim, they all came ashore, and had some beers. I think the water taxi guy told them about our bar's name, and encouraged them to pay with wet cash. They had fun, no harm was done. It's good for business."

"Hum, clever." Pointing toward the palm trees Bill asked. "One more thing, what's with those hammocks?"

"Great for an after-lunch snooze. Just help yourself."

"Thanks, I might do that after I eat.

The tranquil atmosphere of the beach was captivating and Bill enjoyed the beer and sandwich. Afterward he snagged a hammock where he drifted off.

"Hey buddy!" Jeff's voice brought Bill awake. "I don't mean to interrupt your siesta, but if you're not careful you're gonna get fried!"

Bill was startled by the intrusion, regaining his bearing to the here and now. "Oh yeah, I smothered myself with sunblock, but I didn't intend to fall asleep for so long. Thanks, I'll get moving." Squinting up at Jeff, he asked, "Will you be here tomorrow?"

"Sure. dude, I live here. Why?"

"I might be back with a girl—maybe you know her. Molly; she's a charter boat captain."

"Her!" Jeff's face showed his surprise. "She's a hot ticket, but she doesn't usually go out with strangers. Did you know her before?"

Bill was taken off guard with Jeff's reaction, feeling irregular heart palpitations, and wondering what could be wrong with Molly.

"No, I just met her."

Jeff said scratched his head. "You must have golden balls or something; that chick ain't the kind to get connected to no one."

The conversation was baffling to Bill. Getting up from the hammock, and looking at Jeff, he smiled. "Thanks for waking me up. I'll be seeing you."

Now what? Bill wondered. That was just too bewildering. All he'd come here for was some peace and quiet. He could easily just sail away, but he really wanted to see her again.

He headed up the hill. The open expanse of sky and sea below was making his climb go quickly. Enclosed by the dark tunnel of trees surrounding him, his mind was drifting back to his trek with Molly. Why was he so attracted to Molly? She was so different than Shirley. Concentrating on their differences he realized they both had a common thread. Shirley had been quiet but kind and giving. Everyone had loved her, including Richard. Molly was much the same, caring and giving, and everyone seemed to like her except maybe Jeff.

Bill continued to walk and think. By the time he reached the summit, he realized that he had abandoned Shirley by placing his project at work ahead of spending time with her. It was a painful truth that surfaced quickly, just like the killer shark had suddenly jumped out of the ocean, awesome and unexpected. In that instant, Shirley was gone, but in reality, he had lost her long before that fateful day.

That's why he had imagined Shirley and a man who looked like Richard on that ship—it was his subconscious trying to tell him something.

And now he was lonely, sailing and searching for something or someone. Was that how Shirley had felt? Was that why Shirley had turned to Richard?

It was a hard pill to swallow, but the loneliness he was experiencing was a teaching moment. And now he was presented with a second chance. Molly was a ray of sunshine in his formerly gloomy life that had been consuming him since he'd hit his head and lost Shirley, all in the same moment.

Now the question was, did he have enough courage to put the guilt behind him and grab a bit of happiness. He knew he wanted to spend time with Molly. She was a ray of sunshine infusing him with a shot of vitamin D.

Molly willing, he just had to reach out and grab a bit of happiness. Providing he was deserving of this second chance.

With a heavy heart and the sting of the sunburn on his arms, he turned to the trail leading to the shoreline where his dingy was moored.

CHAPTER THIRTEEN

Another restless night. The familiar sounds of Shirley's screams were there, but instead of the shark, Bill envisioned it was Molly who was trying to drown her. Bill awakened with a jolt.

He lay still, wondering, *My God, which one would I save?*

Unable and unwilling to go back to sleep he headed topside. Somehow star gazing always soothed away his anxiety. By daylight Bill had devised a plan.

At 8a.m. he placed a call to Mike, whose voice indicated he was glad to hear from him. "What's it like in paradise?"

"It's heaven and hell combined."

"How so?" Concern edged Mike's question.

"I'm in the British Virgin Islands, and it's just not what I expected. There are scads of boats, both bare-boats and charter boats; the people aboard them only want to do one thing—party all day and all night. Then cruise ships bring in hordes of people, who spend lots of money. They swarm all over the islands like they own the place. They're on every island raising all kinds of hell. It's not what I expected, or wanted." He paused before adding, "Another problem is I met a girl."

"What, a girl already?" Mike did not disguise his surprise. "What's she like?"

"Oh, she's nice; maybe too nice, and that's a problem. I'm getting in too deep; I just met her, but she's got a hold on me. I've got to get away from her. I'm not ready for this kind of thing."

"What are you going to do?"

"Soon, very soon, maybe even tomorrow I'll be heading to the American Virgin Island of Saint John. From what I hear and read, it's quieter there. I'm sure I'll be able to find a secluded spot for myself."

Mike pushed Bill for more information. "What about the girl?"

"Her name is Molly, and she lives here in Tortola and works as a charter boat captain. I'll still be able to see her if I want as Tortola isn't that far from St. John. I just need to distance myself from her for now."

Bill waited a moment before he spoke again. "Mike would you do me a favor?"

"Sure, what's on your mind?"

Bill's voice was strained. "Would you drive by my old house and check on my neighbor Richard? Just let me know if he's still there."

"That's it, nothing else?"

Bill didn't want to give Mike any more time to probe. "No, that's all. Hey, I need to go now. I'll call you back. Say Hi to Wendy. Take care and thanks." Bill quickly shut off his cell phone before Mike could reply. Then he went into the galley to get some coffee, contemplating his next move.

If Molly didn't show by noon today, he'd leave.

He was still in the galley when he heard the sound of a power boat approaching. The sound stopped abruptly, followed by a loud pounding on the sailboat's hull. He raced up to the cockpit to see what the commotion was all about and found Molly ready to board. Offering his hand, he lifted her aboard. Secretly he was happy that she was there.

Her eyes flashed as she greeted him. "Bill, I'm so glad that you are still here! My friend Tom was nice enough to give me a lift over here, delivering me to you." She motioned to the older black man with salt and pepper hair whose smile covered his face from ear to ear. He handed Molly a duffel bag and some snorkel gear.

"Thanks, Tom," Molly said.

Bill waved a greeting. "Thanks for the delivery; I'll make sure she gets back home safe and sound."

Tom threw him a salute before turning his boat around, speeding away as quickly as he'd arrived.

Molly waved an accusing finger at Bill. "I bet you thought I'd never show up! Now tell me the truth…don't fib."

She was as bubbly as Bill remembered. "The truth is, I wanted this to happen, but doubted if you'd show. We spent such a short time together, and there was alcohol involved, which sometimes causes people to make promises they don't remember."

"All right, I too was doubting if this was right, but when I saw your sailboat I knew it was meant to be." Pressing her hands together as in a prayer she added, "Please, show me around."

Bill's emotions reeled from high to low as he questioned his decision. He was ecstatic yet dubious, then jubilant, but apprehensive. He tried to block it out of his mind. *Screw it,* he said to himself.

"Follow me," he said out loud.

Together they descended through the hatch to the interior of the sailboat. Bill enjoyed showing Molly the layout of the living quarters. "Here's a nice kitchen for the misses, and a formal salon where you could knit; going forward you'll find the captains quarters, and in the stern there's a room for guests. Feel free to leave your belongings in there."

Molly followed Bill around like a puppy dog. "This is a Hunter, right?"

Bill didn't follow the query, "Why, does it make a difference?"

"Mercy no, just that I've been on lots of boats, and this has quality built into her."

"Thanks, I think. Let me get your gear, and you go ahead and explore."

Molly noticed a picture of a petite blond woman on the chart table and picked it up.

Rejoining Molly with her gear, Bill saw her holding the picture in her hand. "Is there a problem?"

Molly held up the picture frame. "Is this a picture of your wife, the one that was gobbled up by the shark?"

"Yes, that's her. She's been gone for over a year now, but I can't put that away just yet."

Reaching out putting her arms around him, she said. "Bill, I'm sorry."

"Don't be, it's just something I have to deal with. Now let's go ashore; we've got things to do."

Slipping into Bill's dinghy, they headed for the dock. Molly looked toward Foxy's and asked, "Would you like a brew for the climb?"

Bill shook his head. "No, I'd rather not. Besides you intoxicate me."

Their journey over the hill went quickly. Bill enjoyed Molly's coquettish glances as she told him about herself. "I grew up in Fall River, Massachusetts; you know, the town where Lizzy Borden lived. She's the one that chopped up her folks with an ax."

"Yeah, there was something about 40 and 41 whacks. Anyway, how did you learn to sail?"

"Oh, my best friend in high school was Debbie; her dad was a doctor, and they had a 42-foot Pearson sailboat. I adored her brother so when she invited me to join them I was right there. Her dad and brother were great sailors, and they taught me. Isn't that cool?"

"I guess so; then how'd you end up here?"

"Debbie and I went to college together; we wanted to become teachers; when we graduated, her dad arranged a chartered sailboat here for us for one week. Two of our other girlfriends came along. While here, I got to know the manager of the charter operation. I guess I impressed him, and he offered me a job. Returning home I told my parents about the job offer. They had just finished paying my way through college and expected me to work as a teacher for a while. Which I did. Two years later I contacted the manager of the charter firm, and he hired me. The rest is history."

Turning toward Bill, Molly asked, "So tell me, how'd you learn to sail? Did your dad teach you?"

Bill hesitated. "No, my dad wasn't a sailor; besides he's gone now. I guess I'm much like you, I learned from being on my friends' boats when we were young. Kids growing up by the water always have some kind of boat."

When they reached the beach, Molly dropped the subject, much to Bill's relief. "This is it!" she exclaimed. "We're here. Let's swim out to the first reef, then we can float with the current, it's easier that way."

Bill was eager to follow her. The sunlight provided good light, and the reef was alive with brain coral, fire coral, and outstanding formations of Elkhorn coral. The sea fans waved with the current, rich with a plethora of colorful fish.

When they surfaced Bill couldn't control his delight. "This is magnificent! The colors are so bright. I've never seen so many coral, or fish in one place. Thank you for bringing me here." He took Molly in his arms. "You are remarkable."

Molly tossed her red curls over her shoulders. "Can we get a beer now?"

"Sure." Pointing at the Soggy Dollar, he added, "That guy Jeff at the Soggy Dollar isn't your best fan."

"Oh, that guy is a jerk! He's from Ft. Lauderdale and was a heavy hitter in the drug trade. His father got him a job out here through some connection of his. There is no way in hell that I would get involved with his kind. There's another place down the beach." Molly took Bill's hand and led him in the opposite direction of the Soggy Dollar.

They spent the rest of the day relaxing in the surf. Returning to Bill's sailboat, they cleaned up and, grabbing two cold beers, they sat in the cockpit rehashing the afternoon. The bright blue sky above and soft sea breeze trickling by them added to their enjoyment.

Bill was conflicted about his plans. He didn't want to leave her now; she was delightful, but he knew he had to move on. Gathering his courage he spoke up. "Molly I've got to talk to you about my plans. They have changed. I'm leaving for Saint John in the morning. Things just aren't right for me here. It has nothing to do with you, but these islands don't have the peace and quiet I need right now."

Molly gasped. "No, no, you can't go so soon, it's not right." Tears gathered in her eyes. "Now's whose being a tease. It's just not right. You can't leave me now."

Feeling guilty, Bill explained. "Molly I have to go, and I'll only be an island away. Please don't make it any harder than it is for me." Bill didn't want to leave her either, but he felt that he must.

Molly reached for him. "Can we please stay together tonight? Maybe you'll feel different in the morning. I still have a few more days to spend with you. Please, Bill."

Bill weakened. "If you wish, I can drop you off on Tortola tomorrow."

They spent a quiet evening together and fell asleep wrapped in each other's arms.

CHAPTER FOURTEEN

Bill and Molly rose early. Both said little to one another. Preparing his boat for the sail to Tortola, he stayed busy with last minute checks on his electronics. Feeling everything was ready, he raised the anchor and motored out of the harbor and set a course toward the west end of Tortola. Their destination was Soper's Hole.

Sitting on the bench seat in the cockpit Molly watched Bill adjust the sails. She was sullen but wanted to break the uncomfortable silence. "Bill, did you know that Tortola got its name from the Spanish? It means turtle dove."

Bill laughed. "That's sweet; now I'll call you my little turtle dove, because you live on Tortola."

Smiling, Molly got up and gave Bill a hug. "That was nice; I'm going to miss you."

Looking deeply into her eyes, he struggled not to weaken. "Molly, don't worry, I'll see you again. You told me that there's a ferry that runs to St. John. Just take it over, and I'll be sure to pick you up."

Sitting back down, Molly frowned. "It all sounds good, but I'm not so sure that it'll work."

Bill wasn't in the mood for confrontation and tried to avoid it at all costs. "Look, I need to get away from the crowds. The B.V.I.'s has been overtaken by the charter boat business, and now they have cruise ships that invade the shores of Tortola; what's next? Gambling casinos? I don't want any part of it."

"Bill, I hear you." She was quiet for a while, then spoke. "When we reach Soper's Hole, I'll guide you through the channel. The buoys and markers of the ferry boat operations can be confusing. Once we get inside the harbor, you'll need to go to Sunsail's dock. That's the charter service I work for. I rent an apartment from them. You can drop me off there."

Bill wanted to clear the air between them but couldn't bring himself to, as he couldn't justify his motive on leaving so soon.

He was afraid of his true feelings and was suppressing his emotions. He needed his space right now.

Working together they navigated the approach to and through the harbor, making it to the dock without a mishap. After exchanging cell phone numbers, they bid one another good-bye.

"Molly, I'll call you. I promise."

With her duffle bag, and snorkel gear in hand Molly jumped onto the dock. Walking away, she turned quickly, waving good bye, unable to hide the tears glistening in her eyes.

Watching her with a somber look, Bill rubbed moisture from his eyes and turned away.

***

Reviewing the passage from Tortola to St. John, Bill was confident of the course. Sailing toward St. John, hoped his searching would lead him to his ideal spot of paradise.

Bill enjoyed being one with his boat. The seas were calm, slowly easing the thoughts of leaving Molly. Reaching for the cell phone in his pocket, he pushed on Mike's number. The phone only rang twice when Mike answered.

"Hey, Mike, how ya doing?"

"Fine. What's happening?"

"I'm on my way to St. John. Like I told you, I'm trying to get away from the crowds. The B.V.I.'s are beautiful but much too busy for me right now."

"What about the girl?" Mike asked. "Did you leave her behind?"

"Yep, I had to. She's too nice. I needed to put some space between us for a while. Things started happening too fast." Changing the subject quickly, Bill got straight to the point of his call. "Did you ever get a chance to drive by my old neighborhood?"

"As a matter of fact, I did that just yesterday. Your neighbor's house looks lived in. Everything was just the same as last time we saw it. What's going on? Why do you need to know?"

Bill chose his words carefully. "I don't really know, just wanted to see if he was still in town. I don't even know why I care." Once again he changed the subject. "Mike, you would love sailing here. It can't be compared to any other place I've been. It's really a true paradise. My course will put me in St. John in just about two hours. I'll have to go through customs again, now I'm heading back into American waters. It's just a formality. The process is easy, almost a joke. That's about it for now, gotta go. I'll call again soon."

"Okay, Bill, but for Pete's sake, be safe. So long." The phone shut off.

Bill put his cell phone back in his pocket, once again relishing in the idealistic conditions that surrounded him. The time passed quickly, and soon he approached the harbor surrounding Cruz Bay. Staying clear of the ferry channel, he easily slid aside the Port Authority dock in front of the customs office.

Bill knew that the ferry from St. Thomas was due to arrive within the next hour and was determined to get away from this dock before it arrived. It was a double decker with large twin engines that churned up the water, causing havoc with any of the boats trying to tie up to the dock.

Walking into the customs building, Bill introduced himself to the Customs officer and handed him his papers. He was quickly processed and paid his fee. Bill left the office but heard footsteps following close behind.

"You're going to have to move your boat now. This dock is for people here on official business. It's not a public dock," the Custom's officer said from behind him.

"Really? There's no one else here, and the rest of the dock is empty. There's enough room for the Navy!"

The Custom's officer looked official in his clean gray uniform. "Sorry, those are the rules. You'll have to move it or get a fine, and I don't want to do that to you."

Removing the lines from his boat, Bill motored it out toward nearby Lind Point. Anchoring his boat close to shore, he made sure it was set in place before launching his dinghy. He looked forward to exploring the small informal town, grabbing a bite to eat, and getting some local knowledge about quiet out-of-the-way places. He knew the National Park on the island was so vast that it encompassed three quarters of the island. First order of business was to find some kind of map.

Walking around the village for a while, he overheard the locals buzzing with excitement about Carnival week being just a week away. In a souvenir shop he found the guide book he was looking for and happily found a restaurant where he read about the island while enjoying some chicken wings and a cold beer.

The Ferry Boat from Red Hook arrived as Bill toured the town, and it remained in its berth waiting for the passengers to board for the trip back to St. Thomas. Passing by the ferry in his dingy on his way back to his sailboat, he noticed it was still empty, but people were lining up on the dock preparing for embarkation.

Climbing into the sailboat's cockpit, he rested on the bench seat, where he continued to thumb through the guide, mapping out his plan of action.

The large engines on the ferry boat came to life, and the noise startled Bill. He tried to ignore the loud noise, focusing on the page he had been reading. But the movement of the large ferry disturbed him again.

Looking up, he froze. A man and woman resembling the same couple he had seen in St. Thomas were staring at him. Only this time they appeared closer, and he saw them more clearly.

My God! It can't be!

He tried to turn away, but his eyes were riveted on the couple, smiling at each other. The man turned away from the woman and leaned over the railing to glare directly at Bill. Unfortunately, the woman started walking away before Bill could get a good view of her face.

"No! No! No! This has to stop!"

Bill looked back at the man who was outright smirking at him. *Jeez, he could be Richard's twin!*

Again he tried to tear his gaze away, but he couldn't do it. *This guy is tormenting me. Why? What's happening? I know Shirley is dead! And Mike said it looked as if Richard was still at his home in Mystic.*

Maybe he was just going crazy. And if he didn't get a grip, he was doomed.

***

Richard was pleased with himself. He turned to Shirley standing by his side. "That was good, Shirley; you did great, just as we planned. Did you see that jerk's face when he saw us? We're really messing with his mind now. That'll teach him a thing or two for trying to drown you."

Smiling as usual Shirley didn't understand what Richard meant; she just knew being by his side made Richard happy.

"All right now, Shirl, let's head below." Pointing to the staircase, Richard led Shirley down to the enclosed seating area. "We'll get close to the exit, so we can get off the ferry first and get a cab back to Charlotte Amelie. Our two-week vacation at the Frenchman's Reef is over, and we can't afford to miss our plane back to the states."

Following his instructions, Shirley descended through the hatchway down the stairs to the cabin below. Richard was reliving the crazy obsession he believed about his father and what a swine he was for drowning his mother. Harassing Bill made Richard feel superior, and the wickedness gave him a rush.

**

The ferry passed by Bill's boat, leaving only a rolling sea behind. Bill raised the sailboat's anchor and set sail in pursuit of the ferry. The speed of the ferry boat with its two large engines was no match for the sailboat, but Bill continued to chase it. By the time he reached Red Hook, the ferry boat was returning to St. John with a new set of passengers.

Bill anchored his sailboat among the others in the crowed harbor and went ashore in his dinghy. The building that housed the ferry boat operations was a large concrete structure. Even though the outside temperature was warm, the air in the building felt cold. Multiple ticket counters lined the walls of the building. Adjacent to the counters were rows of seats. They were placed like those found in airports except they weren't as comfortable. The room was crowded with people, who were standing, sitting, or just roaming around.

Finding the ticket counter for the ferry service to St. John, Bill burst in line and yelled at the clerk. "I need to see the roster for the passengers that were on the St. John ferry that reached there around noon today!"

A professionally dressed middle-age woman sat behind the counter. She was busy processing tickets for the passengers waiting in line. Bill demanded her attention, "Miss, did you hear me?"

The woman's eyes met his. "Yes sir, I did, but as you can see I'm busy; besides, that information is confidential unless you have an official decree signed by a judge." The woman continued selling tickets to the other people waiting in line, who were getting increasingly annoyed by Bill's behavior.

"Where is your manager?" Bill shouted.

The passengers grew more angry with Bill by the minute. One yelled. "Hey, big mouth, leave the girl alone, she's trying to do a job. Get the hell out of the way!"

Two large security guards with fire in their eyes approached Bill. They had been watching his outrage escalate and decided it was time to put a stop to his obnoxious behavior. Reaching Bill they flanked him, one on each side, hauling him aside. Bill felt like a dwarf between them.

"Mister, you need to leave," the officer in charge said. "Your behavior is upsetting our staff and the passengers."

Bill tried to shake loose of the guards. "Let me go. I didn't do anything wrong. I just need some vital information."

"I can call the police," said the larger of the two. "I'm sure they'll take the time to listen to you while you sit in their jail cell. Now calm down and leave the building."

Both guards took Bill by the arms and escorted him to the front door. "Wait a minute, I came by boat, and my dinghy is out back."

"Where is your dinghy?"

Bill pointed. "It's tied right over there."

"All right then, let's go over to it." Pushing Bill along, one of the guards yelled at the dock attendant. "Boy, bring my skiff over to the dinghy dock."

The marine patrol skiff arrived aside Bill's dinghy; and the large guard got into it. "Get into your dinghy. I'll follow you out to your sailboat. We don't need your kind causing trouble here. I assure you that I will remain by your side until you leave this harbor."

Bill had no choice, especially after noticing the gun in a holster located beside the controls of the boat next to the guard's seat. Ending up in jail was not an option. He accepted the fact that he just lost any chance to identify the man stalking him.

CHAPTER FIFTEEN

Bill was confused and discouraged as he was escorted from Red Hook. Reaching Bill's boat, the guard set him free. After tying his dinghy to the sailboat, Bill sailed his boat across the bay to America Yacht Harbor, the same place he had stayed the evening prior to his trip to Jost Van Dyke. Securing his sailboat to the mooring line, he used his dinghy to go ashore where he walked to the same dockside pub and ordered a beer.

Looking around the room he recognized a few men and greeted them with a smile. Fred moved to a seat closer to Bill. "Hey, buddy, what ya doin back here so soon?"

"The B.V. I.'s are beautiful, but with all the visitors on charter boat rentals, it was just too busy for me. I wasn't expecting the challenging part of finding a mooring in the harbors. And rude tourists pissed me off at the Baths during my snorkeling adventure. I'm looking for a more secluded and quiet neighborhood."

"The B.V. I.'s can be a lot of fun if you want to party, but it sounds like that's not your bag. If you want to be isolated you need to go back toward Puerto Rico. There are two small islands off the eastern side of the mainland. The smallest one, Culebra, is an out of the way place. It could be just what you're looking for."

"Sounds interesting; why isn't it over run by tourists like the rest of this area?"

"The islands were used for bombing practice during the Second World War, but the people started a series of protests back in the 1970s. The protests resulted in the U.S. Navy discontinuing the gunnery range, and in 1975 they moved their operation to the sister island Vieques to continue their bombing practices. That lasted about 20 years when the people there revolted. The Navy has posted much of the area on the islands as off limits while they clean up the battery of weapons left there, but they were kind enough to turn some of the land over to the islands as long as they used the land for wildlife preserves. Another down side is the fact there is no fresh water supply on Culebra. Much of it is shipped in by ferry to the town of Dewey. Of course most residents have their own cisterns."

"You guys should be travel agents. It sounds like a place I must visit."

"Yeah, you're right, we should be, but travel agents ain't our bag. Just sitting on our asses behind a desk isn't for us. To get there, you'll sail west. Once you're on the western edge of St. Thomas, it'll be another 12 miles. Ensenada Honda is one of the safest harbors in these islands. The approach is a little tricky though. There are lots of reefs and shallow areas, but if you follow your charts you'll be fine. Just make sure you know what the buoys indicate. There are several good anchorages far in behind the reefs. Trust me, you'll really be away from it all there."

"You've convinced me. I need to get back to my sailboat and chart a course. If I get an early start I should reach that harbor before dark." Bill got the bartender's attention and handed him some money. "Buy these guys a drink on me." He turned back to Fred. "Thanks, if I ever get back this way I'll stop by to fill you in on my travels."

Bill left the pub with yet another new mission in mind.

***

Bill stood on the porch outside the pub, looking over a forest of sailboat masts lining the harbor; past them and beyond his view was the eastern end of Tortola. Taking out his cell phone, he selected Molly's number from his menu but the call didn't go through.

He cursed when he realized the call this morning to Mike must have used up all the charge. Walking back through the pub's door, trying to save face, he said, "A guy walks into a bar."

"You forget something?" Fred asked.

"Nah, I need to make a phone call, and my cell phone's dead. Is there a landline in here?"

Fred held up his cell phone. "Here, use mine, but it's going to cost you another beer."

"You got it," Bill said and reached for the cell phone. Bill went back out on the porch and redialed Molly's number.

Anticipating Molly's answer, he watched the peaceful sailboats floating on their moorings. The phone rang only a few times before Molly spoke. "Hello?"

"Hi, there, it's Bill."

She gasped. "What's wrong? This isn't your number; are you okay?"

"Well, yes and no. I just wanted to tell you St. John didn't cut it. I'll be on my way east in the morning. I plan on trying an island called Culebra."

"All the way over there? Now I'll never see you again. Why are you tormenting me? What possibly could have gone wrong in St. John? It's beautiful there."

"Molly, just bear with me. We'll get together again, but I must move on. I've been told it's a peaceful place where I can be alone for a while."

"Okay, are you sure you are all right?"

"Yeah, everything's okay. I just wanted to let you know of my change of plans."

Molly stalled. "Thanks for that, I think." With a sharp edge to her voice she added, "Be careful, I know you're troubled."

The call ended. Looking at the phone, Bill was tempted to call her back, but there was nothing more to say. Returning to the bar, he slapped Fred's back and handed him his cell phone with a $5 bill. "Thanks. Now I'm outta here."

***

Rising early in the morning, Bill had a renewed spirit of adventure. After untying the mooring line holding his sailboat, he watched the line float away and started the small diesel engine which began to purr; he weaved his way around and through the multitude of sailboats moored in the harbor.

Entering the channel between great St. James Island and Cowpet Bay, he set his course south of Buck Island, leading him to open water but keeping him clear of the cruise ship lanes.

Clearing the channel markers, he shut off the boat's engine and raised the sails. It was quiet, and he was in the most beautiful cruising area in the world. A fresh breeze kept the boat on a perfect reach. Standing behind the helm he felt the constant wind brush against his body, and he marveled at the splendor of the sea. Sea birds charged to and fro about the sky, chasing each other, some splashing into the water in search of fish. One even hitched a ride on the rigging for a while.

His day was uneventful, and he arrived at Culebra shortly after 5 p.m. He was pleased with his navigation equipment, the GPS was spot on, and the auto pilot had followed all the waypoints. Now he needed to use his dead reckoning skills. Reexamining the government issued charts helped him identify the buoys and avoid the reefs and shoals. Sailing into the harbor he could see that the island was an unpretentious little paradise.

Navigating deeper into Ensenada Honda, he searched for the out of the way spot he had been told about. Sailing past the main town of Dewey, he noticed a ferry boat at the dock used to accommodate goods and passengers coming from Puerto Rico. A surprise encounter with the couple stalking him would be highly unlikely here.

Once past the busy activity of the town, he brought in the sails; turned on the boat's engine and moved slowly through the harbor, searching for the coves on the north coast. He was finally relieved to reaching the spot he was looking for. Turning off the boat's engine, he anchored behind a reef, knowing it would provide good shelter.

Covering his equipment, he sat down in the cockpit and sighed. The clear turquoise water glowed in the late afternoon sunlight. At the shoreline, a steep cliff ascended out of the water. It was covered by a subtropical mangrove forest. Further along the shore he saw white sandy beaches and dirt roads without traffic. It was a serene and undisturbed island. He smiled to himself as he envisioned spending hours of rewarding beachcombing on miles of unspoiled sand.

***

Bill slept peacefully; he was relaxed and satisfied with his decision to come to Culebra and happy he'd found a place close to nature. It was what he had hoped to find since he last spoke with Dr. Green, which seemed so long ago.

In the morning, Bill reacted with enthusiasm to the area surrounding him, so picturesque and tranquil. Across the harbor a large ferry boat was docking at the terminal in the town of Dewey, the main town on the island and the hub of activity.

Watching he saw a few people exiting the ferry. There didn't seem to be many visitors arriving. Most of the activity was with men delivering supplies such as food and water. Bill continued watching the commotion and the worker hustling about unloading the cargo from the ferry boat. It took a while for the activity to subside before Bill decided it was time to venture out.

Bill was curious and anxious to explore his new-found home. Climbing into his dinghy, first priming the gas with three hard pumps on the small black ball located on the gas line, then pulling on the ignition rope, the motor started instantly; it hummed as he headed over to the dock in front of a restaurant named The Dinghy Dock. While tying up, he smelled coffee mingling with the scent of newly baked bread, making him hungry.

Entering the place, he found a seat overlooking the dock and harbor. The staff was busy serving the customers that filled the room, but soon a middle-aged man greeted him. "Hi, I'm Mel, and I own this place. You're new here. Are you just passing through or will you be with us for a while?"

Bill eyed the man with an apron covering his t-shirt and shorts. His black hair was tied back, and his trimmed black beard was showing stands of silver.

"Glad to meet you, I'm Bill." He smiled at Mel. "I hope to be around for a while. My sailboat is anchored across the harbor. I'm hungry, what's good?"

"Today's breakfast special is French toast with rum and coconut."

"Don't go any further. I'll have that and a black coffee."

"Good choice; this place is where cruisers like you congregate. You'll get a chance to meet the locals if you stay around."

"Thanks."

Mel left, and a young dark-haired girl returned with a piping hot cup of black coffee. "I believe this is for you. I'll be back for your order; if you need anything else, my name is Jennifer."

"Mel took my order. Check with him."

From his table Bill saw his dinghy banging against the one next to it. Straightening, he focused on the dinghies. *What the hell's going on? There's something under all the boats. Do they have their own sea monster?*

97

"Hey Jennifer," he called out. "Can you tell me what's all that action around the dinghies?"

"Oh, the tarpon are messing with them. Every afternoon during happy hour the tarpon get fed. Those guys are just hanging around looking for handouts." She hurried toward another table where a patron was trying to get her attention.

Bill busied himself watching the action of the fish while he sipped on his the coffee. People filtered into the place, some with computers, others with cell phones. Bill remembered reading that the restaurant had a Wi-Fi connection which people used to keep in touch with the rest of the world.

Jennifer returned to fill up Bill's empty cup with hot coffee. She assured him that his order was placed. Bill relaxed while he waited for his breakfast to be served. When it came, it delighted Bill's palate, and he ate with gusto.

Seeing his empty plate, Jennifer returned to clear the dishes. "Is there anything else I can get for you?"

"No, that's it, just a check. Do you mind if I stay here for a while?"

"That'll be fine. It'll give you a chance to meet some of our locals. You might hear the rumors about the abductions of several women on the island of Vieques."

"Sounds like something I should know about. Fill me in."

"Well, it's been going on for some time. Every so often a woman disappears, and no one has been able to discover what happened to her. No clues or traces of their whereabouts have ever been found. It's a real mystery and very uncomfortable for all us here. We wonder if it will start happening on Culebra."

"What's being done? If everyone so concerned, why don't you notify the FBI?"

"That's part of the problem; the local police want to handle it themselves and don't want any interference from the U.S. government. I don't think you know it, but the Navy messed up this area for a long time, and the people here have a lot of hostile resentment toward the U.S."

"Oh, really? Don't you think they could help find some clues and try to end the problem?"

"I can't say, maybe, maybe not, that's just the way it is around here. I'll get your bill, sorry to have burdened you with the news on your first day here."

Jennifer left Bill sitting at his table, thinking *you can't get away from crazies even in paradise?"*

***

After paying the tab, Bill sat at his table looking at the activity in the harbor. He was lost in his thoughts when a handsome, clean-cut man in his early forties approached him. He had brown hair, stood about 5'8" tall, was clean shaven, and dressed in casual attire. "Hi, my name is Brad; you look like a newbie, and I just wanted to welcome you to Dewey. Do you mind if I join you?"

Wanting to know more about the area, Bill agreed. "Have a seat, I hope to stay around for a bit. I've been to St. Thomas and the BVI, but was disillusioned with both. I'm looking for a quiet out-of-the-way spot to relax for a few months."

"You've made a good choice; those other islands are just too commercialized, but that's what draws the tourists, and the islands need their money. You'll find a bunch of expats here, along with some hippie types who act like it's still the sixties, along with some unique, and delightful individuals who can't be categorized. The attitude on Culebra is live and let live.

"How long have you lived here?"

Brad grinned. "My girl and I have lived here a couple of years. We are planning a big wedding soon. If you're still around you're welcome to come to it."

"Thanks, I might do that. Where do you and your girl stay?"

"We're at a beautiful quiet villa across the harbor. It's a hostel. They rent rooms and are looking for long-term renters. They have a dock that can accommodate up to eight boats. The largest slip will hold up to a 40-foot boat."

"Do you own your own boat?"

"Yes, sir, my girl and I have a 32-foot Sea Ray that we stay on. They made an exception for us as we help them with the maintenance. The owners are retired. We do all kinds of odd jobs and take care of the dock."

Bill's was eager to know more. "Sounds like a place I'd like. Do

99

they have water and electricity on the dock?"

"They have a cistern; you know there is no fresh water on the island. The water supply is brought on ferry boats from the mainland."

"I heard that but keep forgetting. My boat is equipped with a desalinization unit, so that isn't a concern of mine. Where'd you say this place was?"

"Just follow the channel as if you're leaving the harbor. You'll find it by the front of the bay."

Bill was intrigued. "Thanks, Brad, maybe I'll see you there."

Brad took the hint and stood up to leave. "Good luck, Bill, I'll be looking for you."

After leaving the restaurant, Bill stood by his dinghy to watch the Tarpon in the water and found himself thinking about the hostel. He was happy with his anchorage but knew he shouldn't isolate himself completely. Deciding to take a dingy ride, he set out to see what the hostel offered.

It was a leisurely half hour trip to the mouth of the harbor. Following the channel markers, Bill arrived at Marker 6 and headed toward shore. A large sign welcomed him to the Hostel Casa Culebra. He guided his dinghy up to the dock where the atmosphere seemed quiet and comfortable. The dock would be a perfect spot for his sailboat.

Pulling up to the dock he was greeted by a tall lanky person dressed in a two-piece pink bathing suit. With large hands, the person was built like a man and walked with an uncoordinated gait on long legs. Bill couldn't tell if the person was a man or a woman. He or she had a receding hairline but the hair on the back of the head was long and tied into a ponytail with a pink bow.

When the person spoke, it was with a pleasant feminine voice. "Hi, would you like me to help you tie your dinghy to the dock?"

Bill stared at the strange get up on the person when he realized he should respond. "Sure, let me hand you a line." Holding up a rope, he gave it to the helpful character. "Thanks."

"Here, let me help you out." The person extended an oversized hand.

Bill shook his head. "No, I'm fine." Once on the dock, Bill asked, "Do you own this place?"

"Oh, no, I'm Sammi, and that's spelled with an *i*. My boyfriend, and I help the owners. You'll find Mickey and Gertie inside. This is a real nice place; you'll see."

Trying not to laugh, Bill walked toward the building at the end of the dock. The hostel was a small complex which seemed to be well constructed. Entering the building he saw a hippy looking, gray-haired man with a matching gray beard sitting at a table. He was casually dressed in shorts and a t-shirt and wore flip-flops on his feet. His attention was on an opened boating magazine.

Bill interrupted his concentration. "Excuse me, I'm looking for Mickey."

The man whose glasses sat at the edge of his nose peered over the top of the lenses. "That'll be me. How can I help you?"

"Well, I just met Miss Spanish Virgin Islands out on the dock; she sent me here to talk with you about your place."

"Sammi?"

"Yep, that's the name, spelled with an *i*."

"He's a real character, loves to dress like a woman, and that's okay, he's as nice as can be. He and his friend Brad have lived here on their boat at the end of the dock for some time. They help me and the missus out around our place. They're decent people, just somewhat eccentric, but then aren't we all in our own way?"

Bill nodded. "You've got a point. I'm new to the area, and I met Brad at The Dinghy Dock in Dewy. He recommended your place,. so I took a ride over here to see for myself."

"We have apartments, seven of them, and they're fully furnished. Each is equipped with a large balcony. It's a quiet place, no place for rowdy types, and no smoking allowed. We have an open gazebo, a small library and game tables for people to gather and visit. Our goal is for you to enjoy the rhythm of Culebra and be at peace with nature. Occasionally we'll get a bunch of people who want to rent a number of the rooms for a week or so, but for the most part, it's just us or a transient sailor or two."

"Sounds ideal; would you mind if I stayed on my 36-foot sailboat and tied it to your dock?"

"We don't cater to live-a-boards."

"Why's that? I'm alone; what's the difference if I rent an

apartment or tie my boat up to your dock? If it's the money, I'll pay you a reasonable fee. I plan to be around here for some time."

Mickey got out of his chair, "I'll discuss it with my wife. Make yourself comfortable, I'll be back."

Bill didn't sit down, instead he walked around, eyeing the surroundings. The hostel was a great place, back to nature, just what the doctor ordered. A large work shop in the back of the building housed the apartments. There were seven numbered parking places in the back yard. The floating dock was in good condition. He scanned the perfectively clear water when he heard a woman's voice behind him. Bill turned around to face a pleasant, petite and slightly chubby woman with short curly salt and pepper hair. She wore glasses, and her face displayed a wide grin.

"Hi, I'm Gertie; Mickey tells me that you are interested in staying at our dock on your sailboat. As he told you, we don't usually allow that. We have made an exception for Sammi and Brad, because they help us maintain our facility. What's your name?"

"Bill. Bill Adams."

"Good; Bill, we've decided to give you a chance, but there will be no dumping of waste from your boat into the water. You must use our facilities for that, which comes with an extra charge."

Bill was pleased. "Just draw up a rental agreement contract. I'll be back with my boat in a few days. How's that sound?"

"Sounds good to me, see you then."

Satisfied with the arrangement, Bill walked back to his dinghy. Looking toward the Sea Ray, he caught sight of Sammi and waved from dingy as he headed back to town.

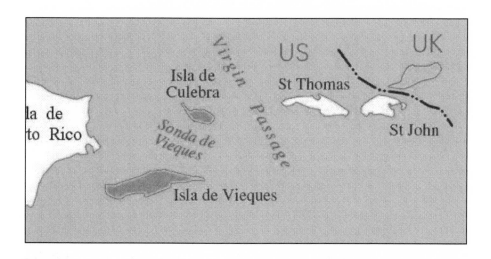

The U.S. Virgin Islands, officially the Virgin Islands of the United States, is a group of islands in the Caribbean that is an insular area of the United States located east of Puerto Rico. The islands are geographically part of the Virgin Islands archipelago and are located in the Leeward Islands of the Lesser Antilles. It is the easternmost point and territory of the United States.

Puerto Rico, officially the Commonwealth of Puerto Rico and briefly called Porto Rico, is an unincorporated territory of the United States located in the northeast Caribbean Sea, west of Isla de Culebra, Isla de Vieques and St. Thomas.

CHAPTER SIXTEEN

Bill took his time returning to his sailboat, taking in the sights, and sounds surrounding him. The water was crystal clear, and the air felt inviting with a light breeze, just enough to create a growing feeling of tranquility. He was content with this spot. It was as he envisioned it, a place for him to reflect on life, to bring a purpose to it.

Leaving the main channel, Bill aimed his dinghy into a small picturesque bay. Hidden within the beautiful blue water and white sandy cove was a fabulous high-end marina and resort, The Club Seaborne. The dinghy slowly putted by until its small motor began kicking up sand.

"Damn it;" he sputtered as he ran into the shallows. Pressing a button on the motor he raised the propeller. Taking the oar out of the oarlock, he pushed the oar deep into the sand and kept pushing on the oar until the small boat was free. Turning the boat around and putting the propeller back down, Bill got under way again, retracing his course past the splendid marina and the mega yachts that filled the slips. He considered the grandeur of the moment and was content to enjoy the solitude of a quieter area.

Bill delighted in his aimless wandering and looked through his guide book for some of recommended sites. There were numerous beaches scattered about the island. At a quick glance he noted ten. Also, there were three smaller islands off Culebra offering spectacular snorkeling.

Returning to his sailboat, Bill spent the next few days getting his bearings and relaxing at the beaches around Dewey. As he became more familiar with the area, he eased himself into a morning routine. First thing on the agenda was breakfast at The Dinghy Dock with its mouthwatering menu and access to Wi-Fi.

However, there were no cell towers on the island, so he couldn't call Mike or Molly.

Bill entered The Dinghy Dock and sat at a table close to a window so he could keep an eye on his boat. Dressed in his usual attire covered by a white apron, Mel was busy visiting his customers, checking to see if they were satisfied with their meals.

Soon he arrived at Bill's table. "How's everything going, Bill? Are you still planning to hang out with us?"

"Mel, you've got me. This place is great. I'm sticking around."

"In that case, feel free to use our Wi-Fi connection anytime. We're glad to have your kind here."

Bill wasn't quite sure what his kind was, but it seemed to please Mel, so that's a good thing. The following morning, before setting out for his tasty breakfast, he placed his securely protected laptop in his dinghy.

Taking a seat at his favorite table by the widow, he looked forward to seeing Jennifer's friendly face, and she arrived within moments. "Good morning, Bill."

"Good day, sunshine. I'll have the French Toast special and a coffee." Jennifer was efficient but didn't have time to visit. As soon as she took his order, she scurried off.

Bill set up his laptop, established the Wi-Fi link, and wrote Mike a note.

Hey, Mike, I'm living on the island of Culebra off the eastern shore of Puerto Rico. Seems I've found the place I've been looking for. Think I'll stay here.

He re-read the message, and satisfied with the content, he pushed *send*. Mission accomplished: the most important thing for Bill was to keep in touch with Mike. He was the only person in the world that he could rely on.

Reaching into the deep pocket of his shorts, Bill removed a folded piece of paper with the e-mail address of Sunsail's charter boat operation on Tortola. Composing the new e-mail, he placed Molly's name on the subject line.

During their last conversation, he had promised her that he would keep in touch. He had enjoyed her company and had to admit to himself that he missed her. however, he carefully guarded the door to his heart, afraid of tempting fate.

As he composed a letter, he was careful to conceal his feelings of the special connection he had developed for her, but inside, those feelings were impossible to dismiss. After finishing the bit of news, he proof read it:

Sunsail charter boat operation@aol.com
Molly Tynin, Charter Boat Captain

Hi, Molly, just want to let you know I've found my ideal place here on Culebra. I'll be keeping my boat at a dock that belongs to the Hostel Casa Culebra. It's a quiet, comfortable spot close to the mouth of Ensenada Honda Bay. I wanted to call you, but my cell phone does not work here. I'm at The Dinghy Dock restaurant in the town of Dewey where they have WIFI access. I'd like to hear from you.

Bill

Hesitating for a moment before sending the message; he wondered if she would respond. He knew she was disappointed with him, which was evident by her curt reply after their last conversation. Thinking she wouldn't want anything to do with him, he dismissed his negative thoughts and closed the laptop. Wrapping it back in the towel, he left The Dinghy Dock to return to his sailboat.

He was anxious now and ready to move to his new location. Hauling the anchor, then raising the main sail, he navigated his boat on a leisurely cruise through the bay, a relaxing journey. After arriving at the Hostel, he skillfully maneuvered his boat parallel to the floating dock. Mickey ran alongside the boat to help with the lines. Within a few minutes Bill's sailboat was secured in place.

"Thanks, Mickey, you made that easy."

"Just part of the services we offer!" Mickey grinned.

Bill pointed to the empty slip at the end of the dock. "What happened to the Sea Ray?"

"You mean Brad and Sammi's boat?"

Bill nodded. "That's the one."

"They went to Vieques, to help with a maintenance project being conducted at a high end resort. They go there a few times a year when the resort has a major construction project or an upgrade. The pay is too good to refuse. The W Retreat and Spa on Vieques is a mega-resort plush with luxury. They cater to the rich and famous. Quite a change from the rustic environment of the rest of the island. It is located on a low cliff right on the beach. It boasts three lavish restaurants, a lounge, fitness room, a spa, tennis courts, a business center and infinity pool. With all those amenities it's vital that the complex be keep in the best condition always. Don't worry, though, they'll be back this way soon. Now get yourself settled, and let me or Gertie know if you need anything." With a wave, Mickey headed back to his complex.

Checking the lines, Bill secured the boat's halyards, his regular routine to prevent them from banging all night and upon inspection, his work met his satisfaction.

Finished for the day, it was time to chill out in the cockpit with a cold beer. Settled into his Captain's chair, he propping his feet up and opened the Soundings Magazine for an enjoyable read.

The following morning Bill decided to skip breakfast at The Dinghy Dock. Instead, he roamed around the hostel, taking in the picturesque tranquility of the undeveloped hamlet. The array of strange sea birds flying by intrigued him. He planned his days activities while sipping a cup of coffee and listening to the birds chirping.

Back on his sailboat, he opened the hatch of the sail locker on the starboard side of the cockpit, moved some lines aside and lifted out a folding bicycle. Anticipating an exploration of the beaches at this end of the island, he assembled the contraption before collecting articles he might need and stored them in a small basket secured between the handle bars. A towel, sunscreen, and a pair of binoculars topped off the storage area.

Then Bill gave each tire a few pumps of air with the portable pump for good measure. Putting on a hat, he rode his bike off the dock and onto a dirt road which was rough; he found himself pumping extra hard at times, telling himself that he needed the aerobic exercise.

The area surrounding him was sparsely populated and relatively isolated. When he came upon a well-worn path leading toward the water, he pointed his bike toward the vacant beach, no more than a small strip of sand. Ashes in the fire-pits still held the smell of a recent burn.

Water quietly lapped the shore. Resting the bike on its side, Bill took his binoculars from the basket, adjusted the strap over his head, kicked off his sandals, and walked toward the surf.

Taking a closer look through the binoculars, he could clearly identify the islands of Cayo Norte and Culebrita, where a lighthouse sat on its highest point. It's doors and windows were gone, and part of the roof was collapsed. The weather and time had taken their toll on the once stellar building. Making a mental note, he vowed to take a closer look. From his view point it appeared as though there would be some awesome sights from the top of the old structure. The other island was in a northerly direction. He was unable to see much of the area but had heard that snorkeling on the south side of Cayo Norte was not to be missed.

Returning to his bike, he slipped on his sandals and pushed it along the path to the dirt road. Climbing back on the bike, he pedaled along the road, which curved around the outline of the shore.

Further along the road he found another path heading toward the shoreline—it was densely overgrown and riding on his bike toward the beach was not an option. Bound to investigate, he continuing on foot. Making his way through an array of prickly bushes, he received several nasty scratches on his legs. Cobwebs covered the pathway, causing him to constantly wipe them away from his face. Finally, he reached a completely deserted stretch of white sand.

The surf was rough, too rough for swimming, especially without seeing another living soul for miles around. Bill was determined he wasn't going back through the briar patch without having a look around. The beach was crescent-shaped, and for someone seeking total isolation, it would be a great place to relax with a good book.

Walking along the water's edge, the clear, clean sea with white froth rushed on shore. The current was swift, giving him the impression there must be a strong riptide. He continued along the shoreline which was littered with an abundance of shells. Beachcombers would be in seventh heaven with all the shapes and sizes of colorful mollusk shells and sea glass scattered about the shore.

Kicking sand into the air, Bill relished his ultimate freedom. Looking into the surf, something caught his eye, causing him to do a double take. Something was bobbing about in the waves. He lifted his binoculars up to his eyes, so he could get a better view. At first glance, he thought it was a manatee, but it wasn't moving. His curiosity forced him into the surf. The undertow griped his legs, which caused him to hesitate. Just a few more steps, and he'd reach the object, but the water was getting deeper. Good thing it was warm.

Finally, he discovered the remains of a drop tank used on military bombers, probably an auxiliary tank from an airplane used to carry an extra fuel supply. This area had been used as a training range for the Navy. Jennifer at the Dinghy Dock had explained to him how much the locals resented the Navy's abuse of the island.

The Corps of Engineers had posted signs on the potentially contaminated areas on the island. Not finding any signs here, Bill felt that the tank was not a threat to the people or the environment.

The tank was half submerged in the sand, and as he slogged in the surf around the tank, Bill went even deeper into the water, its force causing him to lose his balance. He fell into the surf where the force of the waves slammed him head first into the tank.

Grasping the tank for stability, he was able to stand up and resist the strong undertow. Holding the tank with one hand, he rubbed his injured head with the other. Once again he lost his footing and fell back into the water.

With a free hand, he bracing himself on the tank once more before noticing that his hand was covered with blood.

"Damn!" His head pounded with pain, and the saltwater stung the scratches on his legs.

Although his discovery was intriguing, drowning was not an option, and he slogged back to the beach and through the jungle of brambles. Back at the bike, he wiped himself down with the dry towel and headed back to the hostel and his sailboat.

CHAPTER SEVENTEEN

Bill felt better in the morning, as he recovered from the scratches, and bruises from his expedition through the jungle. The big lump underneath the hair on his head throbbed. The ice pack he placed on it last night was nothing but warm water now. The scratches on his legs itched more than they hurt.

He hoped the Advil he just took would work quickly. Looking around the galley he debated on whether or not he should start a pot of coffee for himself. The more he procrastinated the more the tasty breakfasts at The Dinghy Dock seemed a better option. His mind was made up. He'd go there for breakfast, and while there he could check for replies to his e-mail messages.

His laptop was still wrapped in a plastic cover. Taking hold of it, he placed it on the bench seat in the cockpit of the sailboat, while he prepared to launch his dinghy. When the dinghy was alongside the boat he took his delicate package, placing it gently aside him and headed toward the town of Dewey.

As usual The Dinghy Dock was packed with small water craft tightly crowded together, bobbing on their lines while the Tarpon swam below them. Bill waited patiently for a couple in a Carolina Skiff to leave. Waving to them as they passed by, he hastily took the vacant spot. Clutching the laptop, he entered the restaurant, packed and abuzz with conversations competing with the tingling of dishes.

Finding a small table, he sat down. He was beginning to recognize people's faces but hadn't taken the time to befriend any of them. All in good time.

A new waitress approached the table. "Hi, I'm Annie, and I'll be your server today. Would you like a cup of coffee?

"Sure, I like it black," Bill said, smiling back at her. "I haven't seen you here before, are you new?"

"Oh, no. I usually work in the afternoon. What about you? Are you passing through or staying with us?"

111

"I'll be around for a while. I live on my sailboat and currently rent dock space at the hostel."

Annie stopped in mid-pour, the coffee pot suspended above the half-filled cup. "Isn't that where Brad and Sammi live?'

"Yeah, same place."

Annie finished pouring and reached for a small bowl of coffee creamer from the next table, using its placement in front of Bill as a cover to learn closer. When she spoke, her voice was low and shook a bit. "I hope you're not traveling with any women?" she asked.

"No, but what if I was?"

"Then I'd be warning you about the one called Sammi. He's a strange one, dressing like a woman all the time. But he likes women almost as much as he likes Brad, if you get my drift. I heard he tried to molest a woman tourist when she lagged behind her tour group. The only reason she didn't get raped or even kidnapped was because another person on the tour noticed she was standing too close to a person who was dressed like a woman but obviously wasn't a female. The tour guide rescued her just as Sammi was trying to pull her into a shack behind the store the group had been visiting."

Bill was always skeptical of local gossip. "Maybe the tourist was the hysterical type," he said, trying to dismiss Annie's information.

"Nope," she said, standing up straight but still speaking in a low voice. "It's just one of many stories about those two. Now," she said, her voice resuming its normal sound, "what would you like for breakfast?"

Bill was relieved when the waitress headed to the kitchen with his order. He now had time to check his email and he reached for his laptop. Two new items appeared at the top of the email. The first was from Mike, who started off with a brotherly lecture followed with words of caution. Then Mike touched a bit on some work projects and some plans he and Wendy were making for the weekend. Finally he turned to the news of his recent trip to Richard's house in Bill's old neighborhood. It seems that the yard was not being cared for as in the past and looked shabby, as though no one was home, or perhaps someone was ill and unable to keep up with the maintenance. It ended with, "I'll keep you posted."

Bill gazed numbly at the screen, spooked by Mike's information about Richard's house looking unoccupied. A wave of paranoia clawed at him, and he zoned out with its intensity.

Annie returned to his table offering more coffee. When Bill didn't answer at first, the waitress simply leaned forward to top off his cup.

Her shadow caused Bill to jump in his seat. "Huh? Oh, I didn't hear you there for a minute. Thanks." The aroma of the fresh coffee teased his brain into awareness, and to cover his embarrassment, he raised the cup to his mouth. The hot tasty liquid almost scalded his lips, causing him to swallow quickly.

"Your breakfast will be out in five," Annie said before moving to the next table with refills.

Just enough time to read one more email entry. It was from Molly who surprised him with the news that she was planning to visit him for a week. And that she was arriving in Culebra the following morning! She instructed him to monitor his VHF on channel 16, because she would need a lift. "Pick me up at the mouth of Ensenada Honda."

Holy crap! What's happening? I finally find a place that seems ideal. A perfect place for me, and now I'm having overwhelming thoughts of persecution by Richard and on top of that, I have a compelling desire to be with a woman I hardly know.

Where was Dr. Green when he needed her! She was no longer within driving distance, and he panicked for a long moment. Then his pulse slowed along with his heartbeat as he realized that Molly was the only person he was vaguely comfortable talking to here in the islands.

No way was he going to turn her away this time.

Without belaboring a response, he quickly typed his answer: "Molly, I'll be awaiting your call. Bill." Taking in a deep breath, he closed the laptop, knowing his breakfast would arrive shortly.

***

The next morning Bill couldn't stay still, and pacing back and forth on the dock next to his sailboat didn't help. He didn't want to wander far from his radio for fear of missing Molly's call. As the morning wore on, he still hadn't received a call or signal from Molly. He checked the VHF to verify it was set on channel 16, the Coast Guard channel boaters used for official business. The dial hadn't moved.

Heading to the galley to pour himself another cup of coffee, Bill heard the distinctive drone of an airplane's engine, and it concerned him. The airport on Culebra was north of Dewey, but he sound came from just above his boat. Someone may be in trouble, he thought, and just as he was about to head up top, he heard Molly's voice over the VHF.

"Bill Adams, this is Molly. I'm here!"

Bill grabbed the microphone from the VHF cradle. "Molly, I hear you. On my way."

Jumping into the dinghy floating alongside his boat, Bill turned toward the mouth of the harbor where he spotted a green and white Cessna 172 float plane dancing on the water.

Bill cut the speed on his outboard motor, allowing the dingy to come to a gentle stop. In the next moment, the float plane came to a stop a mere few feet from his dinghy.

The fuselage door swung open to reveal Molly's curly red mop whipping around in the ocean breeze.

"What took you so long?" she asked with a wide smile.

Bill's heart pounded with pure happiness. "I didn't know my special delivery package was arriving by air. Nice touch."

A familiar face appeared behind Molly's shoulder. "Bill, you remember Tom? He dropped me off at your sailboat when you were anchored in Jost Van Dyke."

"Nice to see you again, Tom. You seem to be Molly's transportation specialist."

Tom grinned, showing a set of pure white teeth. "I do my best to help Miss Molly."

"Tom lives on a houseboat anchored off Buck Island. He has a boat, this plane, and a bicycle. Prepared for any circumstances."

Tom laughed. "Speaking of circumstances, I'm due back home— got some folks coming for an afternoon barbeque. So just ease your dinghy closer," he instructed Bill. "I think Molly's eager to see your new digs."

As Bill maneuvered the dinghy close to the plane, Molly handed a duffel bag and snorkel gear to Bill who stowed it up front, giving Molly room to lower herself down into the boat where she settled in next to Bill.

"Okay, Tom, you're off duty. I'll see you back here in a week!

Thanks for the lift."

As Bill guided the dinghy away from the floats, Tom eased the plane forward, the engine purring and the propeller whirling. Soon one float lifted up, leaving the other skimming along the water for brief seconds. Then the craft lifted into the air and turned toward the BVI.

Then Molly gave Bill a big hug and pulled back to take a good look at him. She immediately noticed the scratches on his arms and legs. "What happened to you? Looks like you got into it with some coral."

"Not quite coral, just some very mean briers."

"Briers? What were you doing in briers? Picking berries?"

Bill laughed. "Forget it. What's important now is that you are here!" He knew that his eyes were sparkling with joy.

Molly laughed also. "I'm so glad you asked me to come to see you here. After reading your note, I couldn't wait another minute. You'll have to fill me in on all your adventures."

"Who invited who?" Bill teased. "I'm glad you're here, too. There are so many places to explore around here. I haven't seen many of them, so it will be great to experience the sights together. I want to warn you, though, night life as you know it doesn't exist on this island. It's not like the BVI's where life is a nonstop party"

Molly smile was a ray of sunshine. "I'm not worried; we'll make our own night life!"

Bill changed the subject quickly to avoid answering her. "Here we are!" he said as he slowed the dinghy at the entrance to the marina. Let's unload your gear onto my boat, then I'll show you around the hostel."

"Perfect!" Molly's spontaneity and warmth was contagious. "I've never been in these waters before. Not far from Tortola, and from what I can see, this place doesn't seem that much different."

"Well, a word of warning; there is no water supply on this island so you won't be able to bathe while you're staying with me."

Molly wrinkled her nose. "Tell me you're lying."

"No, it's true, the first part, that is. Water is transported from Puerto Rico on the ferry boat, plus the islanders have cisterns to catch the rain water. But the peaceful, quiet nights, with uncrowded harbors make up for any inconveniences."

Wide-eyed, Molly turned to look Bill in the eyes. "All that's well and good, but the BVI's have that, too—it's just a matter of taking the time to find that certain spot. They have some beautiful places off the beaten path. Besides, you know as well as I, the tourists like the noise, and excitement."

"Okay, you win; if this was another time in my life, I'm sure I would have enjoyed it as much as the others. But I do like it here. It's just what I need right now, and soon you'll see it suits me just fine."

Molly nodded at him and turned quiet for a spell, taking the time to inspect the island's sights and sounds. "There sure are a lot of birds flying around."

"Yes! Look up!" Molly looked in the direction Bill was pointing. "There goes a flock of terns, just one of the many species of birds that live here and also in the a bird sanctuary near here. I'm not sure exactly where it's located, but by the looks of it, the whole island should be part of it!"

Bill slowed the speed of his dinghy as it approached his sailboat. "Molly, just tie the line to the dock behind my boat," he instructed.

Molly expertly got a line from the bow and waited as Bill shut the motor off and allowed the dinghy to float smoothly into the dock. Jumping out, Molly quickly wrapped the line around a cleat, securing the smaller boat to the dock.

Bill handed her the duffel bag and snorkel gear before getting out of the dinghy and then carried her belongings onto his sailboat.

After descending into the cabin, Molly glanced around, seeing there were no changes since her last visit. Shirley's picture remained in clear sight.

Bill escorted Molly to the aft cabin. "You can put your stuff in here."

Molly frowned. "I don't want to be isolated back here! I thought I'd bunk with you."

Bill took in a deep breath before replying. "Look, Molly, I'm not ready to be intimate with you just yet. I simply want to enjoy our friendship for a while."

Molly studied Bill's serious face for a few long moment before answering. "Okay, I agree, but can we cuddle like we did in Jost Van Dyke. Wasn't that nice?"

Bill's face relaxed. "Maybe just snuggling, but nothing else. Really, Molly, I'm not ready. I still have unresolved issues."

"I can see that," Molly said in a very quiet voice before marching herself into the forward stateroom to unpack her belongings.

CHAPTER EIGHTEEN

Walking hand in hand along the dock, the two headed to the marina office where Bill introduced Molly to Mickey and Gertie. Molly was curious about the hostel and took the couple's offer to show them around the place. Finished with the tour, she and Bill returned to his dinghy, taking the boat out to the bay, making their way to the town of Dewey.

Taking Molly to Flamenco Beach was Bill's main goal as the beach had a reputation as one of the most beautiful beaches in the world. They spent the remainder of the afternoon relaxing in the surf and enjoying the beach.

Leaving just before sunset as the air began to cool, they headed to Mamacita's restaurant which Bill said was a quiet place to eat. When Bill opened the door to the restaurant, the sound of soft music ushered them inside.

"You're right, Bill, this is the perfect place for an intimate dinner," Molly said as they toasted their reunion with a glass of sparkling white wine.

The following days went by quickly. Bill and Molly spent their time sailing his boat to the smaller islands surrounding Culebra. They hiked to the light house on Culebrita and snorkeled around Cayo Norte. The beaches were spectacular, and the variety of sea life enchanted them.

The time they spent together seemed almost too perfect. Bill couldn't stop himself from developing a bond of trust with Molly, and slowly he opened up to her. When she asked him why he left St. John so quickly, he was able to confess his paranoia of the couple that appeared to be stalking him since his arrival in St. Thomas.

"You've got to understand," Bill said, "there was never a trace of Shirley's body to be found. Not even the floatation cushion I tossed to her. The incident seems so bizarre, and now for this couple to be reappearing—it's like they are taunting me."

119

Molly was understanding and supportive. "I can understand how freaky it seems, but Bill, you've got to move on. You mustn't dwell on something that may be just a coincidence."

"See, Molly, I can tell that you don't understand. I can't let it go! I must know who those two are, or I won't be able to move on with my life."

Molly reached out a hand to touch his face. "Bill," she said softly as she looked into his eyes, "if by some remote chance that the woman is your wife, it is obvious that she's moved on. She is with that Richard guy, isn't she? What good is it for you to know anything more? She's already gone."

Bill regretted bringing up the subject, but he had wanted to get it off his chest, and he trusted Molly. But now he just wanted to change the subject. "See that beach across the way?" he said, pointing at a beach along the coastline of Culebra.

Molly nodded, realizing Bill's wounds were deep.

"That's where I got all torn up from the damn briars. While I was there, I found a drop tank submerged in the sand. It must have been discarded by the Navy when they were using the island as a bombing range. You might be able to get a view of it by using the binoculars."

The binoculars sat next to the helm. Molly picked them up and adjusted them for her sight. "I can't make it out clearly," she said, lowering the binoculars. "I know! Let's take a trip over there. We've got the time, and I'd like to see what you're talking about."

"We can't take the sailboat; the surfs much too rough there."

'Then let's take the dinghy. Are you game?"

"Sure," he said, happy that Molly had allowed him to change the subject. "Let's do it." Then he had second thoughts. "Wait, Molly, are you sure? It'll be tricky, and you'll probably get wet."

"I said I'm in. And who doesn't mind getting wet when you live in paradise! Let's go!"

The dinghy skimmed above the waves. Approaching the beach, Bill accelerated the speed of the small boat over the choppy waves, surfing on top of them and ending up beached on the sand. "That was quite a ride!" Molly exclaimed with exhilaration. "For a moment there I thought the water was ready to come over the sides of the dinghy."

"Yeah, it's really not a safe approach," Bill admitted. Good thing its low tide, so the undertow shouldn't bother us too much." Bill was as exhilarated as Molly.

Walking along the beach, they headed toward the spot where the tank projected up from the sand.

"It looks like it could be a submarine standing on its head," Molly laughed.

Bill agreed. "I hadn't thought of that."

"You didn't? You told me you were a design engineer who worked for the Navy developing submarines. I bet you could do something with this thing."

Bill contemplated her suggestion. "You know, Molly, that's not a bad idea. I could use a fun project. I'm going to need something to keep me busy after you leave. I'll have to see if Mickey will let me bring this tank to the hostel. He might even have some tools I could borrow." Molly took a seat on the sand as Bill walked around the tank, contemplating Molly's suggestion.

Time passed quickly, and soon Bill realized they'd spent quite a lot of time on the deserted beach. "I think we'd better go now. It's going to be a wet ride out of here. You'll need to sit in the center of the boat and hang on tight."

Hand in hand, they returned to the dinghy which sat high and dry on the sand. Dragging it to the water's edge was a struggle, but soon they had it floating in the water.

Molly climbed aboard, situating herself in the center, while Bill continued to shove the little boat out, struggling against the oncoming surf. He gave it one final push before jumping in and quickly starting the motor.

In no time, they were cruising along the shoreline until the dinghy was on plane. Aiming the bow into the waves, Bill increased the motor's power, and they plowed their way through the salty swells.

Waves of water splashed them in the face each time the small boat crashed down hard on top of the surf. By the time they reach the sailboat, both of them were drenched.

Finally aboard the sailboat, Molly searched for a dry towel, finding one in the cockpit. Wrapping herself in the cloth, she whirled about to see that Bill, still sitting in the dinghy, was soaking wet. She burst out laughing. "That was a bit much!"

"Yeah, I know, but remember, you're the one who wanted to see it." After putting the dinghy on the davits attached to the sailboat, Bill dried himself off and tried to unwind, which was not easy as his mind was busy fantasizing about plans for the tank.

They spent hours exchanging ideas on what to do with it.

***

The following day Bill approached Mickey. "I'm thinking of working on a submarine project, and I was wondering if I could use some of the free space you have in the back of the hostel?"

Mickey didn't grasp the outlandish idea. "You want to build a submarine? Are you insane?"

Bill wasn't a braggart and rarely elaborated on the breadth of his knowledge, but he was enthusiastic about his idea. "Look Mickey, I know a lot about engineering; in fact, project development is my specialty. I'll have to improvise many things to make my plan work, and of course, it will really only be a prototype. I enjoy challenging projects. "

Mickey was hesitant. "Well," he said, finally relenting, "there's plenty room in the back, and it doesn't sound like the project will harm anything. Okay, kid, go at it. Just one question; how are you planning to get the thing here?"

Bill hoped that asking for another favor wouldn't make Mickey change his mind. "That's another matter I need to discuss with you. I'll need some help removing the tank from where it is now. You see, it's half buried in the sand, and I can't drag it out with my boat, because the surf's much too strong there. I'll need to hack a path through those damn bushes, then dig it free, and somehow haul it back here."

"Well, when you figure it out, come back and see me."

"But, Mickey, I thought you could help. You have shovels and a come-along. We could use that jet-ski trailer stored over there. I'll use my lines. The only thing missing is a machete. We'd never get through that path without one."

Mickey heaved a deep sigh. "Okay, Bill, but if we get it back here, and you just let it take up my space, I'll fine your ass and kick you off my property. Is that understood?"

"Sure, Mickey, that sounds reasonable. Thanks."

"All right, let's go see what we can find in the shed. We can start off early tomorrow morning and get that thing back here."

At daybreak, Mickey, Bill, and Molly sat in Mickey's pickup truck and headed for the beach. They brought with them a power saw, a machete, two shovels, a come-along, and plenty of rope. The jet-ski trailer was in tow behind the truck. When they reached the overgrown path, Mickey started whacking off branches, clearing the path with the power saw. Bill followed with the machete to fine-tune the passage. Molly's task was pulling the trailer which carried the rest of their equipment.

Reaching the beach they saw the tank still stuck in the sand.

Mickey scanned the area with his eyes. "This isn't a restricted area, so you're in luck. I'm sure the Corp of Engineers don't even know it's here."

The tide was low again, but the surf continued its unrelenting barrage of breakers against them. Mickey and Molly started removing the sand from around the tank. Together they dug a trench and rocked the tank back and forth.

"Hey, Mickey! Throw me the rope," Bill directed. "I'll wrap it around this sea almond tree—this big mother ain't gonna move. It's as good as an anchor, and it'll never budge under pressure."

But the tank wouldn't move. Molly and Mickey continued digging deeper and rocked the tank harder while Bill cranked the come-along. There was no sign of movement, but they kept at it.

Starting to show signs of fatigue, Mickey grunted. "Hey, you two, I'm an old man; you're killing me."

Molly darted him a concerned glance. "Mickey, we can't give up yet! Can you just push harder, just for a little longer?"

Mickey rolled his eyes but did as Molly asked. He gave one final thrust using all his might—and in the next instant the tank moved. A moment later, the sand released its suction hold. The waves helped move the tank forward, allowing Bill to pull it onto the beach.

Together Bill and Molly tied the tank on the trailer, while Mickey sat down to rest. Once the tank was secured, they gathered all their equipment, and with everything tied down, they pushed the trailer toward the truck.

When the trailer was hooked back up to the truck, Bill turned to

Mickey. "Thanks, Mickey, we couldn't have done this without your help."

"Well, then, let's get out of here."

Back at the hostel they sat in the community gazebo and told Gertie about their adventure. Then Mickey caught sight of the 26-foot Sea Ray approaching the end of the dock.

"Time to get back to work," Mickey said and ran down the dock to help Brad and Sammi with their lines.

***

Returning to the sailboat, Bill and Molly spent a quiet evening together. In the morning, they were snuggling in each other's arms, but soon Molly expressed concern. "What time is it?"

With a quick glance at the clock, she said, "I've got to get ready to meet Tom!" Seizing her towel, a t-shirt and a pair of khaki shorts, she dashed off to the shower room.

After enjoying the warm water flowing over her, she stepped out of the shower stall to dry off. She pulled on her shorts and was just reaching for her shirt when the door opened and Sammi stepped inside.

Molly gasped and immediately pulled her t-shirt over her bare breasts. "What the hell are you doing in here? This is the women's shower!" she cried out. "Get out of here now!"

Sammi grinned, his gaze focusing on her chest. "Nothing to fret about," he said almost casually, "there's no one here but us girls." With a smirk on his lips, he advanced toward her. "And there's no cause to be so unfriendly."

As he reached to grab Molly, she surged away from him and screamed as loud as she could. "Don't you dare touch me, you pervert!"

Sammi was not fast enough to catch Molly as she darted around him and out the door, only to run headlong into Brad's arms.

Panicked, she hit him in his chest with her fists and managed to break away..

Bill was loading Molly's gear into the dinghy when he heard the engine noise of the sea plane. He barely heard a woman's scream. Looking up he saw Molly running down the dock toward him, clutching her shirt to her chest. Tears ran down her cheeks, and the next thing Bill knew, she was throwing herself into his arms.

"Hey, you missing me already?" Then he noticed that her body was shaking violently. "What's this all about?" he asked, noting her hands clutching the t-shirt to her chest.

Bill held her in a loose embrace and gently wiped the hair from her eyes. "What going on?'

"Oh, God! The man from the Sea Ray—the one who dresses like a woman—came into the shower room, and I was only half dressed. I was surprised that a man would be allowed in there. I told him to leave but he didn't. He was undressing me with his freaky monster eyes, and then he tried to grab me." Molly paused to take in a big gulp of air. "I was too fast for him and ran out the door—where the other freak from the Sea Ray was waiting. He seemed out of it, almost as if he was possessed!"

Bill was astonished. "What did he say to you?"

"Nothing!" she wailed. "It was his look—it was horrible. I'm sorry, Bill, it was ghoulish."

"Okay, Molly, calm down. I'll go talk to him."

"Oh! No! Don't do that. I just want to go, to get out of here. Take me to Tom, please!"

"Okay, okay, get finished dressing, and I'll get you to the plane."

By the time Bill took Molly out to meet Tom, she had composed herself and sat quietly in the dinghy.

Tom greeted them with a wave from the cargo hatch of his plane. Moving his dinghy to the plane's side, Bill lifted Molly's duffel bag and snorkel gear up to Tom.

Then he turned to Molly, who was looking back at the marina with open fear in her eyes. "Please don't stay away too long, Molly. I'll write you. Tell me you'll come back."

"Bill, I can't promise, but I'll keep in touch." She gave him a long kiss before turning to Tom. "I'm ready," she said.

Bill lifted her up to Tom, who assisted her into the aircraft. Moving his dinghy away from the plane, Bill watched as it winged its way across the water before lifting off.

Now what? he wondered. Everything had seemed so right. How could it all go so wrong this quickly?

CHAPTER NINETEEN

"Secrets create power. Power determines how we live."

James Grady

As the seaplane circled the bay below, Molly felt a lump in her throat and a pain in her heart.

Reaching a safe altitude for flying, Tom looked over at her. "Why the tears, Miss Molly. I have a feeling you're not just sad to leave."

She took time to wipe her eyes with a tissue before speaking. "I think I just ruined it for Bill. There's a couple of weird guys staying at the marina, and one of them came on to me inside the ladies shower room. I'm sure that Bill is going to confront him, and I know the weirdo is going to cause him lots of grief. To make matters worse, the owner of the hostel, Mickey, likes the two guys. If Bill pressures Mickey about the two, I just hope Mickey doesn't kick him out."

Tom was quiet for a moment. "I think Bill can handle himself just fine. Now tell me what's going on between you and Bill."

"Why? Everything is fine."

Tom continued to probe. "I know you, Miss Molly, there's something else, isn't there? You know you can tell me. It won't hurt a bit."

Molly's tears began flowing again. "Well, yes, Bill has lots of baggage regarding his dead wife. He believes she may still be alive, and he feels that she and her boyfriend are stalking him. Bill needs my help, but he won't accept it. I know I can help him get over her." She paused a moment before adding, "I wish she would appear. If she'd show up, Bill would know for sure she didn't drown, and he could put his guilt to rest."

Tom was confused. "His wife is dead, but she may be alive? That doesn't make any sense. I think you should forget Bill. There's no future for you with someone like him. He'll just have to sort things out for himself."

"But Tom, I can help him. I know I can."

"Miss Molly, look at you; you not just sad, you're freaked out. I've never seen you this way. It's just not your nature. Now go back to work, have fun. Things will work out. They always do."

Nodding, Molly agreed. "You're right, Tom."

It was a beautiful day for flying, with a light wind from the east holding steady, and the plane glided smoothly through the air. The blue sky and the turquoise waters were colored patches on an artist's pallet.

Adjusting the power to the plane's engine, Tom circled around his houseboat floating at anchor off Buck island. Bringing the plane in low and slow, he landed and was soon anchored beside the boat.

"We're here already?" Molly said with surprise.

"We aim to please," Tom said with a smile.

"Guess time got away from me."

Tom didn't waste any time in transferring Molly's gear to his speed boat before heading toward Souper's Hole.

When Tom pulled up to the dock in front of Molly's apartment, she slipped him some cash and thanked him for the special favor of getting her to and from Bill's mooring. "See you later for a brew at Little Richards?"

He nodded. "Take care of yourself and remember my suggestion." He waved good-bye and sped away, leaving a trail of foaming water in the wake behind his boat.

***

Wanting to know what went down in the shower room, Bill marched over to the Sea Ray and yelled out, "Sammi!" over the loud sound of rap music spouting provocative lyrics. Moving closer to the Sea Ray, Bill knocked his fist on the hull. "Hey, Sammi, are you in there?"

Sammi appeared on deck dressed in a frilly white dress that barely covered his vital parts. "Oh, it's you, Bill. What's up?"

Controlling his anger was not an option for Bill. "That's what I want to know!" he practically sputtered. "What did you do to my friend Molly? She was frightened to tears."

"Molly? Are you talking about the cute little curly-top girl with red hair? Was she staying with you?" Sammi's face revealed no concern or guilt.

"Yeah!" Bill yelled. "You know damn well she's my guest—you saw us together on my boat last night. What the hell did you do to her?"

"Bill, I don't know what you're talking about." Lowering his voice, Sammi continued. "You gotta believe me, Bill, nothing happened to her. Look at these feet. They're size 13. You know it's hard to find sandals to fit these babies. I just went in to the shower room as she was leaving. As I tripped over these clodhoppers, I toppled her over. I didn't mean nothing by it. She just ran away and didn't let me explain."

Looking at the hemline line of Sammi's white dress, Bill's gaze continued down the long spindly legs, over the knobby knees, and ending at his oversized feet.

"You do have very large feet," Bill admitted as he noticed Sammi's toes sticking out beyond the end of the sandals. His toenails were covered with bright pink nail polish.

Bill shook his head in disbelief. "I wasn't there, but Molly's version of the incident is quite different than yours."

"Um, I'm sorry, Bill," Sammi stuttered, "but honestly, it was an accident, okay? I gotta go now." Leaving Bill standing on the dock, Sammi moved quickly, disappearing inside the cabin of his boat where the music was still pounding.

Not satisfied by Sammi's explanation, Bill stomped away and decided to talk to Mickey about the incident. He found him behind the hostel inspecting Bill's drop tank.

"Hey, Mickey, got a minute?"

"Sure, I was just looking over the tank. I can't see how you plan to make this thing into a submarine."

Not ready to reveal his plans on converting the tank into a submarine, he got right to the point. "That can wait. I have a problem that I want to discuss with you—it has to do with July's centerfold. You know, the one who lives on the Sea Ray."

"Oh, you mean Sammi. What's wrong?"

"He went into the lady's shower room while Molly was in there, frightening her to tears. I don't know what really happened, because their stories of the incident are completely different. But do you really think it is appropriate for Sammi to be going in there? He may think and act like some female bimbo, but you and I know that's not the case. You need to make other arrangements for him. It could get you in a lot of trouble, especially when you have other woman guests."

Mickey tilted his head to one side, appearing to consider Bill's suggestion. "You know, Bill, I never gave it a thought, but you're right. I'll tell him from now on he'll have to use the outside shower."

Bill wasn't done yet. "Sounds promising, Mickey, but what about the lady's room? That could cause some problems, too!"

"I'm not sure that would matter. There is only one throne in there, and besides, the door locks."

"Mickey, get a grip; it's just not right." Bill persisted.

"Well, I could tell him to use the handicapped bathroom." He paused for a minute to think it over. "Yeah, that's what I'll do."

The veins on Bill's neck stuck out, and his face turned scarlet as he thought about how upset Molly had been. "Just put *For the Flamer* under the handicapped sign."

"Hey, that's enough!" Mickey said. "I know they're a little eccentric. You've known that since your arrival here. So cut me some slack! They help me out around here, and they do a damn good job. Now go do some abracadabra with that junk tank you got here. End of story!" Mickey stomped off, leaving Bill seething with anger.

"Eccentric! I'd say that's an understatement," he yelled at Mickey's back. "Something happened to Molly! Something alarmed her enough to cause her to panic!"

Mickey disappeared around the corner of the building without another word. Bill had the urge to jump into his boat and leave this place behind, but then he remembered the tank and the project he had planned for it.

"Damnit all to hell," he muttered under his breath. All his options swirled around in his head. Finally he remembered that Mickey said he would make changes, changes that on retrospect seemed fair. He'd stay for a while to see how it worked out. Then he'd contact Molly. By then maybe she would reconsider and return for another visit.

But right now, he had more pressing issues. What was he going to do with the tank? Culebra had nothing to offer him in line of research and development. Using his imagination and knowledge, he was sure he could make this project work. Failing was not an alternative.

CHAPTER TWENTY

Back at his boat, Bill stewed over this new set of issues. He had come to Culebra to relax, to get away from stress while working on getting his life's priorities back in line. Not to get involved with a woman and an unrealistic enterprise.

The rap music coming from the Sea Ray irritated him, so he went below to sit in the salon and reflect on his situation. But he was restless and couldn't stay put. Looking at his laptop still wrapped in its security blanket, he grabbed it and went topside. Pulling his dinghy around, he placed his parcel safely inside, then climbed aboard and took off.

Ending his ride at the now familiar Dinghy Dock, he lifted his bundle up and went inside to his favorite table where he set up the laptop. Jennifer saw him and scurried over. "I haven't seen you around, Bill; I thought you might have moved on."

Looking up at his favorite server, he grinned. "I was entertaining a friend of mine from Tortola. We had a nice week together, but it's over now. She's gone back to work." Not wanting to say more than that, he changed the subject. "How's life with you?"

"Everything is good here," she said, but Bill caught a whiff of concern in her voice and raised his eyebrows in question. "Bill, do you remember when I told you about the missing women on Vieques?" He nodded. "Well, there's a report that another one has gone missing. There is no sign of her. Last they knew she was going to the Bio Bay, but she never returned. That sounds so creepy. Kinda like a serial killer is on the loose. It's really a mystery that they haven't found even one body nor any clues to indicate foul play."

Bill didn't want to listen to more drama; he had enough of his own. "I'm sure they'll bring in the big guns soon. Someone should have seen something suspicious. How many are missing?"

"Maybe three or four, could be more, all gone without a trace."

Noticing that Bill's attention had turned to his computer, Jennifer moved away. "Sorry to bother you, but I thought you'd like to know."

"Vieques sounds like a good place to stay away from. Say, Jen, I'd like to order lunch."

"Coming right up. I'll get you a menu."

After placing his order, he composed a note on his laptop to Mike, explaining his current unsettling situation involving the submarine project. He knew he should mention Molly but decided to close. Shutting down the laptop and wrapping it back up, he waited for his lunch to be served before returning to his boat.

Bill spent the next few days at the beach, doing nothing much while trying to sort out his dilemmas. By midweek he was ready to do something—almost anything would do. Stopping at the Dinghy Dock on his way back from the beach seemed like a good alternative to his brooding; besides, stopping there gave him a reason to check his mail. Opening up his laptop he found a long note from Mike. He questioned Bill about his association with Molly. He was curious because Bill had failed to mention her in his recent email. In a brotherly manner he cautioned him about the relationship.

Bill grimaced. *Thanks, Mike, enough said.*

Next, Mike made an interesting suggestion for using the tank.

Why not disregard the idea of a highly technical submarine project, because it has all indications of failure. Why not build a wet sub? It's a feasible alternative that could be fun for divers like yourself.

Thinking of all the coral reefs in the area. Bill envisioned the intriguing concept. What a great idea! Continuing to read Mike's note, Bill started to design the wet sub in his mind. He could design it to carry two divers. It'll go faster than a person could dive, helping the divers conserve their air. It could be used to transport other items like fish, lobster, or extra gear. The potential uses were numerous.

Bill went back to Mike's note.

It appears that Richard is home. His lawn is well manicured, and there is a car in the driveway.

The news came as a welcome relief to Bill, and he hoped he could close that chapter of his life.

***

In the days following Mike's note, Bill plunged headfirst into his wet sub project. He made an opening at the top of the drop tank, allowing two scuba divers to easily access their seats. By attaching two flexible fins to the rear of the tank it would increase the sub's mobility. When that was finished he focused on designing the steering wheel, which would control the direction of the wet sub. His goal was to make its maneuverability unimpaired when going up or down, turning from side to side, or just hovering in neutral buoyancy. He would need more equipment, such as trawling motors, 12-volt batteries, and tanks to hold the pressurized air. These things weren't available in Culebra, so he started spending hours at The Dinghy Dock researching on the internet.

Sammi and Brad made a point to stop by and check on Bill's progress. Sammi had accepted Mickey's recommendations for separate areas for his bathroom and shower room without question. Currently he and Brad were in the mist of making wedding preparations. It was to be an elaborate affair, including a white horse-drawn carriage which would escort Sammi to church.

Brad beamed with excitement as he told Bill about the couple's plans. "You know, this wedding is going to be a fabulous affair. Sammi is some special girl. I love her to death."

Bill was installing the steering wheel in the wet sub and listened with a deaf ear as Brad continued to describe the plans, which Bill thought was a bunch of crap.

"The wedding will be at the Christian Community Church; its non-denominational, you know. We can't pinpoint a date yet, because there is a delay by the government in completing our paperwork We'll be having our reception at The Dinghy Dock. You know, Bill; you're invited to join us in our celebration."

Bill was on his back working on the steering wheel cables. Looking up from inside the drop tank, Bill forced a smile. "Sure, Brad, I'd like that."

"Okay then, I'll let you know when we're good to go. Right now, I've got to meet the ferry boat from Fajardo when it docks today."

Overenthusiastically, he explained, "I ordered Sammi a beautiful white gown. I can't wait to surprise her."

Bill liked the frequency of the ferry line service from Puerto Rico. "That ferry sure helps this island survive. I found some of my parts in a place not far from Fajardo. They have everything I'm looking for, but they want cash, so I'll be making the trip soon myself."

Brad agreed. "Yep, it's a help, but their schedules ain't that reliable. Living here don't make much difference though. We ain't going anywhere anyway." Turning, Brad walked toward the old red shed Mickey used for storage and picked up one of the bikes leaning alongside. "I gotta go now. See ya later, Bill." Hopping on the bike, he pedaled away.

Bill scratched his head. "Oh well, different strokes." Returning his attention to the wet sub, he focused on the task of building the sub. He was a perfectionist who must do it right the first time which he believed prevents wasted time and effort. And it kept his adrenalin alive.

***

Sitting on a bench in the ferry boat, Bill anticipated the blast from the ferry's horns as it docked in Fajardo. Entering its berth, the large boat shuddered as it bumped into the dock. Grabbing lines, the men on the dock hurried to tie them to the cleats. As they did, Bill heard the horns he was expecting. Now he was another step sooner to completing his undertaking.

After arriving, Bill would call his supplier, who was to deliver the parts to him at the ferry dock. Using his cell phone for the first time in months, he entered the number. The call was answered immediately.

"Hello, this Bill Adams, is Martin Zamarripa available?" While waiting for a reply, he heard someone speaking in Spanish. Soon he heard a man's voice.

"Hello."

"Martin, it's Bill Adams, I'm here at the dock. How soon can you get my parts over here?" He paused. "A half hour sounds good. I'll just grab a bite to eat while I wait"

The port was a busy place, humming with all kinds of people milling around. Some were leaving the ferry with luggage in hand.

Others were waiting to board it. Industrial workers loaded supplies to be transported to stores and businesses on Culebra.

Searching for a place to eat, Bill spotted a concession stand selling lunches. Reading the menu he decided on a Roti. Finding an empty bench close by, he enjoyed the curry flavored meat and potato sandwich.

Pleased that his cell phone was working, Bill called Mike, who took his call right away. They spent the next 20 minutes catching up on things. "Life is good here on Culebra. Hey, thanks for the wet sub idea, I'm making great progress. You'll have to come see it when I'm done. Once I get these parts, it will be ready for a test run." Keeping an eye out for the delivery truck, Bill saw it pulling into the parking lot. "Hey Mike, I gotta go, my parts just arrived…later."

Martin helped Bill load the parts into a storage area on the ferry. "Thanks," Bill said, grateful for the help. After paying his bill, he slipped Martin a tip. "If I need more parts I'll send you an e-mail."

"Sure, anytime. Good luck with that wet sub of yours. If it works as good as you say, I'll put one in my shop and see if I can get people interested in it. You never know what people are willing to spend their money on."

Mission accomplished, Bill was ready to return to Culebra. Knowing the ferry service's schedule was unreliable, he had no idea how long he would have to wait. Looking around from a comfortable seat on the ferry, he watched the action on shore but soon became bored waiting and his thoughts turned to Molly. He hadn't had any contact with her since she had left in a hysterical state almost a month ago.

Punching in her number, he nervously ran his fingers through his hair. Hearing her voice, his lips trembled. "Hi, Molly, how ya doing?"

"Bill, how nice of you to call. I've been meaning to drop you a line, but I've been slammed with work. You're on your cell, does that mean you've moved on again?"

"No, not at all; I'm in Fajardo picking up parts for my submarine. I changed the concept though."

"Huh, why's that?"

"Well, on Culebra there's no technical help or skills relating to an enclosed deep-water vehicle that we had in mind. After talking to Mike, we came up with the idea of a wet sub. You know, something scuba divers can use."

"Wow, that's a shift, but you've piqued my curiosity."

"How'd you like to test drive it with me? After all, it was your idea to build a sub. Maybe not this one, but none the less, you were involved with the scheme from the start. All you'll need is your regulator, vest, and your bag of snorkel gear. We can rent tanks and weight belts here."

"What about those weird guys? Are they still around?"

"Well, yes, sorta, but they're planning a wedding in a few weeks. Following their grand affair, they'll be away on a honeymoon for some time. We could plan the first sea trial while they're gone. That'll give me the time to get the sub finished."

There was silence while Bill felt Molly might turn him down. There was nothing left for him to do to convince her to come. *What's taking her so long?* he wondered, noticing an increase in his heart rate; a bead of sweat from his brow managed to trickle into his right eye. He wiped it away, sitting tight, knowing she was still on the line. Then he heard her say yes.

"You will?" Relief surged through him. "Molly, that's great! I really want you to be part of this adventure."

"Bill, don't get too excited yet; I still have to arrange for coverage of my scheduled charter trips."

"We have time; the wedding is still weeks away. I'll let you know when they set the date. You can make your plans after that."

Hearing movement and noise around him, he saw passengers boarding. Hurrying past Bill, they jockeyed for seats. The ferry was about to leave. "Molly, the ferry is getting underway. Time for me to head back ...I miss you."

***

The days following Bill's trip to Fajardo were filled with work and re-work, but he was determined his wet sub was going in the water soon.

Brad had his own frustrations with the wedding plans. Standing next to Bill while he puttered on his sub, Brad elaborated. "The Administration officials are in no hurry, and if the paper work is not completed by the time of the wedding, the ceremony could be performed, but our marriage wouldn't be legal in the eyes of the law."

Brad paced back and forth by the sub. "I put Sammi's name on the form they gave me, but that wasn't good enough. So, I had to give them the birth certificate which they didn't approve, because same gender marriages are not recognized here. I haven't told Sammi, she'll freak out. She is so excited, and she just loved the dress. Now the lily-livered little preacher wants more money for his performance. I'll do whatever's necessary. This is going to be a very special day for my sweetheart." Brad started toward his boat, adding, "I'll keep you posted!"

Bill stared after him. The memory of Molly's story still concerned him, and he wondered what these guys were really all about. Something about them was not quite right.

Putting the puzzling situation out of his mind, he went back to work.

CHAPTER TWENTY ONE

It was mid-morning a short while after Bill's trip to Puerto Rico when the ferry boat from Fajardo docked in its birth at Culebra. There were few passengers aboard, but the boat's cargo hold was filled to capacity. The ferry's main mission on this day was to deliver needed supplies to the local businesses that relied on the goods from Puerto Rico to support the island's economy.

A few of the locals exited the boat carrying bundles of merchandise purchased in San Juan. Following them was one seemingly isolated couple who appeared to be confused, trying to establish their bearings. The man was casually dressed in shorts and a t-shirt. His dark brown hair was accented with silver strands around his temples. His eyes were covered with dark glasses. His partner, an attractive blond who appeared to be half his age, was similarly attired. She clung to the man's arm while he scanned the area in search of something.

Taking both her hands the man seemed to comfort the woman. "Shirley, we are looking for a green sailboat. I'll need you to help me find it. It should be anchored somewhere in this harbor. Once we see it, we will make our presence known, but only in an elusive way. Okay now, do you understand?"

Shirley nodded. "We want him to see us, but we don't want to talk to him. Why is that?"

Richard had learned from Shirley's doctor that the best way to interact with her was with a calm, caring voice.

After arriving in Mystic from Montauk, Richard had notified Shirley's mom that she was alive. The news made her mom ecstatic, and she insisted that Richard bring Shirley to her home.

Seeing her daughter for the first time since the boating accident, she realized that Shirley was in a traumatized state. Richard told her how a fisherman had saved Shirley from drowning, but he refrained from explaining the details.

His goal was to berate Bill, but all she wanted to do was to make arrangements for Shirley to get a medical evaluation and be treated by a private psychiatrist.

Looking at Richard through her tears, Shirley's mom argued with him. "Richard, what you say about Bill can't be true. If he meant to do Shirley harm, he would have never opened a trust fund for the two of us with the money he received from the sale of her car and half the money from the sale of their house. He would have taken all the money and ran. He told me that the money belonged to us because no trace of Shirley was ever found, and there could be a possibility she didn't drown. He was so sincere. End of story. Right now, my main concern is getting Shirley help."

"You're right! She needs help, and I'll be glad to assist with it, as much as I can, but I'm not buying your story. I know he pushed her off that boat. I know the type, they are nothing but scoundrels."

Together they made arrangements for Shirley to receive intensive therapy, but even with the intervention, her level of improvement remained slow.

"Shirley, please, just help me look for the boat." Richard's tolerance was waning; holding her hand he led Shirley around the town of Dewey. Reaching The Dinghy Dock, they were fascinated by the Tarpon swimming around. "Shirl, what ya say we get lunch here before we get back on the ferry?"

"Yes; I'm hungry," Shirley said quietly.

Entering the restaurant, they seated themselves at a table by a window. Jennifer, the pleasant young waitress, was quick to introduce herself and take their order. Returning with drinks in hand, she placed them on the table.

"What brings you to Culebra?" she asked. "We don't get a lot of visitors here. It's not much of a tourist mecca, like Vieques."

Richard's face was unsmiling. "We're looking for a murderer, and our sources led us here."

Jennifer was astonished. "A murderer? What are you, some kind of P.I.?"

"You could say that."

"Then you need to go to Vieques," Jennifer exclaimed. "They have big trouble there—abductions, at the very least, but probably something worse. Women have been vanishing without a trace. They could use some outside help. Thank goodness we haven't had any problems here on Culebra."

Richard wasn't in the mood for chit-cat. "Look, we're searching for a guy with a green sailboat, do you know anyone like that?"

Jennifer hesitated as a shot of disbelief washed through her. This guy hadn't shown her any credentials, and he didn't fit the profile of a private investigator. "No, sir, I don't know of anyone with a green sailboat." With that said she turned to walk away. "I'll be right back with your meal."

Shirley fidgeted about in her seat, her eyes darting around the room. She was anxious, as if the man they were looking for would appear at any second. She placed her hand on Richard's arm. "It's Bill we need to find, am I right? Now, who is Bill?"

"Shirley," Richard said, trying to hide his irritation, "remember, he's the man that pushed you off the sailboat."

"Oh, that's right. I forgot."

Jennifer returning with their meals. "Is there anything else I can get for you?"

Shirley looked up at Jennifer. "We're looking for Bill, isn't that right, Richard? Do you know him?"

The blonde woman's question took Jennifer by surprise. "I know a few Bill's. Who is it you are trying to find?"

Richard felt compelled to intervene. "Do you know a Bill Adams? He's supposedly somewhere around here. He killed his wife, and now he's on the run."

"Oh, gosh!" Jennifer said. "You can't mean that; he's such a nice guy. You must be mistaken."

"So, you do know him; where can I find him?"

Jennifer took a step away from the two. "Look, I don't know where he stays. Can I see your identification?"

Richard hadn't planned to become this involved, but he decided if he couldn't find Bill, he might as well start a rumor and let the locals spread it. "Nope, don't have any to show you. But thanks for your information, I appreciate it. Oh, by the way, where would I find the police station?"

Explaining that their police officers come to Culebra from the regional police office in Fajardo, she added, "Our police office is located in a building close to the ferry dock but don't expect anyone to be there; they have been known to leave early and not return for days."

Pivoting abruptly, Jennifer stomped off. Returning with their bill, she placed it on the table by Richard. "Enjoy your stay here in Culebra," she said. "So sorry I couldn't help you find your man."

Richard and Shirley left the restaurant, returning to the ferry boat as it prepared to embark on its return trip to Fajardo.

***

Putting the finishing touches on his wet sub, Bill concentrated on fine-tuning the windshield, when Brad happened by to talk with him. "A windshield? Do you need a windshield under water?"

Bill felt saucy. "Sure, it'll keep the water from spoiling my view. You know the sea is loaded with all kinds of creatures that could get in my path. There aren't any traffic signals down there. Now, Brad, don't you think it gives the sub more class? Like the Nautilus or the Calypso. This baby's going to make waves."

Brad scratched his head in confusion. "Sure, Bill." He hesitated for a moment. "I stopped by to tell you that all the wedding plans are complete, so Sammi and I will be having our celebration in two weeks. Keep that in mind."

Bill smiled back at Brad. "Are the two of you going on a honeymoon?"

A smile spread across Brad's face. "Yep! We have the Honeymoon Suite booked at the W. Retreat and Spa on Vieques; you know, it's the place where we work. They gave us the room for a week; ain't that big of them?"

To refrain from laughing out loud, Bill started coughing. "Sounds fantastic!"

"Look, Bill, I just wanted to make sure you knew about our wedding." Turning back, Brad headed toward the dock.

"Thanks Brad," Bill called after the bridegroom. "I'll try to make it."

Bill focused his attention back to the windshield. He couldn't wait to make the first trial dive in the wet sub. He felt like a kid at

Christmas. Knowing that Brad and Sammi wouldn't remain in Culebra after their big day, he would invite Molly to join him so they could share the experience.

But first it was vital that he make a final check of all the parts, thereby giving himself peace of mind. He didn't want any surprises by forgetting a necessary detail. Once he finished he'd put it to rest and head to The Dinghy Dock in the morning to notify Molly that they're good to go. While there he planned to write Mike a note about his successful venture.

The weather the following morning was a dreary stream of rain, heavy at times. It was the kind of day to stay put and read a good book. Bill didn't care about the weather, all he wanted to do was to tell the world about his wet sub. He reinforced the weather-proof cover on his laptop, then he put on his olive green slicker, buttoning it up to his neck, and raised the hood over his head. As an added precaution, he put a big brimmed straw hat over the hood. Now he was all set and got into his dinghy, leaving for his destination in the nasty weather..

The Dinghy Dock was almost empty. A few local town customers were sitting at the tables, enjoying their breakfast. Mel stood by the front windows, watching the heavy rain when Bill appeared through the gray mist, heading toward the dock.

The dock was vacant, giving Bill a choice of places to tie up. Seems everyone else chose to spend the day reading. Wrapping a line around the cleat closest to the doorway, he seized the bundle holding his laptop and made a beeline toward the restaurant.

Mel met him at the door with a towel. "Here, give me that bundle. Take off those rain-soaked clothes, then dry off with this." Mel waited while Bill removed his hat and slithered out of his slick. "When you're finished drying off, use the towel to clean up the puddle by your feet."

Bill was grateful for the courtesy. "Thanks, Mel, that's what I call customer service."

Mel bowed. "Just trying to please those weary sailors who have a compelling urge to trudge through these inclement meteorological conditions to have breakfast at my place."

"Who's having breakfast?" Bill teased.

Playfully raising his fist, Mel walked away.

The place was quiet, as only a handful of the usual crowd was around. After cleaning up the water on the floor he headed to a small table by the front window, his favorite spot. He draped his sopping wet clothes over the back of a chair, placing the towel under it to catch the water dripping off his coat. Bill sat down in the chair opposite it, then removed his laptop from the bundle.

Jennifer watched him as he settled into his chair. Approaching his table, she greeted him with a smile. "Hi, Bill, what brings you out on this soggy, rainy morning?"

"I came to see you. I can't help myself. Plus, I gotta send some messages to my friends. Why don't you surprise me with today's breakfast special?"

"How about a piping hot cup of coffee first? It'll warm the cockles of your heart." She snickered as she lifted the thermal pot in her hand.

Setting his cup closer to her, he said, "Nothing could be better."

Jennifer filled his cup before leaving to place his order. Bill noticed she kept looking at him from across the room. When she circled around back to his table, Bill sensed that something was amiss.

"Hey, Jen, what's up?"

"Bill, I need to know something, and this may sound insane, but— did you murder your wife?"

Bill sat up straight, a scornful look covering his face. "What did you say? Where did you come up with that?"

Jennifer stood her ground. "Look, Bill—just answer my question."

"NO! I did not murder my wife! If you must know, my wife and I were caught in a storm at sea. She fell off the sailboat, and I couldn't rescue her because I was knocked unconscious by the boat's boom. We should have never been in that situation. It was my fault for not monitoring the weather. Her body was never recovered. In fact, no trace of her was ever found. I spent time recovering in a hospital. Now! You need to explain to me why you would ask me such a crazy question?"

"Yes, I need to explain myself," she said, sighing with relief. "Bill, some middle-aged guy and a younger woman were in here the other day looking for you. He told me he was a P.I., but I didn't believe him. He didn't have any credentials to show me, and he looked like a sleazy type. The blond acted weird, like she was on drugs or something. She even mentioned they didn't want to talk to you, they just wanted you to see them. Then the guy said you killed your wife! The whole thing was batty, and I was suspicious of their intentions."

Bill was shaken. "Thanks, Jen, trust me, I'd be thrilled to hear that my wife was alive. The incident still eats me up inside. Tell me what happened to the couple—are they still around?"

"No, I'm sure they left on the ferry boat returning to Fajardo. Bill, I'm so sorry. I didn't mean to upset you, but I needed to ask and tell you about those people. I'll take care of your breakfast order and get you another towel."

Bill's heart beat madly, and he fought to control the rage surging through his body. *How do they do it? How could they have traced me to Culebra? What's going on? They seem to enjoy tormenting me, but why? How dare they haunt me?*

He booted up his laptop and wrote a lengthy e-mail to Mike. First, he told him of the progress he was making with the wet sub. Then he described Jennifer's questions, his fingers flying over the keyboard. He spurted out a number of profanities while conveying the recent happenings. Lastly, he asked Mike how Richard could possibly know where to find him?

Finishing the note, he hit send just as Jennifer returned. She dried the table before placing his breakfast in front of Bill. The expression on her face seemed sad.

Bill looked away, and she left. Needing to calm down before composing his note to Molly, Bill ate his hot meal. The food was comforting, taking away some of his foul mood. Sipping his coffee, he relaxed a bit. His anger slowly subsided. Focusing on what he should write to Molly, he typed her a short note. Inviting her to be part of the christening of the wet sub made him feel better.

He paid for his breakfast, packed up his belongings, and headed back out in the rain. Once in the dinghy, Bill released the line around the cleat on the dock, allowing the wind to catch the small craft, and it started drifting slowly away from the dock. After clearing any obstacles in his way, Bill started the motor. The rain's force was strong, and it was coming down in sheets, making his visibility poor. Getting out of the rain as fast as possible was not going to happen. By reducing his speed, his sight improved, and the intensity of the rain hitting his face was less. If it would only wash away the thoughts of the man who was tormenting him.

Concentrating on finding the channel markers was his top priority at the moment. Buckets of rain poured in, flooding his boat. Seeing the hostel's channel markers gave him some relief, and he soon arrived safely at the dock. Laptop under his arm, he jumped on the dock and made a dash for the sailboat's hatch. Once in comfortable clothes, he settled down with a good book, but his thoughts kept returning to the guy haunting him.

He certainly looked like Richard, but why would his ex-neighbor spend all this time and money to track him down? And accuse him of murder? It didn't make sense. And neither did the presence of a blond woman. He hadn't been able to get a good look at her, but he knew it couldn't be Shirley. If it was, someone in the Coast Guard, the police force, or even Shirley's mom would have attempted to notify him. None of this made sense.

CHAPTER TWENTY-TWO

It was a beautiful sunny Saturday morning, and the sights to behold were beyond one's imagination. Sitting in the cockpit of his sailboat sipping a cup of coffee, Bill watched the commotion on the dock by the Sea Ray. Mickey and Gertie were dressed in their finest clothes as they waited for Sammi to step down from the boat onto the dock. The grandeur of his six-foot six stature was enhanced by his size-thirteen feet enclosed in white sateen stiletto heels.

Sammi's lanky legs wobbled under a white gown adorned with pearls and lace. His long hair was tied up with a cluster of white baby rosebuds accenting a tulle veil covering his head.

Mickey gripped Sammi's arm to prevent him from falling into the water. Gertie followed behind to keep the gown from tangling. When Sammi reached solid ground, everyone relaxed.

Continuing the parade, the trio aimed toward the white horse-drawn carriage waiting on the street in front of the hostel. The white carriage was decorated with white carnations, and the driver wore a white tuxedo. Reaching the carriage, Sammi exclaimed, "I'm so nervous!"

Gertie used motherly words of encouragement. "Don't worry now, hon, the worst is over, you'll be fine."

Stepping up into the carriage, Sammi's shoe got caught in the long white gown, and he tumbled forward. Only quick movements on Mickey's part prevented the bride from falling on his face. Once Sammi was settled, the horse started moving forward. Mickey, Gertie and Brad followed in their truck.

Already dressed for the event, Bill mounted his bicycle to trail close behind the parade. Sammi's arrival at the church was spectacular. Cheers filled the air, and the accompanying applause was booming.

Sammi's ascent up the steps leading into the church was thankfully uneventful. Waiting in the vestibule, Sammi stood alone while the guests filed in looking for their seats.

Once everyone was settled, including Bill, the organ began to play.

Proceeding down the aisle, Sammi joined Brad waiting at the altar. His 5-foot 8-inch stature was dwarfed by the bride. The odd appearance went unnoticed as Brad looked exceedingly handsome in his black tuxedo. Mickey and Gertie took their places on the other side of the preacher. The ceremony was professionally performed, concluding with the exchange of rings and the traditional kiss.

Following the formalities, the wedding procession quickly left the church, stopping to pose for pictures outside.

The waiting horse and carriage transported Brad and Sammi to the reception at the Dinghy Dock. Along the way, the bride and groom popped pills. Soon the carriage pulled up to the restaurant where Mel greeted them.

In no time at all the reception was in full swing. Bill made his appearance, and after congratulating the couple, he edged toward the back door.

The party goers quickly became out of control. Men were mooning each other, and some of the women in the crowd began flashing their breasts. Sammi's behavior became unruly when he started groping a large breasted woman who was flashing him. Shoving her into a corner, he attempted to remove the rest of her dress.

Mel heard her screams. "Get off me, you animal! Help, somebody help me. This is insane!"

Mel yanked hard at Sammi's hair to stop the assault. The woman spit at Sammi before running away.

Mel had no alternative but to stop the mayhem. "Everybody out, NOW! The party is over."

***

All was quiet at the hostel on the morning following the wedding. Looking at the empty space at the end of the dock, Bill thought the happy couple must have set out on their honeymoon during the early morning hours. He planned on picking Molly up at the airport by using Mickey's pickup truck for transportation, and he appreciated Mickey's kind offer.

Bill was thrilled that Molly looked forward to assisting him with the christening of his wet sub. She planned on arriving on Culebra aboard Cape Air, a small commercial flight operation servicing the islands in the area.

During the week prior to her arrival, Bill kept himself busy painting the wet sub a bright yellow. Adding a finishing touch he put a big black smile resembling that of a bottle-nosed dolphin on the front, giving it a special flair.

He left early for the airport because he was unfamiliar with the facilities there Parking the truck in the shade of a tree, he grabbed his binoculars and walked toward a small wooden building with a red "Customs" sign.

Entering, he looked for directions to the fight operations for information on the arriving and departing flights. Molly had promised to bring champagne but offered little else in her e-mail note.

"May I help you? You look bewildered," the young clerk asked as Bill walked up to the Cape Air desk.

"Yes, I'm here to pick up a friend coming in on Cape Air which is due to be arriving soon. Can you tell me if it's on time?"

"Yes, sir, we have a flight coming in from San Juan in about 10 minutes. Is that the one?"

"I guess that's the one."

"Are you sure?" the clerk asked. "The next Cape Air arrival isn't due until 4 this afternoon."

"It's okay, I'll wait for this one. Thanks."

"Sir, if you go out through the doors to your right, you'll be able to watch for the plane. It'll be coming down the runway on your right."

Bill went outside and with his binoculars, he searched the skies to the west. Seeing nothing, he started pacing in front of the building. Looking at his watch didn't help.

Finally he heard the drone of airplane engines. Raising his binoculars he saw a twin-engine propeller-driven plane approaching the runway. Within moments the craft was on the ground, taxiing toward the building behind him. The ground crew ran to meet and quickly secured the stairs next to the plane's front door, which swung open.

Passengers appeared and descended the stairs. A group of young couples crowded one another, exchanging friendly banter, slapping each other on their backs, and raising their hands with high fives.

Watching their antics caused Bill to smile. They were acting as if they were a bunch of best friends, who were happy to be on Culebra.

Next to exit was a silver haired gentleman accompanied by a slender dark-haired beauty. They radiated sophistication and wealth, NS Bill imagined they owned a yacht moored at the Club Seaborne.

Waiting for more people to appear, he stayed there looking at the stairs for a few more minutes. Where was Molly? His shoulders sagged with disappointment, and he turned to go

He hadn't taken two steps when he heard someone call his name.

Doing an about-turn he saw Molly, who was smiling and waving at him. She was all grace and beauty as she practically danced down the stairs. Running toward Bill, she held her arms open.

Feeling his heart flutter, he smiled and stepped toward her, his arms open to meet her.

Embracing him she planted a kiss on his check. "I'm so excited! I can't wait to christen your sub. Are you ready?" Molly was a bundle of joy. Not waiting for an answer, she took her backpack off her shoulders and pulled out a bottle of champagne. "I'm ready!"

Bill smile covered his face. "Only one? I thought you'd bring a case."

"I would have if I knew you wanted more!" she pouted.

Picking her up, he twirled her around. "Stop that right now, young lady. I just think it's a waste of good wine to break a full bottle of champagne over a ship's bow."

Molly giggled like a school girl. "We'll do whatever you want."

Two men driving a cart full of luggage headed toward the terminal building. "Let's get your bags and dive gear; then we can get on with it."

Walking hand in hand they aimed toward a white wooden lean-to located just outside the terminal's back door Watching the two men dressed in gray uniforms throwing luggage onto racks they waited while the rowdy crowd of young passengers collected their belongings. Finally, Molly grabbed her duffle bag while Bill hoisted her dive equipment onto his shoulder and led her to Mickey's truck in the parking lot..

"What made you go to San Juan?" Bill asked once they were seated in the truck and driving back to the hostel.

Molly winked. "You'll see later."

Arriving at the hostel, Bill parked the truck next to the wet sub. Its yellow paint glistened in the sunlight.

"Bill, she is beautiful!" Molly jumped out of the truck, ran to the sub and caressed its hull. "Oh, my, Bill, she is a masterpiece. And I love her smile! What are you going to name her? Show me everything!"

Molly's excitement surprised Bill, and watching her explore his work energized him. Her questions were numerous, detailed and enthusiastic.

Molly sat inside the wet sub, pretending to drive it. Looking up at Bill with admiration, she said, "Let's go try her out!"

CHAPTER TWENTY-THREE

"How did you ever find this place?" Molly asked Bill who guided the borrowed truck and trailer onto a dirt road with signs posted by the U.S. Navy. "This is a restricted area, off limits to the public."

"We'll stay just outside the restricted area. This is off the beaten path—limited exposure to the public. We don't need tourists gawking at the sub.

Parking the truck close to a sand dune, Bill grinned over at Molly. "Are you set? We'll take her off the trailer and slide her in the sand 'til we reach the water."

"That'll be easy," Molly agreed. As she stepped onto the warm sand, Molly caught sight of something on the shoreline.. "Look, Bill, what's that over there?"

"Looks like a heap of rusted scrap."

Bill followed Molly who ran along the surf line.

"Look, Bill. It's an old Army tank." The rusted heap was partly submerged in the water. "They were built rugged, weren't they?"

"They're built for war. But, come on, we have a christening to get to!"

Molly grabbed Bill's hand, and together they ran back to the trailer. Soon they were pushing the sub over the sand to the water's edge.

"Should I get the champagne now?" she asked.

"No, I want to take the sub down first. And I hope you don't mind, but I want to drive it alone, just to make sure everything is ship-shape," he said as they donned their scuba gear.

Molly nodded at Bill. "I understand why you have to do a solo dive. Besides, I'll be busy with this!" She pulled a camera out of her dive bag and held it up. "Surprise! I got this Go Pro so I can record your maiden dive." She placed the camera on her head.

"First champagne, and now this!" Bill exclaimed and leaned forward to give her a quick kiss.

Bill climbed inside the sub, and Molly gave it an extra hard thrust. The wash of a wave receding from the beach helped pull the sub into the clear blue water. In the next moment, the sub slipped silently beneath the surface.

Submerging herself in the clear warm water, Molly swam after the yellow craft which was already about 200 feet ahead of her.

With visibility a good 300 feet in the crystal clear calm water, Molly started filming as Bill maneuvered the sub.

Molly could clearly see the sub but couldn't close in on it until Bill lowered it to around 30 feet below the surface. There he hovered in neutral buoyancy, just above the sandy ocean floor.

Swimming alongside the wet sub, Molly filmed the test voyage, giving Bill a thumbs up. He then signaled that he was ready to move forward into deeper waters.

Bill tested the craft's maneuverability, making it sway side-to-side before making it roll effortlessly into a loop. Everything worked like a charm; all that Bill had envisioned was actually happening. In fact, the sub's performance proved to be beyond his expectations, given his limited work facility and equipment. His impromptu, inventive imagination surprised Bill himself.

He did one more deep dive before surfacing. As he broke through the water, Molly was there, filming.

She turned off the camera and removed her regulator. "That was fabulous! I recorded all your stunts. Now put this on. It's light weight and is equipped with a bright two-mode dive light and a rechargeable battery that will burn up to 210 minutes. The light will alternate between spot light to a flood light for maximum versatility."

Bill was impressed. "Where did you find this?"

Molly was thrilled that he liked her gift. "In San Juan. It's yours to keep. Put it on your head and take me for a ride."

Turning the wet sub around, they shoved it back into deeper water. Scrambling aboard, they settled into their seats while the wet sub began to submerge. Their merriment enhanced the adventure, and they did not focus on where they were heading. They filmed the underwater sites surrounding them. More rusted pieces of military debris appeared scattered along the ocean's bottom.

The sub's depth gauge registered 50 feet below the surface. Bill was impressed that the air level in his tank was hardly moving; with only a few bubbles from his tank floating upward.

A dark shadow appeared to their right. Changing course, Bill headed directly toward it. As viability cleared, they caught sight of a large armored tank sitting comfortably on the sandy bottom. Barnacles encrusted every visible area. Surrounding the tank were countless colorful fish, and two contented nurse sharks napped in the shadows underneath the wartime relict.

Bill hoped the Go Pro was capturing the beauty of the scene.

While circumnavigating the tank they came across four 55-gallon barrels lying on their sides, nestled in the sandy bottom and abutting the artillery tank.

Looking out of place, the barrels appeared to be recent additions. The two explorers looked at each other with wonder. Each barrel was riddled with holes, as if they were drilled there purposely, letting the water filter into them.

Resting the wet sub on the bottom, Bill let it idle and motioned to Molly to follow him. Together they swam out of their vehicle and moved closer to get a better look at their discovery.

Focusing the Go Pro's spotlight into the holes didn't give a clue as to the contents of the barrels.

Bill thought if he removed the covers on the barrels, he could find out, but he couldn't bulge them. Molly followed Bill back to the wet sub where he logged in the location of the tanks on the dive gage's GPS.

Rerouting the wet sub's direction, he discovered they had inadvertently traveled north into the heart of the Navy's restricted area. He took the sub up to the surface to get his bearings and after adjusting their heading, they arrived safely back on shore and out of the restricted area.

"What do you make of those barrels?" Molly exclaimed while removing her gear. "I don't think they are part of the tank; they look too new. I wonder how did they got there."

"I don't think the Navy put them there, but what's inside of them has to be something heavy for them not to float to the surface. And why would they be buried in 50 feet of water if there wasn't something to hide?"

"Exactly!" Molly replied. "Good thing you got it on film. We can view it with a fine-toothed comb, and if necessary, report it."

"Molly, that's not so easy. This area is off limits to the public. We could be arrested for trespassing on posted Government property."

"But, Bill, we didn't trespass on purpose. And besides, whatever is in those barrels could be valuable, maybe even something the Navy has been looking for.

"Well, for now we have more important things to do. Let's get the champagne and celebrate a successful dive."

They carted their gear and the Go Pro back to the pickup. While Molly went to the cooler with the champagne, Bill inspected the wet sub for possible damage. Seeing none, he relaxed and sank into his own little world, watching the changing shades of blue extending out into the ocean. Smiling, he dug his feet dug into the buttery sand and basked in the contentment of this special moment. All the turmoil he had experienced during the past year faded away.

Bouncing back over the warm sand, Molly held up the chilled bottle of champagne. "Here's to the yellow submarine."

She handed the bottle to Bill, who deftly popped the cork, which flew into the sky. Foaming bubbles ran down the side of the bottle as Bill poured the fluid over the wet sub's happy smile.

"I christen thee the *Molly T.*"

"Oh, Bill!" Molly gasped.

"Well, it was your idea, wasn't it?" He smiled at Molly.

"Not all of it."

"But your spirit moved me to create it." He gave her a quick kiss. "Thank you for being here with me. Now take a swig."

"Out of the bottle?"

"Yep, I don't see anyone with fancy stemmed glasses coming toward us. Watch me, it's not difficult." He raised the champagne bottle to his lips for a sip. "Cheers to us! We make a good team."

Molly wiped tears from her eyes. "It's your day!" Flinging her arms around him, she added, "Congratulations!"

Holding her tightly in his arms, Bill pressed his lips to hers, the splendor of the moment overwhelming him. The champagne bottle tilted, leaking white fizzy suds on them like a fountain. Bill quickly righted the bottle. "Now take a swing like a big girl."

Her eyes sparkled as she complied. Together, they frolicked in the surf like carefree children, pausing at times to finish off the champagne. Happy and mellow, they noticed the sun dipping to the west.

"This was the best day ever," Molly declared as they drove slowly back to the hostel.

CHAPTER TWENTY-FOUR

The island of Vieques is a secret paradise, and the sweetness of the land can be felt as soon as you step foot ashore. Beachcombers flock to the white sandy beaches, searching for shells and sea glass. The sparkling blue water plays host to sailors, scuba divers, and charter fishing tours. The local fishermen sell their prizes to the restaurants that line the Malecon, making it a joint effort of the islanders to help each other, and everyone wins.

Wild horses roam freely about the island, and deep within the interior is a jungle hiding remnants of another world. The island life is a buzz with boutiques, restaurants, and opportunities for unforgettable adventures. Accommodations can be found at bed and breakfast inns, private homes, multiple hotels, and the world famous five-star resort, The W. Retreat and Spa.

At the W. Retreat, Brad and Sammi enjoyed the lap of luxury in their honeymoon suite, awakening each morning with breakfast served to them in a king-sized bed adorned with silky white satin sheets. The hospitality offered to them was beyond the imagination for the couple who had met in a dirty dark, smoke-filled bar in north central Florida. Attracted to one another, the bizarre duo united forces by mowing lawns and repairing mobile homes. One day they noticed an advertisement offering a boat in exchange for helping around a marina.

Mickey and Gertie hired them, and soon the two lovers were living aboard an old boat that they fixed up in their spare time. All went well until a hurricane trashed the marina and every other boat, including Sam and Brad's.. Insurance companies were overwhelmed with claims, and the two con artists convinced the insurance adjuster their wrecked boat was worth far more than his estimate. Their outlandish claim was paid in full. Mickey and Gertie tried the same scheme and received a similar windfall for their damaged marina. Searching the internet, they found a hostel for sale on the island of Culebra.

Brad and Sammi soon followed, and the normally dirty, sweaty, maintenance workers started a new phase of their lives.

"We've come a long way, baby," Brad told Sammi as they enjoyed the view from their balcony. "But our honeymoon here with the rich and famous has to come to an end."

"Let's celebrate one last time," Sammi begged. "See that girl down there? The one who's all alone in paradise? She's begging for company."

"Okay, honey," Brad said, "she can be your wedding present. Let's invite her to see the plankton tonight."

Brad and Sammi were accustomed to the natural beauty the island offered, especially the Bioluminescent Bay said to be the brightest in the world. Single celled plankton create an eerie bluish light when touched. The dazzling results were a tourist attraction available every night by boat.

"She might even like to dive with the plankton," Sammi said. "Tourists always like seeing the electric-blue flashes in the dark water. Let's get dressed. It's time to share some Mojitos with our new girlfriend."

Soon Brad and Sammi were sauntering with the blond who had looked younger from the distance, but she was alone on vacation and had no issue with hooking up with two gay strangers. She walked arm in arm between Brad and Sammi along the shoreline where vendors at small kiosks sold gifts, mostly arts and craft items.

Brad and Sammi were familiar to many of the vendors as they often helped out at a mojito kiosk, giving the owner, Joe, some time off. Today, though, Joe was happy to serve Brad, Sammi and their new friend unlimited free drinks.

***

Awakening at dawn, Bill wasn't ready to open his eyes just yet. He enjoyed the soothing sound of soft rain bouncing off the deck above, allowing him to float into reality as he thought about the rain. *A passing early morning shower, not a bad thing, it'll wash the salt off the hull.*

He remembered that he planned to take Molly to The Dinghy Dock for one of Mel's special breakfasts and to follow up on Mike's e-mail while he was there. He was eager to know Mike's ideas on how Richard was tracking him down.

Smelling the aroma of fresh brewed coffee drifting into his cabin sparked his desire to get up. Turning over to ponder the unrumpled side of the bed, he wished that he was ready to take the next step with Molly. But he wasn't ready for intimacy just yet, because his baggage still overwhelmed him at times. But that didn't stop his desire to get lost in shared passion.

He sighed. It would just have to wait.

Quietly slipping into his shorts and a t-shirt, he strolled into the salon. Molly's back was turned so she was facing the ship's hull while she poured coffee into a cup.

"Good Morning, something smells inviting," Bill said.

She turned toward him with a vibrant smile, and he realized anew how special she was.

"Hi, sleepy head, are you ready for some java?"

"You never seem to disappoint me, plus you're always full of vim and vigor."

"Well, for one thing, I'm still on a high from yesterday. Bill, you are awesome! That wild dream of yours really came true."

"Hey, cut it out, I'm no hero, but I do appreciate your enthusiasm. I'm pleased with the sub's performance myself, but there's still work to be done."

Hesitating, she asked, "Do you mean the barrels?"

"A project always needs refining, and, yeah, the barrels are part of it," he admitted. "Because we were in restricted water, how we approach exposing our find needs to be carefully calculated."

"Oh, Bill, why so serious? We don't have to tell anyone about the barrels. For all we know there's nothing special left in them. But let's watch the Go Pro video." She gave him a quick kiss on the cheek. "Just relax, everything will be all right."

Marveling at her free spirit, he smiled before focusing on the coffee. "Are you hungry? Let's go get breakfast. The shower has passed."

"Do you want more coffee?"

"Nah, I'll wait, but why don't you take one to go. When we reach the Dinghy Dock I'd like to e-mail Mike to see if he has any news about Richard's appearances. I'm going out to dry off the seats in the dinghy. Meet me there."

Pouring some coffee into an insulated tumbler, Molly dumped the rest down the drain and joined Bill on the dock.

The Dinghy Dock was crowed as always. Jennifer escorted them to a table for two. After feasting on rum-soaked French toast, Bill patted his stomach with contentment.

"That was sinfully delicious," Molly said.

Bill pulled his computer out of its case. "Molly, please excuse me for a while, I need to see Mike's news."

"Sure, I'll watch the tarpon play."

Booting up his computer, he opened his mail, and found Mike's note.

Richard must be monitoring your cell phone conversations. He probably got clearance from his friend at the Mystic Police Department. Remember Sargent Carlson? Don't forget, he thinks you pushed Shirley off the boat, and he's not about to forgive you for that. He's obsessed with making you suffer for such a murderous act. Maybe it's time for you to come back home and confront him directly. That would end your torment.

Bill thanked Mike for his discovery and felt better prepared to handle situations in the future. He continued telling Mike about the wet sub and described how it well it worked. Closing the computer, he looked around the restaurant to see Molly and Jennifer deep in conversation.

"Okay, that's enough chit-chat, ladies," he teased them. "It's time for us to leave."

Molly joined Bill and said, "See you next time Jen,"

On the ride back to the hostel, Molly told Bill how frightened Jennifer was about all the disappearances of the women on the island of Vieques. She also mentioned Jennifer's o ther concern, how Bill's wife could vanish without a trace.

"She getting an uneasy feeling about your story, too," Molly added. "I told her that you still are confused about your wife's fate."

"Yeah, she's talked to me about those missing women, too. I don't know what it is, but she's obsessed about them; their disappearances scares the hell out of her. About my wife, Richard planted an element of doubt when he told her I killed Shirley."

Returning to the hostel, Molly went to the shower room to get a towel she had left behind after bathing last evening. While she was there, Bill busied himself attaching the Go Pro camera to his television.

Finding her towel Molly rushed back toward the dock and nearly knocked Mickey down. "Oh my, I didn't see you there. I'm sorry, Mickey, are you all right?"

"I guess so. What's the rush?"

"Nothing really, just lost in my thoughts."

"It's good to see you back here, Molly."

"Thanks, it's good to be here. Our dive was a major success. It was nice of you to allow Bill to work on the sub here. It really turned out to be fabulous." She paused. "I want to thank you for making other bathing arrangements for that Sammi person, the one that dresses like a woman. He is an odd one."

"Yeah, somewhat, but he means no harm. Molly, while I've got your attention, I want to caution you about Bill."

Molly turned rigid. "Bill? What's up with Bill?"

"A Captain Maurino Rodriquez from the Regional Police Department in Fajardo paid me a visit the other day. He asked me a few questions about Bill's background. Someone from up north stopped by his office and told the captain that Bill killed his wife."

"That's ridiculous! Bill never killed anyone! So, what did you tell the man?"

"Never mind what I said. Do you know for sure that Bill didn't kill her? Were you there?"

"Mickey, don't be absurd! NO, I wasn't there! But I know Bill, and he's suffering from Post-Traumatic Stress because of the incident. He feels remorse over his wife's disappearance. You do know that he almost died, don't you? Well, for your information Bill was found unconscious on the deck of his boat and was flown to a hospital and admitted to ICU. When released from there he went through a lengthy recuperation period."

Raising up his arms, Mickey said. "Molly, calm down, the cop was just doing his job, especially with what's going on over on Vieques. I'm sure you've heard about all those missing women."

"I thought we were talking about Bill. He's carrying this grief around because his wife's body has never been found. He's never had closure, damn it!"

"Bingo! The women from Vieques have never been found either. So is there something in common here?"

Molly was exasperated. "Look, Bill didn't kill anyone. Get over it! If I were you, I'd be watching Sammi; there is something troubling in his behavior. He's one scary mother!!"

Stomping off with her towel, she mumbled, "I'm not going to upset Bill with such trivia." Climbing aboard the sailboat, she slipped down the hatch and displayed the towel. "I got your towel back. Are we ready for the first viewing of the *Molly T?*"

"We're all set. I even made us some popcorn."

"I knew I smelled something good."

The Go Pro recording was spectacular. It captured the vivid colors of the water, fish, and coral as brightly as in real life. Placing her hand on Bill's knee, she said, "I feel as if I'm still there."

"If that was the case, this popcorn would be soggy."

"Stop it! Bill, look at you go, that sub is something else. If the Navy ever sees this, they'd be sorry they let you go."

"We're coming up to that submerged tank; let's take a good look at those barrels. It's perplexing. I'm sure the Navy didn't put them there. Look how the two barrels on this side are encrusted with barnacles. They have holes around the bottom, which allows water to flow inside."

The Go Pro continued to play when the barrel without barnacles came into sight.

Bill stopped the video. "Molly, did you see that?"

"No, what did I miss?"

Backing up the recording, Bill slowly started moving the video forward. "Look, there's a crab at one of the holes. There! There it is! What is it eating?"

"Oh, no, no, no! It's someone's finger! See the red nail polish on the fingernail!"

"It can't be!" Bill exclaimed. Rewinding the last segment, he went through it frame by frame. Sure enough, caught in the crab's claw was the decaying flesh of a decomposing finger showing signs of red polish on the nail.

Molly got up from the sofa and ran to the head. Bill heard her retching.

And my troubles begin anew.

No way could he ignore the whole incident. He had an obligation to report their find. He would just have to take whatever punishment they imposed on him—for what? Venturing into a restricted area? Finding a woman's body in a barrel?

He shivered as if he'd just been dropped into an icy sea—then mourned that it was just another part of his life's drama which was turning more outlandish by the day.

CHAPTER TWENTY-FIVE

Bill heard Molly fumbling about in her cabin, but he wanted to wait a few more minutes before interrupting her. Time passed, and still no Molly. Anxious, he walked toward the aft cabin to check on her. He found Molly with all her gear piled in a heap on the floor in front of her.

"Bill, I need to go! I didn't sign up for this. Your wet-sub is fabulous, and I wish you well with finding someone to help you solve the mysteries that are in those barrels. I can't and WON'T be part of it! So please, if you will, take me to the ferry dock. I'll go back to Fajardo and get a flight back to Tortola."

Her stunning words upset him. "Molly, you don't have to go. You can stay a little longer. Gee, you've only been here a few days."

Molly's impish style had disappeared, and Bill saw a frightened weary stranger in front of him. He took a step toward her, but she stopped him. "Bill, please, things are way too serious. Mickey told me the cops stationed in Fajardo were here looking for you. It had to do with something related to your wife's death, and Jennifer told me she was suspicious of your story. Now, will you take me to the dock, or do I have to beg Mickey for a ride?"

Bill's jaw dropped, outrage filling his face. "That bastard! He's gone way over the top!"

Moving aside quickly, Molly retorted, "See what I mean. You need help, but not from me! I'm not going to be sucked into a murder rap. I'm out of here!!"

"Molly, please!"

When she stood her ground, he knew he was defeated. There was no winning this battle. Picking up her gear, he motioned for her to follow him. "Let's go. Get in the dinghy." Jumping in as instructed, Molly sat on the bench seat in the center of the boat. Bill followed with her gear in tow.

Leaving the hostel, the only noise heard on the dinghy ride was the sound of the small motor's hum and the splashing of the propeller

167

gliding the boat through the water, plus a few squawking gulls passing above them.

Reaching the ferry dock, Bill killed the motor. Placing Molly's gear on the pier, he felt her glaring eyes assault him as she climbed out of the dinghy.

"Later, Bill." Bending down, she awkwardly struggled to pick up all her gear, then walked away.

Watching her leave him as the dinghy drifted away from the dock, he muttered, "Damn it, Shirley! Why are you tormenting me? If you only would have left a trace of yourself behind."

***

Mike knew that Bill would never return to confront Richard, so he took the task on himself. Stopping by Richard's house, he walked up to the front door and rang the bell. Unsure if anyone would answer, he tried just the same. It wasn't a long wait when the door slowly opened. The casually dressed man stuck his head out the door, appearing as if he had just been roused from a sound slumber.

For a moment Mike felt a surge of guilt and doubted his intentions. "Hi, Richard, we've met before; I'm a friend of Bill Adams." Waiting for a reply, Mike wondered about the man's strange behavior. Then he reminded himself that Richard's actions of vengeance and the strange sightings had the makings of an unstable stalker.

Appearing dazed for an instant, Richard took a moment to become focused. "Oh, you! What the hell do you want here? Get lost!"

Shoving his foot forward, Mike tried to prevent the door from slamming in his face. "Hey, just hear me out. I won't be long."

Richard relented. "Spill it out, what do you want?"

"Well, first of all, I am curious to know if you've ever heard from Bill's wife Shirley?" Mike was deliberately trying to push Richard's buttons. He'd been rehearsing the situation over and over with Wendy and was trying to read Richard's body language.

Richard's voice was deep and thunderous. "Shirley? Pete's sake, man! We all know that your friend killed her. Have you forgot, he pushed her off that boat of his." Richard was clearly agitated, and he clenched his fists.

Mike was surprised at the clues Richard was broadcasting—the

168

tightness around his mouth, his fists tightening. He had to stop himself from smiling. It was obvious, his question had pushed more than one button. "Then I assume you haven't seen her, right?"

Locking his arms across his chest, Richard continued. "I don't believe in ghosts. Do you?"

The traffic in the street was light, but Mike looked around to check if there was anyone close by. Not seeing anyone he pushed his point harder. "So, have you seen her, or haven't you?"

"Hey, wise guy, I've told you all I know. You're harassing me, plus you're trespassing on my property. Now leave. I have connections with the police department."

"No, no, wait, there's something I need to know. I'm asking you this because my friend Bill said he heard that you came to visit him on the island of Culebra with some blonde woman."

Forcing a crooked smile, Richard replied. "Oh, so you heard, that's perfect!" He clenched his jaw. "That no good SOB should be in jail."

Not wanting to give in just yet, Mike stalled. "Wait just a minute, Richard! What about you? You're the one who seduced Bill's wife, weren't you? You and Shirley were having an affair. It wasn't Bill at all. You both did your dirty little deeds behind his back. Then you somehow convinced Shirley that she needed to leave Bill and move in with you. You're nothing but the worst kind of scum-bag. Now leave Bill alone. He loved Shirley, but he was busy making a living while you and Shirley were making whoopee! And what about your friend Sargent Colman with the police department? Are you hitting on her now?"

Mike caught himself just before he was going to mention the cell phone conversations.

Richard's face was beet red, and he was more than furious. Mike knew it was time to leave, because he didn't want to be attacked by Richard, who was in good shape for a middle-aged man.

Raising his voice to a screech, Richard was unabating. "Look, mister, what I do is my business, not yours. Get out and don't EVER come back!" Richard slammed the door shut, rattling the frame.

Mike was relieved and could not help but smile. *Richard knows something about Shirley, but what could it be?*

Maybe it was time do some sleuthing of his own.

***

Richard stood rigid, leaning his back against the front door. His heart was racing, and he felt faint. He was just thankful that Shirley wasn't there. That would have been a disaster. Shirley was in respite care at the private behavioral health facility near her mother. Shirley's counselor had recommended a short stay there, one beneficial to both of them. Shirley was gradually regaining some memory functions, which caused her to become agitated at times. Richard was trying to cope, but he was tired of it all, getting weary of the stress.

Agreeing with the professionals, he accepted the respite services. Another thing on his mind was the need to discuss a guardianship for Shirley with her mother. His investment with Shirley's care involved a great deal of time and effort. Because it looked like her recovery was likely to happen, he felt an urgency to protect himself from any backlash from Bill. The inscrutable truth would soon be hard to conceal.

To make things worse, now Bill's meddling buddy Mike had become someone to be reckoned with. "Who does that punk think he is, coming around here? He's going to pay for it. Wait and see, it's not over yet."

CHAPTER TWENTY-SIX

*"Take Sides. Neutrality helps the oppressor, never the victims.
Silence encourages the tormentor, never the tormented."*

Elie Weisel

Rising in the east, the sun's red and orange hue cast a reflection on the clear water below. Sitting on the dock in front of her apartment, Molly felt a soft breeze teasing her rosebud curls. Perching herself on the edge of the dock with her feet dangling below, she swayed them back and forth. Her mind was deep in thought, so much so that she didn't hear the squawking gulls or the clanging from the halyards of a sailboat anchored in the harbor. A large sea cow she usually treated to fresh water was floating patiently below, but the water hose remained curled around the piling.

So deep in thought, Molly didn't even notice the familiar sound of an outboard motor of a boat arriving at her dock.

"Miss Molly, what are you doing here?" The inquiry startled her. Molly had asked Tom to check on her place while she was in Culebra.

She gathered her wits before responding. "Oh, Tom, I left Culebra early, which was a big mistake, and now it's too late to change it. I really messed things up."

Tom shut off his boat's engine. He handed Molly a line attached to the bow of his boat, and she cleated it to the dock. "Miss Molly, it sounds like you've had more trouble with Bill."

Shaking her head and inhaling a deep breath, she said, "It was a fabulous time, his wet-sub is superb, and it was a flawless trial run. He even christened it the *Molly T.*

"Then I don't understand why you're sitting here all alone only a few days into your visit."

Taking another deep breath, she continued. "It all went to hell when I freaked out. It should never have happened. Bill needs me now more than any time before, and I've abandoned him."

Tom was sympathetic. "What is it? Tell me what's bothering you."

"That damn neighbor of his in Connecticut made a visit to Culebra and started rumors. The jerk goes to Fajardo to tell the cops that Bill killed his wife. Then he indicates that Bill could be involved with the missing women on Vieques. Everyone's watching Bill with suspicion.

"To top things off, during our wet-sub dive we discovered a bunch of barrels lying on the sandy bottom beside a World War Two tank located about 50 feet below the surface. We recorded the dive on the Go Pro I gave Bill. Later, while watching the video, we discovered that at least one of the barrels contains body parts. A woman's hand! I was so horrified with our discovery that I left. I didn't even say good-bye. Now I regret it, but there's no way I can apologize."

Bending down on one knee next to Molly, Tom put his arm on her shoulder. "You can go back. I'll take you. You know I never thought the relationship would go very far, and I didn't think it was good for you, but somehow Bill has entered your heart. You need to tell him you care."

"I know, Tom, but I'm not sure he'll want me back. I was mean and nasty to him, and it wasn't his fault. But he needs my support, and I'm a witness to his discovery. If he was the killer, he never would have taken me to that location. He was as shocked as I was to see that crab eating a human finger! But I had just heard about the missing women on Vieques, and I panicked."

"Get your luggage; I'll fly you back. First, we'll circle his boat—he'll know it's you. I'll call him on his VHF. He'll come for you, I know it."

Molly hesitated. "Tom, are you sure? I'm so afraid he'll reject me. He doesn't need more torment."

"Get your stuff while I give the manatee some water."

"Oh, I forgot all about it being there, thanks." Molly ran toward her apartment. "I'll be right back."

***

An early morning rain shower passed as quickly as it began, leaving behind a thick gray mist. Bill wasn't in the mood for breakfast at the Dinghy Dock. In fact, he was in a lousy mood and moped around the salon, dragging his feet, feeling dejected. He couldn't shake the terrible ending of one of the most glorious days of his life. He wondered what the hell happened to Molly, his playful companion? How could she change her personality so drastically? She owed him an apology.

Just another reason not to go to the Dinghy Dock. He knew he might e-mail her a nasty note; it was best not to do anything for a while. Instead, he poured himself a cup of coffee from the pot he had brewed earlier and climbed up the steps to the cockpit to sulk.

The air was heavy with humidity, and bubbles of perspiration covered his skin. Just another nuisance to contend with. Bill knew the sun would break through the clouds soon, and a cool sea breeze would start to dry things off. Hopefully, the sunshine would improve his mood. For now, he felt like a broken man.

Peering through the gloomy mist, he shook his head at the terrible turn his life had taken. The smell of rain lingered in the air as he wondered what to do next? He felt so alone, like when his parents were killed in that freak bus accident. *There's no one here for me, I know it's up to me to figure this out, it just seems so hard getting started.*

He knew, though, that he could not run away from this. He thought about how he'd felt about Shirley's disappearance. Whoever was in that barrel must have a family somewhere who needs to know what happened to their loved one.

He took another sip of coffee. He knew that things get easier when faced with a reason to proceed, but still, taking that first step was difficult. Felling the warmth of the sun as it rose higher, Bill knew the mist would soon be gone.

His depressed thoughts were disturbed by the loud engine whine of a fast approaching airplane. His boat started to vibrate as the sound intensified. Bill's mind sensed impending danger.

Suddenly panic overwhelmed him—something was wrong, the plane's going to crash! Looking up at the sky, he saw the pontoons of a seaplane just above the sailboat's mast. Then its wings tilted left and then right as if to wave. He sagged with relief. It was Tom! Bill's heart lifted with a thought—was Molly on the plane?. He reached for the VHF radio mounted near the helm, which constantly monitored channel 16. He waited a for few minutes until he heard Tom's voice. "Seaplane pilot to Bill Adams."

"Bill Adams here, is that you, Tom?"

"Yes, sir, and I have a passenger. She would like to know if you would come out to talk with her?"

He hesitating just long enough for Molly to doubt he would respond. "I will, but I expect an apology from her, for her obnoxious adolescent behavior. I'll be along once you land."

Taking his time; Bill didn't want to appear too anxious. In fact, he was questioning why even go. He couldn't tolerate her drama queen existence any longer. Every time she gets the least bit upset she goes ballistic.

Getting aboard his dinghy, he started the outboard, and the boat splashed through the water of the bay. As he approached the seaplane, his dinghy bobbed about in its wake. Tom and Molly crowded each other in the plane's open hatch. Guiding the dinghy below them, Bill shut off the motor.

Molly was first to speak, "Bill, thank you for coming, I'm sorry for my behavior. If it's all right with you, I'd like to help with reporting our discovery."

"Not so quickly, Molly. Not all is well. I have my own problems. I don't need you to constantly agitate my state of mind. I'm sure you were a handful for your father. Especially after he paid for your college education, and you thumbed your nose at him by living a Bohemian life, sailing around the Virgin Islands."

"That's not fair!"

"Well, I'm not your father, and I won't deal with your melt downs, so if you really want to help me, then grow up!"

Both remained quiet for a moment before Molly replied in a soft voice. "Bill, you're a great person! You've been handed a bunch of crap from everyone, including me. I am sorry for adding to your stress. I want to help you with this, and I vow to support you in whatever way I can."

Staring into her eyes, Bill replied, "That sounds like a canned speech. Actions speak louder than words. I just don't know, Molly; how can I trust you to keep your word?"

Looking beyond Molly, Bill motioned to Tom. "If you two want to hang out here for a while please do. I need time to think. I'll be back within the hour; if I don't return you better leave."

"Whatever Miss Molly wants, that's up to her."

Starting the dinghy's motor, Bill pointed the boat's bow south. After slipping out of sight, he stopped the boat and let it drift. He knew he had been hard on Molly, but his pent-up feelings just exploded into some type of madman's tirade. Knowing he must sort things out, he weighed his options.

Back aboard the seaplane, Molly was as determined as ever. "Tom, I'm not leaving, I'm staying right here. You know I can't leave him; I'd never forgive myself."

Floating on the water the plane rocked peacefully in the serene quiet of the bay. No one spoke. Soon the sound of a small motorboat closing in gave Molly hope.

"Molly, I think I've over-reacted. I should have looked at it through your eyes—it's not every day someone finds a barrel containing body parts, especially with a person who has been accused of murdering his wife. You have always believed in me, so it's my turn to believe in you. I need your support; so, please, join me, and together we'll figure this mess out."

Molly's smile rivaled the sun's rays peeking out of the clouds above them. "Oh Bill," she cried out. "I won't let you down." Seizing her belongings, she gave Tom a hug and lowered herself into the dinghy and Bill's waiting arms below.

CHAPTER TWENTY-SEVEN

Bill pointed the small outboard boat back toward the hostel; a maddening silence filled the air as neither one spoke. Bill felt his body flush, and he wiped away the perspiration beads forming on his forehead. Taking a sideward glance at Molly, he noticed her hand was placed over her heart.

"Molly," he finally said, "thank you for coming back. I do need your help. Something unfathomable has happened, and we have an obligation to report our findings."

Molly began to relax. "Thanks for breaking the ice. My heart was racing, and it was worrying me. I'm sorry about my behavior. I promise to stand by you."

Bill's face turned grim. "You know, Molly, whatever we discover in those barrels is not going to be pretty. So please consider not witnessing the contents when the barrels are opened."

"I'll take you up on that. I don't want to lose my head over this; no more freaking out. I promise."

Smiling now, Molly seemed sincere, but Bill still doubted if she had the stamina to face possible accusations and intimidations. "That's my girl."

Reaching his sailboat, Bill tied the dinghy to the swim platform. "Let's unload your bags, then we should head toward the police station. You said Mickey told you the name of the cop who came snooping around asking questions about me."

"I think it was Rodriguez, but you can check with Mickey."

"Nah, I'll take your word. The less Mickey knows about my business the better."

"I won't be long," Molly said and hurried to stow away her gear.

Bill waited for her topside. Within moments Molly bounded back up on the deck. "I'm ready, so let's get going."

Jumping back into the dinghy they sped away. The sun was high in the sky, but the cool southerly breeze drizzled salt spray on them. It was another delightful day in the tropics, and the small boat skipped over the sparkling water.

Sitting next to Bill, Molly moved closer. "So what's your plan?"

"I haven't formulated one in my head yet, but the first thing I want to do is to set the record straight with Richard. I didn't get a chance to tell you what Mike did, because we were so involved with the wet-sub."

"So," Molly said impatiently, "tell me what happened!"

"Easy girl! Mike's good intentions turned on him. He went to Richard's house and confronted him for harassing me, which upset Richard. A few days after the encounter Mike found the tires on his car slashed. After replacing them, he filed a complaint with the local police.

"The following week while driving to work he felt his car start to shimmy. When he pulled off the interstate, he discovered the lug nuts on all four tires were loose. If one of the wheels fell off while traveling at 65 miles an hour, he could have been in a serious wreck."

"Bill, that's terrible, and Mike thinks Richard did it?"

"Yes, but he has no proof."

"What about fingerprints?"

"Molly, I'm sure Mike is following up on the incident reports. He thinks we should set some type of trap. Maybe get Richard to return here, confront him, and make him stop all these games. Plus, I'd like to know who the blonde woman is."

"Sounds too risky," Molly exclaimed, "that guy is vindictive and somewhat unbalanced. There's no way of knowing what he might do to you and Mike if he's pushed into a corner."

"I know, but things are out of hand, and he must be stopped. Once we have a formal plan, we may have to work with oversight by the authorities."

"That sounds better. Do you think the blonde lady is Shirley?"

"I'd be surprised if it is. First, it can't be her, she's not like that, and secondly, I'm sure someone would have notified me if she was alive."

Guiding the dinghy up to the dock close by the police station, Bill grabbed the piling and wrapped a line around a cleat. They were soon walking toward the office. The sign on the door posted office hours:

178

Monday – Friday 8 AM to 5 PM. Knowing not to trust the sign because the hours of the police station were unreliable, he tried the door, which opened.

Entering the rather barren office, they saw a woman sitting behind a desk busy working with her computer. A large potted plant of wandering ivy with its leaves cascading down to the floor surrounded the corner behind her. The woman appeared to be in her fifties, her salt and pepper hair wrapped tight in a bun; she was dressed in a black and white uniform. The name displayed on the desk was Mrs. Chadwick, Secretary.

"Good afternoon," she said. "What can I do for you two?"

"I need some information," Bill said. "I understand that a Captain Rodriquez from the Fajardo Police Department was here recently asking questions about me. Could you tell me when he is planning to return, because I'd like to meet with him?"

"Your name, sir?"

"Bill Adams. I'm an American visiting Culebra."

"Yes, sir, the Captain doesn't come to Culebra often. Your best bet would be to go to the Fajardo Police Department; he's sure to be there."

"Thank you. Another question I have is how do I get in touch with someone from the Corps of Engineers?"

Mrs. Chadwick was perplexed. "The Corps of Engineers? May I ask why?'

"I just wanted to know more about the restricted areas on the island."

Mrs. Chadwick spoke sternly. "Mr. Adams, there are many signs posted on all the beaches outlining the restricted areas. What else would you need to know? You know that YOUR United States Navy is responsible for all the destruction they caused on our island."

Bill tried to stay cool without revealing his true intentions. "I just would like to speak with someone in that division."

Mrs. Chadwick did not hide her annoyance; she twitched about in her chair, her demeanor turning from professional to one of irritation. "The Corps of Engineers office can be found in the city of Ponce in Puerto Rico. You can find it in the Plaza de las Delicias, which is a short taxi ride from Fajardo. A large white building houses the government seat, and it represents the many municipalities of Puerto

Rico. It's the regional hub for various government entities."

Her snippy tone told Bill it was past time to leave. "Thank you, Mrs. Chadwick. Just remember, the U.S. Navy is out there protecting you and me every day."

Smiling and turning toward the door, Bill escorted Molly out of the office. Before leaving Mrs. Chadwick behind, he said. "Here's to the boys in blue," and as he walked away, he began singing "Anchor's away!"

Outside in the sunshine, he turned to Molly. "Looks like we'll be setting sail to Fajardo. Are you up to it?"

CHAPTER TWENTY-EIGHT

Setting sail at daylight for the 26-nautical-mile trip to Fajardo gave Bill peace of mind by allowing time to take care of any unforeseen mishaps that could occur. He estimated it would take them five to six hours under sail, giving them an arrival time of early afternoon. Standing behind the helm, Molly sailed the ship for most of the trip.

Enjoying the break, Bill admired her skills. The boat held a perfect reach for most of the sunny and breezy day.

Approaching the mainland, they sailed into the Villa Marina where Bill had prearranged for the dockage. The facility was a large full-service marina featuring the latest in technical equipment. Bill completed the check-in procedure quickly, and leaving the sailboat, they walked to the police station, located a few miles from the marina on Victoria street.

Arriving at the station, Bill was able to set up a meeting with Captain Rodriquez. The conference was congenial. During their discussion Bill explained the situation on his sailboat the day Shirley was washed overboard and gave the Captain references to verify his story if he desired.

The Captain was apologetic, and told Bill his obligation was to follow through on questionable activities, especially in light of the missing women on Vieques.

Bill refrained from mentioning the barrels and the probable contents that he and Molly had discovered on Culebra, wanting first to discuss the matter with the Corps of Engineers personnel.

Leaving the police station, they hailed a cab which drove them to the city of Ponce. They arranged to be dropped off at the Plaza de las Delicias, which contained an elaborate display of buildings with a colonial flair. Lion sculptures decorated each of the four corners of a central square.

They found a large white government building nestled among the others. A sign outside the entryway listed all the departments within the premises.

Once inside they followed the corridor to the office of the Corps of Engineers. The hallway was dingy with soiled finger prints on the walls. Walking down the hall, they passed very few people heading toward the exit, it didn't seem to be a busy place. They followed the directions for the Corps of Engineers office. The room's interior reflected the hallway's decor—stuffy with no windows; a rusted ceiling fan circulated slowly above them, barely moving the air.

A pleasant looking young woman sat behind a reception desk adjacent to the doorway. "Hello, how my I assist you?"

Bill wasted no time in asking to meet with one of the staff members to discuss the restricted beach areas on the island of Culebra.

The woman directed them toward the waiting area while she notified an officer. Bill and Molly sat down on what appeared to be wooden kitchen chairs and waited for further instructions.

Molly made a face, pinching her nose. "This place smells nasty."

"It's musty, maybe moldy? We better not stay too long."

The woman reappeared, followed by a gangly built man with long unkempt hair and a beard that could use a trim. His uniform consisted of a gray shirt and trousers. His black shoes were scuffed, and one was untied.

Bill and Molly rose.

"Good afternoon. "My name is Roger Poole, please follow me." He escorted them to a small cluttered cubical behind the reception area. It was as bleak as the outer areas, and his desk looked as disheveled as his appearance. "Please have a seat. You are Bill Adams, and who is your friend?"

"This is Molly."

"Glad to meet you both. I understand you wish to discuss the restricted areas on Culebra?"

"That's right. You see, we inadvertently strayed into a restricted part of a beach on Culebra."

Before Bill could continue, Officer Poole's voice became loud and domineering. "You know you have no business in those areas! It is posted for a reason! You both could have received grave bodily harm by setting foot there. It is impossible for our department to patrol that vast area of contamination. An adult as yourself should have known better and adhered to the law."

Bill was stunned and tried to make peace. "Yes, sir, it was an error of my judgement, but it was not intentional."

The officer's verbal attack continued. "Look, sir, I could fine you right now for trespassing on posted property, but since you admitted your crime, I'll let you off this time. But if you ever violate the restrictions again, your fine will be doubled; that is if you don't blow a leg off in the meantime!"

Bill knew he was fighting a losing battle and quickly decided that he didn't want to disclose his information to such a bitter, power-hungry jerk. Standing up, Bill motioned for Molly to follow suit. "I'm sorry to have disturbed your afternoon. I'll make sure that I don't wander into that area again; good day, sir."

Gripping Molly's hand, he lead her out of the office door in front of the secretary who watched them in amazement.

"That was over the top!" Molly exclaimed once they were in the hallway. "Now what?"

"Let's get the hell out of here. I need some fresh air."

The outside air was clean and clear, and a soft breeze filtered by, swaying the fronds on the palm trees. Lots of people milled about the plaza.

Looking around, Bill saw a building with a large sign advertising ice cream. A long line of people waited at the service window, anticipating their turn to be served. The ice cream stand was a nice addition to the beautiful plaza, and it drew a crowd.

"Let's get an ice cream cone," Bill suggested. "Then we can discuss our options and devise a plan."

"Yes," Molly agreed with a quick smile, "something tasty to brighten up our afternoon. Make mine strawberry."

Finding a bench shaded by two royal palm trees, Molly waited for Bill, who returned with a cone in each hand. They sat together in a companionable silence and lapped at the ice-cream. Wiping the ice-cream drips from their faces and fingers with napkins, they were forced to quickly finish the cones.

"That guy in there was so full of himself," Bill said, still seething from his encounter at the Corps of Engineers office. "He is the worst kind of environmentalist. His only goal is to patrol the area. I'm not sure if he really wants to protect the people or even the environment. To top it off he loves the power that goes with it. So be it, I have another idea, let's try the U.S. Coast Guard. They have jurisdiction over all the U.S. territories around here. I don't know why I didn't think of that before. Come on we're going back to the boat. This time I'm taking the Go Pro with us."

Hailing a cab just outside the plaza, they returned to the sailboat. The taxi cab driver gave them directions to the U.S. Coast Guard Station which was adjacent to the Costumes House in Fajardo, not far from the ferry dock.

Bill slipped down to the salon and found the GoPro on the counter. Back on deck, he held it above his head. "Thanks for the present, Molly," he exclaimed. "Come with me, I need some good luck."

Arriving at the Coast Guard station, they clambered up the stairs of a traditional styled, large white saltbox building with a red roof. They entered through a heavy white door, setting foot inside a large bright room with many open windows overlooking calm turquoise waters. The view of a myriad of colorful boats of all sizes and makes moored in the harbor pleased them and gave them hope this experience would be better than their earlier one.

Maps of the local area were displayed on the inner walls, and VHS chatter added to the ambiance. A large-screen weather map was mounted on a stand behind them. Everyone was in uniform, all acting professional and engrossed in their work.

Approaching a glass-enclosed office, Bill waited for his turn to speak with someone inside.

"Hello, do you have an appointment?" A woman asked as she slid the glass window open.

"No, I'm an American spending some time in the area. My name is Bill Adams, and I have been living on my sailboat docked on Culebra. While scuba diving there I recently made a discovery I'd like to share with someone in charge. I have a video recording on my Go Pro that I know the Coast Guard would be interested in."

"What was it you discovered?"

Bill didn't want another uncomfortable encounter. "Miss, I really think that the Commander should hear this first."

Sensing the urgency in Bill's voice, the receptionist directed them to seats in the adjacent waiting room. "Please, find a comfortable seat, and I'll try to find someone who will be available to meet with you."

"Thanks." Wandering into the waiting area Bill and Molly settled into a soft leather couch, which still had the new leather scent. Sinking down in the cushions, they watched the activity around the station.

Soon a stately man with a head of white hair dressed in an officer's uniform appeared before them. "Mr. Adams, I am Commander Wilfred Gildersleeve. How may I help?"

"Glad to meet you, sir," Bill said, coming to his feet. "I am Bill Adams and this is my friend Molly Tynin. We were diving in the waters around Culebra, trying out my wet sub in a depth of about 50 feet when we discovered some barrels near a sunken tank."

The Commander's eyes narrowed with curiosity. "Barrels, what kind of barrels?"

"Well, sir, they appeared to be 55-gallon drums. I have this video with me, and I would like to share it with you."

The officer saw the Go Pro in Bill's hand. "You must have something of importance to come to me with a video, Mr. Adams." Commander Gildersleeve instructed them to follow him.

He escorted them into his office, which wasn't plush by any means; instead it was rather professional and modest, containing a desk, a few chairs, and an array of plaques displayed on the walls emphasizing his distinguished medals and awards.

Handing his GoPro to the Commander, Bill explained, "Sir, it would save a lot of time if you would start watching the video we made. After you view it, we will gladly explain and answer any questions you might have."

Commander Gildersleeve raised his eyebrows in question and wasted no time in uploading the video from the Go Pro onto his computer, sinking into his chair as he pushed play; the recording started.

Watching the wet sub maneuvers seemed a bit odd to him, especially with the level of Bill's concern. When the film revealed the 55-gallon drums alongside the tank, he sat up straight.

"You may want to slow the pace of the video down a bit, this is where it gets intriguing," Bill warned him.

Following Bill's recommendation, the Commander adjusted the speed of the video just as the crab with the finger in its claw appeared. "What the hell? Is that what I think it is?"

Stopping the video he backed it up and froze the frame. "You said you were diving in Culebra not Vieques?"

"That's right, sir."

"That is a woman's finger in the crab's claw, isn't it?"

"That's what we thought. We never touched it though. In fact, we didn't notice it until we started watching this video when we got back dockside."

"You do have the coordinates of these barrels, don't you?"

"Yes, but I've been told by Officer Roger Poole of the Corps of Engineers not to ever go near there again."

"Does he know about the barrels?"

"No, sir, I never got the chance to tell him. He just berated me about being in a restricted area. That's when I lost interest in sharing my information with him, so we left his office and came here."

The Commander's anxiety was evident. "Screw them, I need to get my men in the water now! What's with that yellow thing you're riding in?"

"That's my wet-sub. I designed and built it."

"You built that thing? I'll be doggoned."

"Yes, sir."

"I'm making it my top priority to examine the contents of those barrels. Currently, we are conducting an ongoing investigation of the missing women from Vieques. Homeland Security and the Fajardo Police Department are also involved. You did the right thing by coming here. There is a remote possibility these barrels could be connected to their disappearance. A clever murderer would hide incriminating evidence in some obscure location like this. I'm overriding the Corps of Engineers. My men will provide the oversight for the operation and make sure no one gets hurt while in the area. But it is imperative that we discover exactly what's inside those barrels."

The Commander closed the video on his computer and swung round in his chair to face them. "I'm keeping this. Do you have the coordinates of the site?"

"Yes, I have that information recorded on my dive equipment

which is on my sailboat. The boat isn't that far from here; it's in a slip at the Villa Marina."

"Good, I expect you and Miss Tynin back here within the hour."

Bill and Molly stood as the officer came around his desk to open the door to his office. He paused. "I'm curious about your wet-sub; what is its speed through the water?"

"Well, I don't have a gauge for speed, but it can go twice the speed of a diver, maybe somewhat faster."

"That's good, and you keep it on Culebra?"

Bill was surprised by the Commander's interest. "I'm staying at a dock I rent from the hostel there and store it by their shed."

"If you don't mind, I'll have my crew stop by with a Coast Guard Cutter. They can place the wet-sub on our vessel. You're welcome to come along and give my men instructions on its operation. Just keep in mind that this is a top security mission. Under no circumstances can you tell anyone of this matter. And know that a breach of security could lead to your arrest and a possible felony conviction. But I trust you, and I'm thinking I might need your assistance, Mr. Adams. Where did you get your experience?"

"I was involved with a special submarine design project while working for the Department of the Navy in New London, Connecticut."

"Ahh," he said knowingly. "I know New London well; I received my training there. Are you some kind of engineer?"

Bill smiled with a beam of pride. "Yes, sir. And yes, I'm happy to show your men how to operate my sub."

"Great," the officer said and shook first Bill's hand and then Molly's. "I'll see you soon, then, with the coordinates, and we can get this show on the road."

Bill's face broadcast his pleasure as he and Molly walked back through the open expanses of the work station full of people working and monitoring the VHF channel.

Outside, Bill gave Molly a quick hug. "Damn, I'm so glad someone is finally listening to us!" Bill drew Molly to him and kissed her on the cheek. "Thanks for standing by me. You're the best!"

"Bill, I didn't say anything!"

"I know, but you were there to support me, just as you promised."

In response, Molly kissed him back, then taking his hand in hers, she led him down the red steps. "Let's get those coordinates! And after that, you and your yellow sub have an important mission to accomplish."

CHAPTER TWENTY-NINE

On Vieques, Brad and Sammi continued to enjoyed the pampering they received from the spa employees. They lounged around the pool and hobnobbed with the wealthy clientele. Sammi received many skeptical glances, but it never became an issue.

The eve of their departure came all too soon. While preparing to take their belongings out of the room, the chief of the maintenance staff asked them to stay. He explained his urgent need to ready the grounds for some distinguished members of Caribbean bureaucrats who would convene at the W Retreat and Spa in the coming weeks. The meeting was bound to generate news coverage and expose the plushness of the hotel to the world.

His request gave Brad pause. "What do ya think, Sammi, another week on Vieques? Why not?"

To top things off there would be a new moon the following week, providing the darkest sky over the Bio Bay. The lack of moonlight makes a spectacular display of the millions of bioluminescent dinoflagellates. The extreme darkness was bound to increase the tourist activity, and it would be profitable for their side business of selling mojito's. The honeymooners were happy to oblige and quickly completed their relocation back to the Sea Ray docked in the luxurious five-star marina on the premises.

***

A faint rumble of thunder drifted away, and the few black clouds remaining raced across the sky to a new destination. The rain drops slowly diminished, and the sky was adorned with a fabulous array of color. Bill was on the deck. "Hey, Molly, you got to see this!"

She was in the salon fetching a towel.

"Hurry up here, there is a brilliant rainbow across the harbor."

The late afternoon thunder storm had cooled the air, providing

189

relief to the steamy humidity over the mainland.

Molly made it to the deck just in time to admire the sky before the colorful splendor started to dissipate. Bill was on the phone, so Molly waited quietly, wiping up the excess water off cushions and flat surfaces.

Bill paced the deck with his cell phone to his ear. Drops of rain dripped on him from the spreaders above his head. He listened to Mike tell him of his continuing saga involving the Mystic police department, which had recently hit a snag in the criminal investigation involving his slashed tires. "The cops thought they had a lead, but it turned up to be nothing substantial."

Prior to Bill's visit to Fajardo, he and Mike had exchanged e-mails outlining the damages they suspected Richard of initiating. Their plan was to coax Richard back to Vieques so Bill could confront him of spreading false rumors about Bill being responsible for Shirley's disappearance.

"Meanwhile, Mike, you might want to stop pissing people off."

"Yeah, you're right, but that guy Richard really gets under my skin."

"Hey, the best news is that I'll be launching my wet-sub in the Bio Bay on Vieques soon. It should be spectacular. I'll be propelling the wet-sub through the glow of electric blue plankton."

"Way to go, Bill !"

"Yeah, I heard the best time of the month for seeing the bluish glow is during a new moon, which is happening in a week. I'll call you back next week with the details of my journey into the dazzling light show."

Finished with the call, Bill settled on a bench in the cockpit, a gentle warm breeze tousling his hair as it helped to dry up the puddles.

Molly finished drying things off, wrung out the towel, and prepared to hang it over the side of the boat. Feeling playful, she wound up the towel and snapped it toward Bill. He burst out laughing, "You devil! No one has done that to me in years. Give me that towel before someone gets hurt." Molly's lightheartedness was entertaining.

Grabbing the towel from her, he placed it over the rail to dry. The white hulls of a hundred boats surrounded them, but they were alone in the cockpit.

Turning around he motioned Molly to sit beside him. "We've had a whirlwind of a day and finally got the attention we needed. I have an idea that our discovery will help solve the mystery of those missing women." He placed a gentle hand on Molly's arm "What do you say, bright eyes? Let's go to Rose's for some seafood. We have a full day of sailing ahead of us tomorrow, and we need to eat."

"I'm in," Molly smiled, "and thanks for giving me a second chance. You're my hero."

"Okay, darling, let's go!" Leaping onto the dock with a spring in their steps, they walked hand in hand.

***

After intercepting Bill and Mike's phone call, Richard sat in front of his computer intently investigating hotel accommodations on Vieques. The W. Retreat and Spa was very impressive and pricy, but the plush luxury they offered was too good to ignore. He wasted no time in booking a reservation and then went to find Shirley.

He discovered her outside in the garden pulling weeds. "Hey, sweetheart, what do you say we take a little trip to Puerto Rico?"

Warm affection softened Shirley's face. "Whatever you want, Richard."

Shirley had made great strides in regaining parts of her memory, although her recollection of being washed off the sailboat still remained hidden within her mind. She continued to feel a special affection toward Richard, but when venturing out of her comfort zone, she became confused and easily lost her focus. This annoyed Richard because her behavior was difficult for him to ignore.

Shirley's mother was pleased that Shirley had found happiness without Bill, although she could never condone Shirley having an affair with Richard. Observing his affection toward Shirley, she accepted that he really loved her. She prayed daily, and in her heart she knew there was hope that Shirley would recover her repressed memory. Then the mystery surrounding that dreadful day would be revealed.

Shirley's mom also kept wishing she would hear some word from Bill, but every time she brought the subject up with Richard he became furious. Just maybe she should contact Mike to see if he knew Bill's whereabouts.

CHAPTER THIRTY

The following morning, Bill prepared the *Molly T* for the Coast Guard cutter's arrival. It was a quiet morning around the hostel with sunlight pouring down from all directions. A few sea gulls in the distance squawked at each other, probably fighting for some morsel. A couple of doves cooed sweetly on the branches of a nearby Gumbo-Limbo tree.

The hostel seemed deserted. Mickey and Gertie were not fussing around their property, and better yet, the slip at the end of the dock, home to the Sea Ray, was vacant.

At the shed where the wet-sub was stored, Bill completed the pre-check procedure, pleased that everything was in order. "She should run as good as ever," he told Molly who stood close.

"Here's the blanket you wanted," Molly said. She had retrieved it from the linen closet on Bill's sailboat.

"Thanks. Like I said earlier, it will be easier to drag the sub on the blanket instead of trying to carry her by ourselves."

Molly arranged the blanket next to the sub. Bill instructed her to lift the back while he took the front, which was heavier.

They both struggled to lift it. "Stop!" Molly yelped. "Wait, Bill, this is awkward; I need to get a better grip." She let go, and the back of the wet-sub slammed down on the ground. Bill cringed and set his end down before assessing the problem.

"I'm sorry, Bill; I lifted it before when we were at the beach, but for some reason it feels harder today."

"At the beach it was on the jet ski trailer," Bill observed. "Here, try this." Taking her hands in his, he placed one on each side of the wet-sub. "All we have to do is get it up a few feet. Then it'll be easy."

"Easy for you to say."

"All right, Molly, are you set? You don't have to lift it high, just enough to move it over the blanket. Ready? Lift!" In one quick maneuver, they settled the *Molly T* on the blanket.

"Good going, now we can drag her." Each held an end of the blanket, cradling the sub in the middle while sliding their yellow prize along the driveway.

Reaching the grass, they slid it past the gazebo toward the dock. The grass was softer but more uneven, making walking harder on their ankles.

"Perfect, Molly, you did a good job. Thanks. Let's sit down here on the dock and wait for my ride. When is Tom picking you up?"

"Oh, gosh, I forgot to tell you!"

"Tell me what?"

"I decided to stay here until we find out what's going on. While we were in Fajardo I called my boss and told him I was taking a leave of absence. I hope you don't mind."

"If that's what you want, Molly, it's okay with me. Just remember, whatever we find inside those barrels may be gruesome, like something seen in a horror show, and I'm not about to coddle to more babbling nonsense."

"I know. But I figured as long as I don't have to see whatever it is you discover first hand, I promise not to become unstrung."

Bill was skeptical, sitting there gazing into the water, not seeing a thing, just listening to the water splashing quietly against the hull of his sailboat. "Molly, I can't thank you enough for staying by me, but you need to toughen up. Remember Margaret Thatcher? They used to call her The Iron Lady; you need to be strong like that."

"I can do that, Bill, trust me."

Wanting to believe her, he decided to trust her, to give her the benefit of doubt. Besides, he didn't want her to leave. The bond he felt for her grew more resonant by the day. Putting his hand on her chin, he turned her face toward him and kissed her softly on her lips. "I know you can."

Their special moment was disturbed by the roar of diesel engines. A 45-foot Coast Guard response boat, part of the shore based fleet stationed in Fajardo, came speeding down the canal, turning abruptly, settling by the dock. The wake splashed water over their feet, causing them to jump to their feet.

"They're showing off," Bill said, noting how his sailboat rode up and down on the waves washing beneath it.

Four uniformed sailors quickly tied the lines to the dock. They stood straight as an arrow, like tin soldiers all in a row. Each appeared to be over six feet tall with muscular physiques, buzzed haircuts, and tanned skin. All were in their late twenties or early thirties.

Stepping forward, the crew chief introduced himself. "I'm Doug Sheets, and I'm in charge of this mission. You must be Bill Adams."

"Yes sir," Bill said, standing as tall and straight as he could.

Doug had coffee brown skin, brown hair, and piercing brown eyes. "These are my men, Paul, Gary, and Pete. We'll all be involved in this operation, and we work as a team; you do understand that?"

"Yes sir," Bill repeated. "This my friend, Molly Tynin. We've been expecting you."

"Hello, Miss," he said before turning his attention to the wet-sub. "So that's what Commander Gildersleeve wants us to use? It looks primitive."

Bill was offended. "Well, it's just a proto-type. It works better than it looks."

Doug turned to his men. "You guys grab it and bring it aboard. Bill, are you set?"

"Almost; I just need my gear."

"You won't need anything. We have you covered. Hop aboard!"

Bill gave Molly a quick hug before stepping aboard the response boat to watch the crew pick up his wet-sub. With little effort, they stowed it on the deck behind the cockpit, securing it as if they had done it many times before. Doug gave the word, and the men released the lines. Taking his place behind the helm, he started the engines and maneuvered the Coast Guard vessel out of the hostel's channel.

Molly stood on the dock to watch the 45-foot boat crash through the water, leaving a trail of white foam behind.

"Molly!" Mickey yelled, "What was that all about?" He and Gertie stood at the far end of the hostel.

"Oh, well, uh," she stuttered and quickly came up with an edited version of the truth. "While we were in Fajardo, Bill started a friendly conversation with Commander Gildersleeve who's in charge of the Coast Guard Base. Bill mentioned his wet-sub. The Commander was impressed so he sent these guys to take it for a ride." Trying to avoid any more probing, she smiled and waved. "I gotta go, got lots of things to do before Bill gets back. Catch ya later." She rushed down the dock and disappeared into Bill's sailboat.

CHAPTER THIRTY-ONE

Reaching open water, Doug accelerated the Coast Guard craft to a steady 30 miles an hour. The mighty boat splashed through the surf, hugging the coastline until it reached the northern most point of Culebra, studded with large coral heads. Doug guided the boat around the small islands which jutted out into the water above the point. After clearing the hazards, he brought the watercraft safely into Bahia Flamenco.

Following Bill's co-ordinates, he located the spot where the depth gauge indicated 50 feet of water below the vessel. The crew hastily lowered and set the anchor. The sea was calm in the horseshoe shaped bay, making it easy for the men to prepare for their dive. Attaching the wench hook to the wet-sub, they swung it over the deck, lowering it into the water aside the cutter.

The Scuba equipment is heavy and clumsy, making it difficult to navigate out of water. The four men making the dive couldn't wait to get overboard, while the Coastie identified as Paul was to remain on deck to control the wench needed to hoist the barrels up from the sea bottom.

Once all the divers were ready with their inflatable vests, tanks, weight belts, regulators and Go-Pros in place to document the venture, Doug gave instructions.

"Seeing you've been here before, Bill, you lead the way," Doug said. "I'll ride behind you in the sub. Pete and Gary will follow."

Bill agreed. "I'll be leading everyone to the barrel in question, the one we saw the crab holding what looked like a woman's finger."

"That's the one, we'll focus on that one first, then come back for the others. Paul, when we're ready, release the wench from the wet-sub, and we'll make our decent. Gary, you take the wench line with you. Paul, when Gary pulls the line hard three times you begin pulling her up."

"Aye, sir."

"Ready, men? Let's do it!'

The men tumbled off the side rails of the boat, splashing easily into the water. Turning to Doug, Bill gave him the traditional diver "Okay" sign, before he swam into the wet-sub. Arranging himself in the driver's seat, Bill adjusted the ballast tanks. Doug quickly placed himself into the seat behind Bill, who took the sub down. Approaching the sandy bottom, the dark outline of the submerged tank appeared.

Guiding the Molly T alongside the tank, Bill placed it in neutral buoyancy, and it floated above the sandy bottom. The nurse sharks sleeping in their place below the tank. A school of blue-green Parrot fish floated close by, and two large Angel fish eyed the divers, inspecting the intrusion into their space.

All the divers floated around the four barrels still resting near the tank. The barrels were similar in size and shape, most likely all coming from the same location. Around the base of each barrel were numerous crudely formed rounded holes. Layers of barnacles clung to the rims of the holes, on three of the barrels. Only one barrel was still clear of barnacles. Bill pointed it out to Doug, and the divers started inspecting it further. The lights from the Go-Pros didn't reveal anything notable from within the holes.

A slight current of water pushed against the men as they surrounded the barrel. They tried to move it, but it wouldn't budge. The water around them was full of bubbles rising from their regulators as they struggled to move the barrel.

Doug shook his head in frustration. The barrel was extremely heavy, seemingly laden with extra weight. Gary and Pete decided to secure the wench line to the barrel; working together they placed it around the barrel. When they were ready, Gary yanked on the line which instantly became taunt. Working in unison the men rocked the barrel until the line successfully pulled it upward.

Gary and Pete followed the barrel upward. Jumping into the front seat of the wet-sub, motioning to Bill, Doug indicated he wanted to drive. Bill backed away while Doug struggled to fill the ballast tanks. The wet-sub bounced around like a bull at Mickey Gilly's place.

Bill remained put, giving Doug time to figure out how to operate the sub. After a few minutes Bill swam up to the sub and adjusted the ballast tanks, showing Doug the way they worked. Doug kept trying on his own but finally gave up. He swam out of the sub, indicating to Bill that he was heading to the surface.

When Bill brought the sub up, the others were already on board. Removing their dive gear, they attempted to haul the barrel into the boat.

"Hey," Bill called out, "somebody up there give me a boat line for the sub." Leaning over the side, Gary threw Bill a line. After tying the wet-sub to the boat, Bill climbed aboard.

"Hey, Doug," he called out, "I thought you said you worked as a team. Don't you remember the first rule of diving? Never leave your buddy alone! And next time you want to drive my sub, clear it with me; I'll give you a lesson. Seems you could benefit from some one-on-one instructions."

Doug ignored Bill's comments, focusing instead on opening the 55-gallon barrel. A ring clamp encircling the lid which was secured with a tight bolt. "Damn thing won't budge," Doug grumbled. "Pete, get me a wrench and a hammer. I'll whack it free."

Placing the wrench on the bolt Doug used the hammer to move it. It took a few adjustments, a lot of elbow grease, and determination to open the barrel.

With the lid removed, the hideous contents were revealed to the sound of a collective gasp.

"Holy mother of God!" Gary exclaimed. The others remained speechless.

Bill thought he had readied himself for the horrifying reality of finding a dead body inside the barrel, but he never dreamed of such carnage: a decomposing body of blue-gray skin sparsely covering a skeleton, facial skin eaten away, worms crawling out of the hollowed-out eye sockets. The limbs were covered with hordes of crabs, eels, worms, and other sea creatures feeding on the body.

"Where did all those crabs come from?"

"They got in though the holes at the base of the barrel, and now they want to get out," Bill said. Crabs scattered on the deck and swarmed around the men's feet.

"Get those vermin outa here now!" Doug screamed.

Gary and Pete danced around as if standing on hot rocks. Grabbing a mop, Paul pushed the crabs aside, while Pete turned a hose on them.

They floated into the scupper, falling off the boat into the water below.

Bill leaned forward. "Looks like the body was dismembered to fit in the barrel. Do you think there is only one body in there?"

"For God's sake, I hope there's only one. It's hard to tell with all the eels slithering over it." Doug's voice was taut with stress.

"Wait a minute," Bill said. "What's that dangling around the arm?"

Doug paused for a minute while they examined the plastic bracelet. "Looks like one of those things that glows in the dark that kids play with."

Bill nodded. "Yeah, it could be one of those, but you know that scuba divers have to wear glow sticks during their night dives. That's puzzling, I've never heard of scuba divers in the bio bay, have you?"

"No, I haven't, but it's something to check out." Doug turned to his crew. "Gary, you and Pete secure the lid back on this barrel. With all the water draining out, it won't take long for the stench of death to overwhelm us. Forensics has lots of work to do. This body could very well belong to any one of those women missing from Vieques.

Doug turned to Bill. "You may have found a breakthrough in the case. "

"Hopefully it will help in finding the person or persons behind this atrocity," Bill said, "if indeed this is one of the missing women."

An oppressive mood overtook the crew.

"I guess we'll know more after we raise the other barrels."

The crew made short work of bringing up the remaining drums, all of which contained human remains in various states of decomposition.

With their grim finds on board, they hoisted Bill's sub up and secured it before making haste to depart.

When the boat was far enough off shore and away from any nautical hazards, Doug placed it on a plane, taking it up to optimal speed, its hull ruthlessly slapping into the waves, spewing fountains of water high above the bow.

"You know," Bill said to Doug, raising his voice above the sound of the engines, "I don't envy the guy who has to break the sad news to the family members."

"Yeah, Bill, that's a nasty dirty detail, it's not going to be easy even for our Chaplain."

Doug changed the subject. "That wet-sub of yours has possibilities. Its speed is impressive. It's quite a piece of equipment, and it's harder to operate than it first appears."

Bill grinned. "Next time, I'll give you a lesson. I'm sure with a little training you'll get the hang of it."

"If you don't mind, we'll keep it with us until we meet you in Vieques. The Commander wants you to contact him after arriving there. Then he'll fill you in about our objective. Remember, not a word about this mission to anyone, not even your girlfriend."

"Don't worry, Doug, she wouldn't want to know. She saw enough watching the Go-Pro video. She's too squeamish to even inquire."

Returning to Ensenada Honda, Doug idled his boat up the channel to the hostel's dock, pulling in behind Bill's sailboat.

Jumping onto the dock, Bill waved a goodbye and watched as the boat roared out of sight, trailing behind a wake that rocked everything in its path.

Bill's mind was jumbled with horrible images, but he felt an inner peace knowing that Molly was waiting for him. Looking up to the sky for a moment, he envisioned a bright streak of light coming from some hidden place, reaching out to him like a fleeting illusion of faith.

CHAPTER THIRTY-TWO

Walking toward his sailboat Bill smelled garlic, the aroma tickling his nostrils, his stomach growling. The savory smell of freshly baked bread enticed him even more as he made his way to the hatchway.

Molly felt the sailboat sway under Bill's weight and hurried to greet him as he descended into the salon.

"When I heard the noise of the Coast Guard boat's engines I was relieved, knowing you were back. I was worried that my sauce would burn. How'd it go?"

"You know I can't tell you anything, but I will say it was exactly what we thought."

She let go of Bill. "You look upset; maybe you'll feel better after a shower and a glass of wine. I made you a special supper."

Bill smiled. "It smells delicious! Like something an Italian chef prepared. The aroma is so inviting I can't wait to dig in, but I know a shower would help improve my mood."

She turned toward the counter. "Wait, Bill, I have something for you." Grabbing a warm piece of garlic bread, she said, "Open wide."

He didn't hesitate and immediately chomped down on the bread. "That'll hold me!" he grinned and bounded toward his stateroom.

Following his shower, he returned to the salon where the soft sound of music filled the air. The table was elegantly set, and candlelight flickered magically, creating dancing shadows on the walls.

Molly inspected Bill's appearance. "You look great, like that handsome man I know." Handing him a glass of chianti she added, "Here's to you, may your discovery help solve the mystery of the missing women of Vieques."

"I'm not sure that's an appropriate toast, Molly. I'd rather celebrate the fact that you stayed here and made us this gourmet meal; now that's something to celebrate. Cheers!"

They each took a sip of the red wine. Molly was curious to know what transpired during the dive. "Did Doug change his mind about your wet-sub?"

"I don't think so. He did try to drive it but couldn't figure out how to inflate the ballast tanks, so I took over. I don't think he has patience for the simple things. Look, Molly, I know you want me to tell you what happened, but I'm not supposed to talk about the investigation. Let's relax and discuss our sail to Vieques. We should allow ourselves a day to prepare before the Coast Guard gets there. I'd like to see what the Bio Bay is all about."

Sipping on the wine, they were drawn into the moment. Holding up her glass, Molly said, "Here's to us!"

Relaxing, Bill's his eyes radiated contentment and tenderness. "Yes, it is about us, isn't it? Let's make it last; I think I may be falling in love with you."

Molly's eyes welled up with tears, and she trembled. "No one has ever said those words to me. They sound wonderful. It's a Cinderella dream come true, and you are my prince charming. Yes, together we will make it last."

Molly led him to the sofa. "Let's sit for a while; I don't think I can eat anything right now." They sat on the couch in each other's embrace, forgetting about the world around them.

***

Richard and Shirley were packed tightly on a bench seat aboard the ferry boat to Vieques. The boat was rolling and bouncing around on the waves. Richard was grumpy and showed signs of being annoyed with the arrangement, but he knew it was his idea to take the one-hour ferry boat ride for a four-dollar fare instead of paying eighty dollars for one way on a fifteen-minute flight.

Looking out the window on his side of the boat, he patted Shirley's arm. "Looks like the ferry dock ahead. I can't wait to get off this tub full of smelly sardines."

Shirley offered him one of her sweet smiles. "It'll be nice to be on land again."

Richard ignored Shirley's remark. His increasing irritation with Shirley's behavior was escalating, and he was questioning if she would ever get her memory back. Holding on to her arm he said, "Just stay with me as we get off; I'll carry the luggage. After we're off the boat

I'll hail a cab."

It took some time for the ferry boat to dock; meanwhile everyone anxiously waited to deboard. When given the all clear, the mass of people exploded into unorganized chaos. People pushed and shoved as they vied to be first in line. Richard marched Shirley through the unruly crowd. A couple of young teens pushed their way ahead of them.

Richard yelled at them. "Hey, fat boy, wait your turn!"

The teen threw Richard a bird. "What's wrong, old man? Is your arthritis bothering you? Looks like you need a wheelchair."

Richard wanted to slug the kid, but restrained himself. Holding back he watched the teens move themselves through the crowd.

Finally, he and Shirley walked off the boat onto the dock. The fresh air was a welcome relief; the warmth and accompanying soft sea breeze brought with it the scent of sweet smelling flowers. A sandy beach ran along the shoreline and was visible from each side of the dock. It seemed to invite them to take a stroll, but that had to wait.

Across the street from the dock was a line of taxi cabs. The drivers stood beside their cabs looking for customers.

As they moved closer to the cabs an eager cabbie asked, "Taxi, sir?"

Richard nodded. "You bet we do! Take us to the W. Retreat and Spa."

"Good choice, sir. That place is just plain plush; let me take your luggage." The cab driver placed their luggage in the trunk of his cab, while Richard and Shirley climbed into the back seat. They sat on soiled seats, while their feet slid around on sandy foot mats.

It was a short ride to the extravagant resort perched on a low cliff abutting the beach. The ambiance was awesome. Ornate sculptures, beautiful flowers, and palm trees lined the entrance driveway. Their first glimpse of the grandness was one of breathtaking splendor, like seeing the Taj-Mahal, radiating to them a feeling that they were among a very elite clientele in a place of elegance and grandeur.

The driver helped them with their luggage. Richard felt downtrodden, arriving in such a dirty, junky car. He reached into his pocket and handed the cab driver a meager tip. "Thanks, but you need to clean up your cab." The cab driver quickly left, and they turned to the grand entrance directly in front of them.

***

Brad and Sammi spent their week trimming trees and planting flowers around the grounds of the resort. Numerous gardens surrounded the 156-room resort, and each one required a special display of distinctly different sea-side flora. This sparked some creativity on their part, and they counted on it to please their boss.

The infinity pool grounds needed special attention due to the large quantity of chlorine in the water, constantly splashing out onto the shrubs. Their strategy was to take their time working around the pool area, so they could watch the young women dressed in their skimpy bathing suits, sipping on fancy drinks topped with cherries and small paper umbrellas. It felt like a bus man's holiday to them, as they ogled all the young shapely women whose husbands played 18 holes of golf. Then the men followed it up with a stop at the 19th hole, where they drank martini's and told lies about their perfect game, leaving their young beautiful wives basking in the sunshine on lounge chairs surrounding the pool.

CHAPTER THIRTY-THREE

Sailing along the southern shore of Vieques, Bill and Molly headed to the town of Esperanza, one of the two small towns on Vieques. Esperanza was mainly known as a fishing village, noted to be full of friendly people. They searched for an old dock adjacent to a dive center that rented out moorings. There was only enough space for three moorings, and he hoped that one would be available.

They rounded the small island of Cayo Real. "There's the dock," Molly exclaimed, "and I see two empty moorings."

"Great, but right now I need to avoid a reef on our starboard side. Once I get around it, I'll swing above the last mooring, and you get the line."

Grabbing the boat hook and placing herself on the bow, she held the hook in the water as they drifted by the mooring, then she caught the line. Hauling the mooring line on deck, she slipped the loop onto her boat line, and quickly wrapped it around a forward cleat.

"Good job, Molly. This will be a good anchorage for us, and the Coast Guard response boat can tie up to the dock if they want. That will make it convenient for everyone."

Molly frowned. "I'm not sure they would want to stay at that dock; it's in pretty shabby shape. I think there's a newer dock in the next bay they may like better, besides this dock seems to belong to the local fishermen."

"Well that's their call, let's take the dinghy ashore. I want to pay for the mooring before they kick us out."

Jumping into the dinghy, Bill drove it onto the sandy beach. "Looks like it will be a short boat ride to any spot we want to go."

Walking into the dive shop, he inquired about the mooring fee and paid for two days. The scent of dead fish wafted off the dock. Several local fishermen lined the dock, cleaning their catches and throwing the left over dead carcasses into the water, while greedy brown pelicans dove into the water to gobble up free meals.

Bill and Molly linked their arms and walked along a boardwalk above the beach, admiring the laidback enclave as they ambled along the main street of the picturesque malecon of Esperanza. The street was lined with many open-air restaurants and bars. Nestled between them were boutiques, some guest houses, and an information center located in a large historical building.

"Bananas, that's a cute name for a restaurant," Molly said. "Let's stop there for a drink and a snack."

"Sounds good to me. I just got a whiff of something being barbequed on a grill. Smells good, but nothing like your Italian meal."

Entering the building, they sat at a small table overlooking the water. A server approached the table to recite the daily specials.

"We're new to the area what would you recommend?" Bill asked.

"My favorite items are the pasteillos and the amarillos. I'll be back in a minute while you decide."

After reviewing menu, they decided on the servers recommended dishes. Neither of them knew what ingredients made up their choices, but decided it would be fun to give themselves a taste bud challenge.

The turquoise water of the bay was abuzz with small fishing boats, and the water glittered in the sunlight, while small wakes rippled beyond the boats. Bill recognized the hull design of the fishing boats, and he mentioned it to Molly. "The hulls of those boats look like the skiffs they use for fishing off shore in the Northeast."

Molly laughed. "Once an engineer, always an engineer. I was enjoying the parade of fishing boats, not trying to figure out the hull design. I guess I am from Venus."

"Mars isn't such a bad place; it's just got a bad rap, but being here with you is better. It's quite nice here. I'd never given Vieques much thought, and it's different than I envisioned. "

"In what way? It's not different from any of the other islands."

"Not different in make-up, just that it seems much quieter here."

"Well, that could be because it hasn't been discovered yet."

"You're right, so let's enjoy it now. When the world finds out about this place they'll ruin it like they did the Virgin Islands."

Molly didn't respond.

When their food was served, Bill asked the server what was inside.

"The pasteillos is a deep-fried flour pocket stuffed with lobster, and the amarillos are sweet plantains. Enjoy."

"Umm," Molly said after the first bite. "Good stuff."

Sharing their delightful meal was a perfect beginning of their new adventure. Bill watched his boat bobbing around in the water. Small waves kept moving it about as the fishermen began arriving back at the dock with their catches.

"When Richard and his friend arrive they won't have any problem finding my sailboat. We've made it easy for them. I can't wait to bust his charade."

"Have you heard anymore from Mike?"

"No, I meant to e-mail him before we left, but as you know, we were busy." A sly look crossed his brow. "You know what, Molly, I'd better contact Commander Gildersleeve. Can I use your cell phone? I don't want to take the chance of having my conversation monitored."

She handed Bill her phone.

"I need to go outside where there is less noise. Can't afford to miss any important information."

"Sure, that's fine."

On deck, he dialed the Commander. "Hi, Bill, I have received news regarding the contents of the barrels. The autopsies revealed that the victims in the barrels were indeed the missing women from Vieques. We found more glow sticks and the remnants of a ticket for the pontoon ride into the bay. We're currently awaiting the DNA results taken from the last victim."

Clenching his jaw, Bill kept his emotions contained as he thought about the dismembered women in the barrels.

The Commander continued explaining his plan. "We're coordinating a sting operation with Captain Rodriquez and his police force. They will patrol the bay on land. His men will be in plain clothes. We don't want to alert anyone who might abort their kidnapping plans, while we are trying to keep an unsuspecting woman from harm."

Finishing his conversation, Bill returned to Molly who was sitting alone at the table. Sorry to leave you." Handing her the cell phone, he said. "Thanks. That was an earful."

"What did he say?"

"Well, I'm not supposed to tell you, but you need to know. The bodies in the barrels were identified as the missing women. There are some solid clues in there with the bodies which makes them believe there's more than one person involved. Hence both a land and sea operation."

Molly stared out the window. "I guess it's up to you and the Coast Guard men to capture the evil creeps."

"Doug and his crew will meet us at the Bio Bay tomorrow afternoon, and we'll go through the drill before nightfall. Seems there's not enough water to float the wet sub from the ocean into the Bio Bay, so we'll have to portage it over a sandbar at the entrance of the bay which runs seven feet or deeper. That's not bad, and we should be able to see any unusual illumination of the microscopic plankton from just a few feet below the surface."

Bill avoided telling Molly that Doug didn't want her taking part in the mission. But Bill needed Molly to surface the wet sub, nothing more, because Doug was not yet familiar with the ballast system. Bill didn't care if Doug approved, but he wasn't going to bring up that small detail if he didn't have to. And he was certain that Molly would be safe with all the Coasties and police placed strategically in and around the bay.

***

Richard and Shirley left the W. Retreat and Spa in late morning and caught a cab to the town of Isabel Segunda. The town was located just beyond the ferry boat dock on the north coast, not far from the resort. Its layout was that of a typical business district with a plaza, grocery stores, banks, a post office, gas stations, as well as a few shops and restaurants.

"Shirley, do you see Bill's dark green sailboat out there? I know his buddy Mike said he would be here. I wonder if he's playing games with me? That idiot! I've spent a fortune to torment him, and now he's a no-show!"

Shirley looked over the water trying to find Bill's boat, but there were many boats on the water. "I see sailboats, fishing boats, and even a few luxury types, but I can't see anything green." Shirley pointed her finger toward the north, "Maybe if we go up by that pier, perhaps we'd find him there."

"What pier?" Richard looked in the direction Shirley was pointing. "You're right! Let's take a walk up there, the jerk has to be there."

After spending over an hour looking for Bill, the sun's penetrating heat got to Richard. The cool ocean breeze didn't help to him to cool him off. His shirt was dripping wet with perspiration. "That's it, Shirl. I'm done. Let's get back to the resort. It's not a long walk to the ferry dock, there's bound to be a cab there."

***

By the time, they returned to the resort Richard was in a frenzy. He stewed about everything going wrong. Shirley felt the beautiful hotel room closing in around her, and she started to feel like she was in a combat zone. All Shirley wanted to do was to get away from him for a while. "Richard, I think I'll go out by the pool."

"What, and sit in the hot sun? You are nuts, woman."

Shirley didn't like that remark, "No, I'm not!" Looking out the window, she continued. "It's looks so nice and refreshing out there. Don't worry, you know I won't go in the water. I just want to relax in the sun. Maybe I'll dangle my feet over the side. I won't be gone long. Why don't you take a shower to cool down?"

Shirley put on a white bathing suit which looked nice on her slim figure. She covered herself with sunblock, then took a special pool towel with her. Before leaving the room, she kissed Richard on his check.

***

Brad and Sammi looked at the colorful flowers they piled into the wheelbarrow, taking them out and arranging them in special formations to enhance the colorful beauty of the display in and around the pool area. Passing close by to them, they couldn't help noticing Shirley. Brad nudged Sammi. "Check out that babe she's a looker, bet she would be fun to play with, and she's all alone."

Sammi nodded.

Shirley found a lounge chair and spread her towel over it, settling into a comfortable position. She looked over the spectacular view of the ocean, content to be free from the increasing negativity she felt around Richard.

Sitting there undisturbed, she focused her attention on Brad and Sammi working in the garden planting flowers. The flowers were beautiful, and the gardeners seemed to have a knack for arranging them. Shirley found herself wandering in their direction.

Shirley noticed there was something odd about the tall man with a bald spot on the top of his head and a long ponytail growing out of the back of his head, but the shorter man was handsome. Reaching the area where they were working, she stopped to chat.

"Excuse me, but your flower display is absolutely beautiful. I have a garden of my own at home but it's nothing compared to this one. What is your secret?"

A wide smile crossed Sammi's long face. "Why thank you, miss."

Brad was more to the point. "These flowers grow well in the tropics. They are plentiful and healthy, making it easy to create these colorful arrangements. I'm sure that wherever you come from, your area has its own type of flowers that do well in that climate."

Shirley remembered a few details about her garden. "What about the soil and the fertilizer you use? They make a difference, don't they?"

"Look around you," Brad said. "The sky's the limit at this place. Cost is not an object if it looks good to the folks like you who spend big bucks to stay here." Pausing he asked. "By the way, will you be here tomorrow night?"

Shirley thought it was strange question, "Why, yes, I think so...."

Again, Brad spoke. "Well, here on Vieques we have this magnificent Bio Bay that no one should ever miss. Tomorrow night will be moonless, meaning a darker sky will make the plankton glow brighter, and the show will be more astonishing. Just imagine the water sparkling with hundreds of blue diamonds."

"That sounds too good to be true, and I'm sure it would be something to see. But I don't know if I can go."

"Tell you what," Brad said, "Sammi and I are going to be there. We have a little business to run, but you are welcome to join us. I'll even take you on a boat ride so you can have a better view of the diamond light show in the water."

Shirley was impressed. "Really, it sounds beautiful. I'll try to make it."

"By the way, my name is Brad, and my buddy here is Sammi. What's your name?"

"Oh, I'm Shirley. Glad to make your acquaintance."

"So, Shirley, we'll meet you out here around the pool about 5 p.m."

Shirley stalled.

"What's the matter, Shirley?" Sammi asked.

"Well, I think I would like to go, but I'm having a little trouble with my memory now and then. Sometimes I can't remember what I'm supposed to do."

Studying Shirley, Brad spoke quietly. "Shirley, just come out to the pool like you did today. You can remember that, can't you?"

"Yes, I think so. I do like sitting around the pool, but I've been told to stay out of the water, although I'm not sure why."

"We'll leave it at that," Brad said. "Hope to see you then. We must get back to work. Don't want to lose our jobs, you know."

Smiling, Shirley walked back to her lounge chair.

CHAPTER THIRTY FOUR

Just before dawn Bill awakened to the sound of loud voices coming from the adjacent dock. Peeking out the side window of his cabin he saw many local fishermen loading their boats with bait and setting up their rigs for the long day at sea. Rolling over in his bed he noted a lull in the conversations, followed by the drone of many motors pushing the fleet of fishing boats out of the harbor. The wakes from the boats began lapping against the hull of the sailboat, rocking it like a cradle.

Remaining still for a moment, Bill's mind raced so he got up. Glancing in the door of the aft cabin he saw Molly sleeping soundly. Going topside into the cockpit he anticipated a red-yellow sunrise, but he was too soon. On shore the windows and doors of the buildings clamored, as the merchants slid them aside, preparing their shops for business.

Bill slid into the dinghy and rowed ashore, leaving it perched safely on the sandy beach. Strolling up to the poorly maintained main street thoroughfare, he noticed the road was full of pot holes and debris and crowded with foot traffic as the young and old scurried, some going to school, some to work, others like himself in search of breakfast.

Watching the activity he was struck by the bright, cheery greetings the people exchanged with one another. The dusky dawn sky began filtering in the sun's rays, and the warmth of the sunbeams felt good on his skin. He hoped to find an isolated spot to enjoy the tranquility of a quiet breakfast.

Finding nothing of interest along his walk, he considered returning to his boat when he passed by a couple in an open air restaurant sitting at a table under the shade of a palm tree. Inhaling the smell of freshly brewed expresso which was filtering through the air, Bill decided to stop. Leaning toward the couple, he asked. "Excuse me is this place open to the public?"

"This is a private resort, but I'm sure they'll serve you breakfast. Just grab yourself a chair."

"Thanks, I'll do that."

Seating himself at a sunlit table overlooking the water, he ordered a meal. His anxiety over his role in the Coast Guard's covert operation in the Bio Bay was troubling him. The reality of the operation had become more dangerous than he first thought. Recalling the contents of the 55-gallon barrel discovered in Culebra, he knew they would be dealing with psychopaths with sick minds and no moral boundaries.

A rider on horseback passing by distracted him from his thoughts; he watched as the horse and rider trotted off. Finishing his Spanish omelet, he ordered a quiche and some pastries for Molly.

Slowly wandering back, he took in the scenic atmosphere of the tiny village. How could such a happy place be home to the tragic killing of innocent women? If his discovery could help make a difference in the lives of other unsuspecting women, then it would all be worth it.

***

Sitting in the cockpit of the sailboat, Molly sipped a cup of coffee from the pot she brewed for herself in the galley, watching Bill strolling along the shore line, then returning to his dinghy. Within minutes he was back on the boat giving her a kiss.

"What a beautiful morning. Did you get to see the sunrise?" he asked.

"I was a bit late today, but I'm soaking it up now."

He handed her the paper bag containing the pastries and quiche. "Something for your breakfast."

Examining the contents, she remarked. "What a gentleman, and it smells yummy. Thanks."

Bill seemed anxious. "Molly, I've got to call the Commander because I need to know if everything is on schedule."

"Sure, my cell phone is on the counter, by the coffee pot."

***

Later in the morning Bill and Molly took the dinghy out to the mouth of Bio Bay and anchored it. Seeing the sand bar that crossed the mouth of the bay they left the dinghy and headed for it. Walking through the clear warm water, they reached a patch of dry land.

Bill looked over the water of the bay. "At high tide millions of dinoflagellates wash into the bay and are trapped within the bay as the water level recedes. The nutrients found in the bay and its warm water creates a perfect breeding ground for sustaining the microscopic single-celled whirling-tailed organisms." He surveyed the height of the sandbar. "Looks like we'll be portaging the wet sub, there's no way it will float over this bar. When we reach this point, we'll just haul it over, shouldn't be hard. Once we get it in the bay, we'll leave it sitting on the sand bar. It won't go anywhere, and it'll be fine until later."

"That sounds easy enough. I'm sure those strong Coast Guard men won't flinch an eye lifting it up," Molly said with conviction.

After his conversation with Commander Gildersleeve, they decided it wasn't necessary to meet the Coast Guard crew at the dock—they would come directly to the sand bar.

Bill smiled, delighted by Molly's good nature. Walking along the sandbar the roar of large diesel engines alerted them of the approaching vessel. The white Coast Guard response boat came to an abrupt stop close by, spraying water high into the air and creating waves forceful enough to knock the two of them over.

"Those cowboys love to speed," Bill said. "I guess they feel privileged to use all that power."

The sound of an anchor splashing into the water was followed by the silencing of the engine noise. The men on the boat began lowering the yellow wet sub into the water. Placing their remaining scuba gear on, they tumbled backward from the deck of the vessel into the water, and together they pulled and pushed the wet sub to where Bill and Molly stood. Once at the sandbar, they lifted it into the bay. Doug waited on the response boat with a cadet named Henry, who was to stay aboard while the others were diving. Doug waited until everything was set, then he dove into the water and joined the others in the mouth of the bay.

Doug shouted at Bill, pointing his finger at Molly. "What's SHE doing here? I suppose she's giving you moral support! Miss Tynin has no business here." The sea gulls gathered around the large boat started madly flapping their wings, flying away from his tirade.

Ignoring the intimidation tactics, Bill spoke up. "Molly is here because I want her to inflate the ballast tanks of the wet sub once I swim away. Her role is to make sure the wet sub surfaces, that's it. End of discussion."

Bill felt the daggers from Doug's eyes. "Are you daft? Don't you realize the dangers she could encounter?"

Bill was adamant and stern. "Doug, get over yourself. This is my wet sub, and the Commander wants me to use it on this mission, so I will. Now back off."

Wanting to diffuse the discussion and get on with the maneuver, Pete interrupted. "You two better put your tanks on, and let's get this over with."

"You're right, Pete," Bill continued. "Everything we need is in the dinghy. It won't take us long to get ready."

The water in the bay was warm and inviting. A few remaining sea gulls flew above their heads, flapping their wings while heading back toward the town in search of some free handouts.

Sitting in the wet sub, Bill and Molly were ready. Bill slowly submerged the wet sub, feeling the warm clear water engulf his body. Once they were one fathom under the water, Bill guided the sub through the water until they reached the predetermined GPS destination. It was the area below where the pontoon tour boat floats at night, allowing the swimmers to plunge into the water to experience the thrill of the dinoflagellate sparkling all around them. The disturbance of their movement caused the dinoflagellates to generate a stunning light show. Satisfied with his position, he placed the wet sub in neutral buoyancy and waited for the others.

Once Pete and Gary arrived, Bill swam out of his seat, ascending until he broke through the surface of the water. Moving into his seat, Molly engaged the ballast tank control, causing the wet sub to rise though the water. Everyone surfaced and gathered around the wet sub. Pleased with the trial run, they discussed the evening's strategy.

"Damn, Bill," Gary said, "we had a hard time keeping up with you. What's the speed of your craft?"

"I calculate it to be close to 5 miles an hour. About twice as fast as a strong swimmer. It won't take you guys long to catch up. Make sure you have your Go Pro's on your head. You'll need your cameras on and the spot lights engaged. It's gonna be pitch black down there. Now let's get back to the sand bar."

Doug waited at the sand bar for them to surface. Appearing more jovial, he questioned, "How'd it go?" His change in demeanor put the others at ease.

"Everything worked as planned, but it may be trickier in total blackout conditions. We all need to concentrate on our mission; it can become spooky when you are surrounded by what seems to be a cave of darkness. I know, I spent some time on *Alvin,* a small research submarine operated by the Woods Hole Oceanographic Institution. Exploring the Atlantic Ocean at depths of 2 miles can give you an eerie feeling." Changing the subject, Bill said. "Molly and I will head back to our sailboat, and we'll meet you here at dusk."

Doug spoke again. "The crew and I will remain here. Bill, I need to caution you again about the gravity of this mission. You need to prepare yourself for a potentially dangerous encounter. This is not a joy ride. I still question your judgement involving Miss Tynin."

Doug's gaze remained intense, but Bill did not back off. "Thanks for the lecture, Doug. We'll see you later."

CHAPTER THIRTY FIVE

The main dining room of the W. Retreat and Spa was elegant. Chandeliers hung from the ceiling, their sparkling array of glass glittering throughout the room. The sun's rays bouncing off the crystal created colorful prisms akin to an aurora borealis Draping white linen table clothes covered the tables. The place settings consisted of porcelain china and crystal stemware. All this finery invited the guests to dine. The room was encircled by an expansive display of picture windows, and the view through them was spectacular. It overlooked the manicured grounds, which abutted the shimmering ocean waters, giving the guests a feeling of being outside.

Richard and Shirley enjoyed their meal of roast pork, baked potatoes, and Caesar salad. Placing her fork on top of her plate, she looked at Richard. "You know, everything we've been served has been delicious. This is such a nice spot. Now that I'm done with my meal I think I'll change into my bathing suit and go out by the pool. I know this vacation must end soon."

Turning his attention on Shirley, Richard questioned. "Really, Shirley? Are you sure? It's so damn hot out there, I don't know how you can stand it."

Tilting her head. "Richard, it's wonderful. You don't know what you're missing. Why don't you join me for a while?'

Richard seemed preoccupied. "Maybe later. The waiter just told me there is another town on this Island. Right now, I gotta figure out where it is. It's somewhere near the Bio Bay they talk about. I bet Bill is hiding there. We need to find him. He must be punished for deliberately pushing you off his sailboat."

Shirley shrugged. "Okay." She wasn't interested in Richard's obsession. "Well, I'm done. I can't eat another bite, so I'm going to change into my suit. I hope you'll be able to spend some time with me.

"I'll see, Shirley. Let's go now. I'll walk you to the room."

***

After changing into her bathing suit, Shirley didn't waste any time getting to the pool. Settling into a lounge chair, she relaxed.

Brad and Sammi's goal was to complete their job today. Currently they were replanting the last flower bed, which was farther away from the pool, although they could clearly see the activity around the pool. Sammi was on his knees digging in the dirt, preparing the overgrown flower bed for the fresh new greenery. The new batch of flowers in the wheel barrel consisted of brightly colored budding blooms that they coordinated for exposure to the perfect amount of light and darkness.

Shirley watched their activity from afar, not realizing who they were. Relaxing in the lounge chair, she closed her eyes, listening to the constant chatter and the splashing of the people in the pool. Laying on the lounge, she couldn't shake the idea that she was forgetting something important. The constant yearning of not knowing what she forgot bothered her. Reopening her eyes, she focused on the gardeners working in a flower bed almost hidden from sight.

Curious to see what kinds of flowers they were planting today she got up and slowly walked toward them. The walkway angled away from where they were working, so she made her way over the manicured lawn. Sammi was the first to detect someone wandering across the green expanse, which was an unusual occurrence. Realizing it was Shirley Sammi said to Brad, "Guess who's back? Look up, our friend Shirley is coming to pay us a visit."

Turning around Brad watched as Shirley approached and greeted her with a big smile. "Shirley, good to see you again. Do you remember us from yesterday?"

Stuttering. "Ka… ka… kinda. I know you like flowers, and I think there may be something else." A soft sea breeze rustled the flowers and spread their fragrance into the air. Shirley searched her memory.

Sammi held up a pot of impatiens he was about to place in the ground, glancing up at her. "Yes, the three of us are going to watch the plankton shine through the dark water of the Bio Bay."

"That's right, now I remember."

"Shirley, we really need to finish this job and clean up. We'll see you later. Why don't you wait for us by the pool?"

"I'll do that." Turning around she found her way back over the soft

222

green lawn. Once on the walkway she was surprised to see Richard heading toward her. She hurried over to greet him.

Richard was irritated, which disturbed Shirley. With a scolding tone of voice, he quizzed her. "Who were those men you were talking to? I've seen them around the pool ogling the young women; you need to be careful who you associate with. They look like shameful scum."

"Richard, that's not fair; they are very nice, and they like flowers."

"Shirley, you need to go back to our room now! I'll have a word with those two." Shirley didn't move, "Go on, get out of here! Girl, move it!"

Walking away, she went over to her lounge chair, gathered up her towel and begrudgingly left the pool area.

***

Richard waited until Shirley was out of sight before strutting like a rooster over to the flower bed where Brad and Sammi were working. Eyeing Sammi suspiciously, he shouted. "What the hell are you guys doing? You have balls disturbing the guests!" Looking directly at Sammi he yelled, "You're a pitiful freak!"

That did it. Sammi rose from his place on the ground. "Hey, mister, you have no place speaking to me like that!"

Richard pushed Sammi hard on his chest. "You heard me, stay away from the guests, you creep!"

Doing a panoramic scan of the area and seeing no one else around, Sammi sucker punched Richard hard in the gut. Brad attacked from behind, giving Richard two quick jabs in his kidneys. Richard fell to the ground.

Sammi picked up the shovel next to the wheelbarrow they transported the flowers in, and using the wooden handle as a weapon, he whacked Richard in the ribs, then he struck him in the head, knocking him out.

Blood oozed from the wound on Richard's head. Together they threw Richard into the wheelbarrow, quickly moving his body to the maintenance shed where the yard equipment was stored. They dropped the body alongside an empty 55-gallon barrel behind the shed. Leaving him there, they returned to the flowerbed to complete their job.

***

Like a scolded child, Shirley scurried back to their room. Richard's mood changes were getting her down. He became irritated so easily. Sitting in an easy chair, she waited for him to return. After what seemed like hours she decided to return to the pool. Still dressed in her bathing suit, she slipped on a cover-up and left the room.

The bright sunlight welcomed her, it's rays bathing her with warmth, making her feel content. She searched the pool area for signs of Richard without success. Assuming he went for a walk, she settled into a lounge chair.

The sounds around the pool slowly faded away, and she dozed off until she felt someone pulling on her toes. Opening her eyes, she recognized Brad standing there with a bouquet of flowers in his hands.

"Thought you might like these. We've finished our job, and we'll be leaving Vieques tomorrow. But tonight, we're going to the Bio Bay to see the show. You're still joining us, aren't you?"

Shirley was confused by the intrusion. "I guess so. I was looking for Richard, but he seems to have disappeared. That's not like him; he usually watches me like a hawk."

"Maybe he decided to hit a few balls on the links. I'm sure he'll show up later. Listen, Shirley, just stay here. Sammi and I will be back soon, then we'll all go to the Bio Bay. If Richard shows up he can join us, too. Once we get there I'll buy you a mojito cocktail. They are to die for."

Searching the pool area again for Richard, Shirley couldn't find him, so she focused her gaze back at Brad. "Yes, I'd like that."

Making an about-face, Brad strolled to the other side of the pool. Shirley inhaled the fragrant flowers; smiling, she placed them on her chest and closed her eyes.

CHAPTER THIRTY SIX

The sun's light was fading, and the sky became a canvas of purple and pink. Bill and Molly returned to the Bio Bay for their rendezvous with the Coast Guardsmen. Approaching the bay, they saw their wet sub sitting on the sandbar, and the Rescue Boat anchored a short distance away.

Bill suddenly had serious doubts about involving Molly in the recon. His bullheadedness had ruled over reason. He'd never be able to forgive himself if something happened to her. The possibility of losing her was reminiscent of Shirley's puzzling disappearance in the sea and the grief that followed.

"You know, Molly," he said, gently patting her knee, "it will be totally black when we submerge. So make sure your Go Pro's search light is engaged. Once we stop, all lights will be off until we see suspicious movement above. You might experience a claustrophobic feeling; if you start to get anxious try not to let it overwhelm you. Try wiggling your toes. If that doesn't work, just surface. It will only take a few seconds from 7 or 10 feet."

"Bill, I'll be fine, don't worry. I'll inflate the ballast tanks, and I don't think I'll have a problem. You can count on me. I'll be there to help at all costs."

The brightly lit sky slowly changed to a light gray as they pulled up to the sandbar. Molly got out of the boat, where she was soon joined by the others while Bill tied his dinghy to the rescue boat.

It didn't take long for the sky to darken, and by then all the divers were in dive gear ready to go.

"All right everyone," Bill said, "Molly and I will head out in the wet sub. Pete and Gary, you two follow us."

"We got your back," Gary said

Moving into deeper water the wet sub slipped into the darkness of the bay. The blue glimmer of the dinoflagellates followed them through the water. The beaming radiance of the search lights shone brightly through the complete gloom.

The GPS on Bill's dive gauge illuminated the waypoint. Arriving at their destination, he placed the wet sub in neutral buoyancy. Hovering just above the bottom, they shut off their search lights, and an eerie black abyss engulfed them.

***

Sammi and Brad found Shirley on the lounge chair where they'd left her. She was sleeping with the flowers on her chest. Sammi made an obscene gesture with his groin, and Brad nudged her gently. "Shirley, it's time to go. Are you ready?"

Shirley was slow to respond, trying to reacquaint herself to the surroundings. The bright sunshine had given way to gray shadows surrounding the pool.

"Oh, Hi. Is it time to go?"

Brad extended his hand. "Come with me. We have a company car waiting."

With the flowers in one hand, she reached out to Brad with the other. He guided her around the pool.

Shirley stopped abruptly. "Where's Richard? Something's not right. I can't go without him."

Sammi twitched with impatience. Not wishing to mess up their plans for the rest of the evening, Brad quickly intervened. "Richard said he would meet us at the Bay."

"How do you know that?" Shirley questioned."

"I saw him just as we were parking the car. He didn't want to wake you, and he said he was going to your room for something. Don't worry, he said he'll be along. Now let's get into the car."

Brad led Shirley to a late model blue Chevrolet parked by the curb. "Hop in, I'll sit next to you while Sammi drives. It's not far from here."

"Are you sure?" Shirley asked, looking back toward the hotel.

"Don't worry, Shirley, you're in good hands." All Brad could think of was putting his hands all over her.

The road opened up in front of them as night settled in. Sammi guided the car around curves and through a thick forest of trees until they came to a small village. Sammi abruptly stopped the car to allow a horse and buggy to pass.

The bay was located just outside the town where Sammi parked the car, and the three of them promenaded along a dusty dirt road. Voices of happy people drifted across the lawns which were littered with small tents displaying artwork of local artists. Other stands nearby sold t-shirts, custom made jewelry, and all sorts of souvenirs.

Brad stopped in front of the Mojito stand where he and Sammi helped serve the specialty drinks.

"I didn't know you two were still on the island," the owner said. "You guys want to take over for a while? I need a break."

"Sorry, Joe, not tonight, but I'd like to make a drink for my lady friend."

"Sure, help yourself; you know the routine." Moving away, he waited on another customer.

Brad poured the premade drink mixture over ice, then he took a few mint leaves and added them to the mixture in a red plastic cup. He placed the premix back on the shelf, making certain that no one was watching as he produced a hidden bottle of liquid from his pant pocket. Pouring all the substance into the cup, he quickly stirred it with a straw.

"Here you go, Shirley," he said, handing her the cup.

"Thank you. It sure smells good. What's the green stuff? Mint?" She sniffed but did not take a drink.

"It's really refreshing. I know you'll like it, and I'm sure it will help you calm down."

"Thank you, Brad, but I'm not a fan of liquor."

"Just try it, Shirley. I'm sure you'll enjoy it." *Just drink it, bitch!* he thought as they waited for Sammi to return with the tickets for the pontoon boat ride.

Shirley fidgeted, obviously on edge, and she kept looking around for Richard.

"Come on, Shirley, just one sip won't hurt you. You need to relax."

"Okay, I'll just try it." She took a sip. "Mmm, it tastes sweet and sour."

Brad sighed with satisfaction and turned to Sammi who held up three tickets.

Shirley quickly poured some of the drink into a bush of oleanders.

"How's that drink, Shirley?" Sammi asked, and she jumped. "A few more sips of that and you'll lose your fear of the water."

Shirley took another tiny sip. "Now I can taste the lemon and lime. It's not too bad after all."

Sammi handed Brad the tickets. " I'll see you two later. I'm going to help Joe for a while—give him the break he wanted."

When he got to Joe's Mojito stand, he kept walking, going directly to the car. Opening the trunk, Sammi removed a dive bag and slipped away to a secluded part of the bay. At the water's edge, he put on his dive gear and slipped into the lagoon. Swimming out into the darkness was easy for him as he had done it many times before, and he headed to the buoy that he and Brad had placed near the spot where the pontoon boat would drop off its passengers.

Brad and Shirley climbed aboard the pontoon boat and found a seat close to the rear. Once settled, Brad pulled two glow sticks from his other pocket.

"You'll need to put one of these around your ankle," he explained to Shirley, "and the other one around your wrist. It's just a precaution in case we get separated. I'll be able to find you in the darkness."

"What about you? Aren't you going to wear one of these things?"

"Nope, I'll be fine. My mission is to take care of you."

The boat rocked as other guests filed on board, instantly crowding one and other. The chatter of excitement filled the air. When the gates closed, the soft hum of an electric motor signaled departure, and the boat slowly moved away from shore.

As the boat entered the darkness of the lagoon, the water below began reflecting bright blue lights caught in the wake of the boat. Soon they changed into a brilliant electric blue as the boat settled into the total darkness.

Shirley was amazed. "Oh, how beautiful! They do look like diamonds sparkling in the water!"

Coming to a standstill, the boat floated gently on the water. The people on board jumped into the bay, the air filling with excited squeals.

Shirley hesitated, but the joyful cries of the others made it seem like fun, so she agreed to give it a try. With Brad beside her, she splashed into the water.

"Try floating on your back," Brad said, and soon they were

floating away from the boat and the people around it.

"Move your arms like your making diamond water angels."

Completely relaxed, Shirley did as Brad suggested. Her glow sticks shone a bright neon yellow green within the blue glimmer of the bay.

"Brad, this is so much fun!" She giggled as she moved her arms.

Brad caught sight of the bubbles from Sammi's regulator as they reached the surface. "The fun is about to begin."

Shirley felt something brush against her leg. "What was that?" She jerked her head up just as Brad's hands pressed down on her head, shoving her beneath the water.

Feeling Sammi tug Shirley deeper into the lagoon, Brad let go and swam back to the pontoon boat.

***

Just below the surface, Bill and Molly waited for the glow of the dinoflagellates to begin as the frolicking of the people above disrupted their environment. Molly was the first to notice the glow sticks appearing in an isolated area far from the other swimmers, and she tapped Bill's shoulder.

Bill saw the strange activity and the multitude of the dinoflagellates surrounding the green-yellow glow sticks shining through the darkness like neon lights. Turning on his Go Pro camera and search light, Bill darted forward. Suddenly, he caught sight of another diver emerge from the darkness to swim toward the disturbance. And weirder yet, another person swam away from the ruckus.

Bill closed in just in time to witnessed the diver pull the woman under, and in the bright glare from the spotlight Bill saw the diver shove his extra regulator into the female swimmer's mouth.

The woman struggled against the diver, and Bill instinctively reached out to help her. But the other diver's hold on the woman was firm.

Bill kicked the diver in the face with his flipper, the force of the blow breaking the diver's face mask. The jolt surprised the diver, and he lost his hold on the woman.

Bill immediately surfaced with the woman in his arms. She

coughed violently and tried to catch her breath.

"Calm down, you're safe now!" Bill yelled.

Bill heard Doug and Paul arrive in the inflatable. "She's not breathing!" he called out to them.

The two Coasties yanked the woman into the inflatable and started CPR until she regained consciousness. Her body shook, and she convulsed.

Bill pulled himself into the inflatable and struggled quickly out of his dive equipment. "Is she going to make it?"

"She's conscious," Paul said.

Bill leaned forward to take a look at the woman he'd just rescued. "Oh, my God! Shirley! You're alive!"

"Bill, you know this woman?" Doug asked.

"Yes!" With a shaking hand, he brushed dripping water from his brow. "She's my wife."

In a split-second two years of desperation and guilt over losing her to a shark washed over him. He shook with shock, relief and finally anger. "How could you do this to me? Why didn't you try to try to find me, to tell me that you were alive?"

Doug grabbed Bill by the shoulder. "This woman is your wife? This case gets more and more bizarre!"

"Yes," Bill said, still trembling. "She's been missing without a trace for over two years."

"But what about Miss Tynin?" Paul asked as he helped Shirley sit up.

"She's still with the wet-sub," Doug replied when Bill didn't answer. Scouring the inky black lagoon with a huge spotlight, Doug discovered the bright yellow sub floating not far away.

Meanwhile, Bill took Shirley's hands in his, touching her as if she might dissolve right in front of him. "It's really you, Shirley. Why didn't you tell me you were all right? I've relived that day over a thousand times worrying about what happened to you. How could you be so cruel?"

"Bill?" Shirley's voice rasped his name, and confusion filled her widening eyes. "Bill, is that you?" Her grip on his hands tightened. "Oh, Bill, I knew you would rescue me. The...the...shark...it was right there, just an arm's length away. It even brushed against my feet. It

230

circled around me very slow. I was petrified. Then it was gone, no longer anywhere in sight. I just held on to the floatation cushion you threw and waited for you. But you didn't come, and I thought for sure that the shark was coming back..." Shirley started shaking again, this time from hysteria. Then her eyes rolled back in her head, and she slumped into Bill's arms.

"Doug, we need to get her to a doctor right now!" Bill said. "She's going into shock!"

***

Brian, a security guard at the W. Retreat and Spa, always canvased the resort area in a golf cart just before dark. He was in his late thirties and took his job of protecting the resort's property and the safety of the guests seriously. Circling the pool on his way back toward his compound he heard someone yell for help.

Regaining consciousness, Richard hurt so bad he couldn't even force himself to stand up, but he found enough strength to yell for help.

Driving toward the sound, Brian found Richard lying on his back behind the maintenance shed. "My God, man, what happened to you?" the guard asked, bending to touch Richard's injured head.

"Those damn guys you have planting the flower gardens around here beat me up. They were flirting with my gal, and I told them to stay away from her. That's when they attacked me and dragged me over here."

"You mean Brad and Sam? They finished up their planting detail today. I read the register just before I made my rounds, and I saw they signed out one of our company cars for trip to the Bio Bay. The light show should be spectacular tonight, and those two characters like to see it when they're on the island."

"What the hell, man, they must have Shirley with them!" Richard struggled to a sitting position. "Did you hear me? They have my girl Shirley!"

"Don't move, sir. I'll call for help. You need medical assistance." He pulled out his cell phone to call the chief security officer. "Hey, Juan, it's Brian, I'm out by the maintenance shed. We need a medic down here right away. There's a guy who's hurt. He's in really bad shape, so hurry. And you might want to call in the police. It looks like this was a criminal attack."

The medics arrived within minutes, stabilizing Richard, and the police were right behind them. When the medics assured the police that Richard could answer their questions, they grilled him for more information.

The lead medic told the police to hurry it up. "More than likely, this guy will require a transfer to a hospital on the mainland."

As the ambulance drove away, one of the policemen at the scene notified their captain of their findings.

Captain Rodrigues was on duty patrolling the Bio Bay, participating in the sting underway. He ordered an all points search of the area, ordering the apprehension of Brad and Sammi. He also ordered that when the Bio Bay tour boat returned to the dock, all passengers were to be searched before they were allowed to leave the boat.

Juan accompanied the police with their investigation, leading them to the resort's plush marina where the suspects' boat was located.

"You know there was an attempted drowning in the Bio Bay just a few minutes ago," one of the police said. "The man who rescued the woman said two men were trying to drown her. It could be these two. We can't allow them to escape."

They stopped at the Sea Ray. "Do you really think the guys who own this boat are the one's involved? They seem like decent men, if a bit odd." They climbed aboard the Sea Ray and started to look around.

"Look here," Juan said, pointing to a 55-gallon barrel in the cockpit. "It's one of our barrels; we use them for waste products." Juan shone a light on it.

The police officers stepped closer, and the younger one gasped. Inside the barrel were large concrete blocks and a machete with dried blood encrusting the blade.

"This doesn't seem very decent, does it?" the young officer asked, looking Juan in the eyes. "Are you thinking what I'm thinking?"

"You don't even want to know what I'm thinking. But you know as well as I do that we need to find those madmen now!"

CHAPTER THIRTY SEVEN

Watching Bill as he ascended through the water, Molly moved forward into the wet-sub's driver seat, pulling the lever controlling the ballast tank inflation. Looking for signs of the two Coast Guard divers was futile in the dark water. She was almost to the surface when a lone diver swam directly above her.

Sensing something was out of the ordinary. Molly surfaced and left the wet sub. She engaged her Go Pro camera and spotlight and followed the diver, closing in on him quickly. Something about the man looked familiar. His dive mask dangled from his face, and he acted as if he was fleeing. Then his dive mask started slowly slipping away into the dark water.

Pushing her fins with all her might, she rapidly reached the diver who seemed confused. Without a dive mask in place over his eyes, he couldn't possibly know what direction he was heading in the ebony water that surrounded him. Reaching out she grabbed the large fin on his foot, causing him to turn toward her.

The spotlight on Molly's head allowed him to clearly see her. He lunged in her direction and pulled the regulator out of her mouth. Then he took the hose off his extra regulator and wrapped it around her neck.

Molly resisted with all her might, fighting his attempt to drown her, but she needed air! She forced herself free long enough to replace her regulator and rid herself of the hose around her neck.

Escape or die were her two choices. Where were the Coast Guard divers? They were way overdue. As the man lunged toward her again, she doused the spotlight. He'd never see her in the dark without a dive mask.

***

Following the wet sub into the pitch-black water, Pete and Gary were close behind. Their Go Pro spotlights provided visibility straight

233

ahead. Something big came through the darkness and bumped into Gary's ribs, causing him to panic, and he surfaced.

"What the hell happened?" Pete asked as he broke through the surface.

"Something big enough to eat me just butted into me. What was that monster?"

"Gary, get a grip—that was a manatee, not a monster." Pete's spotlight illuminated the sea cow swimming lazily away. "Come on, we gotta get back down there. We've lost a lot of precious time."

"Pete, wait! It's like being in a freaking cave, not knowing what's lurking around the next corner."

"Gary, we don't have time to discuss this. Put your damn regulator in your mouth. Now let's go!"

Gary reluctantly followed orders, and the two divers descended into the raven-colored water. Reaching the waypoint indicated on their dive gauges, they found the area deserted, but from their location they noticed luminous blue trails disturbing the darkness of the lagoon. Pete indicated for Gary to follow him to investigate the cause of the plankton's disturbance.

Drawing closer they caught sight of a female diver struggling to escape from the clutches of a large male.

Pete aimed for the larger figure while Gary pulled the woman away.

Back on the surface, Molly clung to Gary. "Oh, am I glad to see you!" She took in a few large gulps of fresh air. "I'm all right now. Go help Pete. That diver down there tried to kill me!"

Gary wasted no time in heading toward Pete, while Molly inflated her dive vest and bobbed limply on the surface. Her body quaked uncontrollably at the close call. Scanning the area, she saw the Coast Guard crew in their boat close by, and the police force was clearly patrolling the shoreline. Knowing she was safe helped her regain control.

Meanwhile Pete tackled the diver who fought like a maniac. Gary arrived just in time to help take him in custody, dragging him to the surface a few yards away from Molly.

"That's the creep who stays at the Hostel on Culebra where Bill docks his sailboat!" she exclaimed. "This guy and his buddy work part-time at the W Retreat."

"I have an idea that the police have been looking for you," Gary said as he and Pete dragged Sammi toward the shoreline which was lined with police.

"Let me go!" Sammi yelled and struggled, but he was no match for the two Coasties.

"Here you go," Gary said as he heaved Sammi to his feet and shoved him right into Captain Rodriguez's custody. "This guy tried to drown Molly out there. Wonder what else he's guilty of?"

Sammi was quickly handcuffed and stuffed into a police cruiser. Not far up the shoreline, Brad was already handcuffed, his legs shackled. "You can't prove anything!" he yelled.

Captain Rodriguez shoved him toward a second cruiser. "We've got barrels of proof," he said before laughing and laughed bitterly.

***

Molly shrugged out of her dive gear just as Doug appeared out of the darkness.

"Anything to say, Miss Tynin? Gary tells me you almost got yourself killed!" His dark eyes blazed at her. "Maybe next time you'll listen to those in authority and spare yourself a lot of grief."

Molly knew he was partially right, but the man's arrogance rubbed her the wrong way. "If I hadn't been on the lookout, at least one of those degenerates would have gotten away. My Go Pro recorded that monster trying to kill me—that's got to mean something to the Coast Guard and the police."

Covertly she was thankful to be alive. The fight with Sammi had been the most frightening experience of her life. Just thinking about it again made her heart pound and her hands tremble. She pushed away the vision of herself drowning in the coal-black water of the lagoon, her motionless body lying on the bottom of the bay in a shroud of darkness.

"Then I'll be confiscating your Go Pro. Hand it over," Doug demanded.

"I want it back when you're done with it," Molly said, giving it to him. "It cost me a pretty penny." She looked up and down the shoreline. "Have you seen Bill?"

"Bill rescued a woman from Brad's clutches," Doug said. "He

accompanied her to the general hospital in San Juan.""

Molly stared wide-eyed at Doug.

"Apparently, he knows the woman."

"Really? How's that?"

Doug was not a warm fuzzy kind of guy, but he didn't want to upset Molly more than she already was. "Seems the woman is his wife. She was airlifted to San Juan, and Bill followed in a plane he chartered at the Vieques airport."

Molly gasped, covering her mouth with her hands as she tried to calm herself. "Oh, my God, Shirley is alive? What was she doing out in the water? Wait a minute? Was she with the guy stalking Bill?"

"You must mean the man named Richard? Apparently those two guys almost killed him back of a maintenance shed. While he practically bled to death, that guy," he pointed to the car holding Brad, "took her to swim off the bio bay boat. She almost drowned."

Molly sank to her knees, ignoring the scrape of sand and broken shells on her skin.

Questions whirled around in her head. *Shirley was alive! And Bill went with her, even leasing a plane to get to the hospital. Would Bill go back to Shirley? And where does that leave me? Should I stay or go back to Tortola?*

She was torn, despondent, undecided. But she couldn't stay here on the shore with the night closing in around her.

She came to her feet. "I better get Bill's dinghy and take it back to the sailboat. He left it tied to your response boat."

"We'll take you back to our boat," Doug said gently, "and give you a lift. It's too dark for you to travel out there all alone. Besides, we'll be taking the wet-sub back to our base in Fajardo. It won't be out of our way."

Doug's words didn't seem right. "Hey, that wet-sub belongs to Bill. Why are you taking it?"

"Commander Gildersleeve was impressed with its performance. He wants to have Bill design one for commercial use, and he is willing to provide the financial backing."

"Are you sure? That sounds farfetched; Bill didn't mention anything about it to me."

"I'm not aware of their discussion, maybe it hasn't happed yet. All

I know for sure is that we were instructed to return it to our base."

Molly was satisfied. "Well, I guess we'll just wait and see what develops."

After loading everything back on the response boat, the Coast Guardsmen pulled up to Bill's sailboat which floated lazily on its mooring.

Their position allowed Molly to jump onto the sailboat's bow, landing on the hull above the forward cabin. Lowering the dinghy into the water, Gary threw Molly the line which she caught and attached to a cleat on the sailboat's side.

She waved as the Coast Guard crew sped away, leaving the sailboat swaying in its wake.

A deep melancholy settled over Molly. Walking around the deck, she watched the activities in the village, but it did little to change her mood. She blocked out the gaiety and chatter coming from the street.

Exhausted from pacing, she sat down in the cockpit and began to sob.

CHAPTER THIRTY EIGHT

The Emergency Department at the Ashford Medical Center in San Juan catered to visiting tourists, and it was an extremely busy place. The doctors and nurses hurried about with determined purpose. Bill stood in the hallway, watching the activity just outside of a waiting room provided for relatives and friends of the injured or sick patients. Red lights flashed, and beeping sounds from all the electronic equipment filled the air. The P.A. system announcements continued to interrupt what seemed to be controlled turmoil.

Richard's arrival at the waiting room surprised Bill. His head was incased in a large white gauze bandage. Seepage of blood formed a red ball which contrasted sharply with the white dressing. His left eye was severely bruised, and he could barely open it. His left arm was stabilized in a sling.

"What the hell happened to you?" Bill demanded.

"None of your damn business, you low life scumbag. What are you doing here? Trying to make up for your plot to kill your wife?"

"Just in case you forgot, I'm Shirley's husband, and for your information, I didn't murder anyone or attempt to murder anyone. That is just a fantasy you made up in your pitiful distorted mind. Can't you be civil for once?"

"Why should I be? I just got the living shit kicked out of me by two whack jobs. They broke two of my ribs, and it hurts like hell to breath. Then the local spick police force arrested me and fined me for supplying them with fraudulent information, plus they informed me that I'm wanted by the Mystic Connecticut police force for motor vehicle tampering."

There is a God, Bill thought. "Sorry for your bad luck, dude."

Richard sighed. "Tell me, Bill, what's happening? The cops told me that the guys who beat me up attempted to drown Shirley in the Bio Bay, but you saved her. Thank you for that. Do you know how she is?"

239

Bill was about to tell Richard when he noted a sudden onslaught of activity coming and going from the room where Shirley had been taken. Then all activity stopped abruptly.

An ominous feeling overwhelmed Bill as he sensed something was wrong.

The door to the room opened, and a young distinguished dark-haired man dressed in a white lab coat came out. He glanced around at the people lining the hallway outside the crowded waiting room.

"Excuse me, I'm Bill Adams; my wife Shirley is in that room. May I go in to see her now?"

The man's face expressed an uneasy relief, while his eyes drilled into Bill's. "Glad to meet you, sir. I'm Doctor Morales. Yes, you may enter in a moment, but before you do I'd like to speak with you privately."

The doctor escorted Bill to a small room where he shut the door behind them. The walls and floor of the room were barren. A few folding chairs in the center of the room were arranged in a circle. Pointing to the chairs the doctor said, "Please have a seat."

Bill was about to settle into a chair when the door burst open, and Richard charged in, ranting, "What's going on? Don't you two leave me out in the dark." He jabbed Bill's shoulder with his good hand. "You can't hide from me, asshole!"

The doctor looked dumbfounded and annoyed by the intrusion. "Do you know this man?'

"Unfortunately I do. It would be best if you let him stay. Trust me, it'll be much easier."

Doctor Morales took a chair and composed himself. "As you are aware, Mrs. Adams was involved in an attempted drowning where she inhaled a great deal of water from the bay. She also ingested a mind-altering drug usually referred to as ecstasy or a date rape drug. which didn't help matters. I am sorry to tell you that she slowly and silently drowned.

Bill and Richard stared at the doctor, who continued his explanation. "What she passed away from is a very rare problem. You see, inhaling water can irritate the lungs and cause swelling which hinders the lungs' ability to provide oxygen to the blood stream which in turn supplies the lungs and other organs such as the heart with the necessary process that is vital in keeping us alive. The medical term for this condition is pulmonary edema.

"From the history I believe you, Mr. Adams, supplied earlier to the intake nurse, I noted she had experienced another catastrophic water-related trauma sometime in her recent past. All these circumstances culminated within her body today, resulting in major organ failures. I am sorry to tell you that she has expired."

Bill wasn't sure he understood the doctor's explanation. "What did you say?"

"Mr. Adams, your wife has died." The doctor stood up. "I'm sorry for your loss. If you need to speak with a Chaplain, please discuss it with the nurse. You are free to enter the room now to see your wife."

The doctor quickly left the small sitting room. Bill sat quietly, as he tried to absorb the news. Shirley was dead? Shirley was dead. He felt sadness, but no remorse. Truth to tell, he had gone over a similar scenario many times in the past two years. He'd already gone through all the stages of mourning for her.

Richard jumped to his feet and screamed. "You got your way, you no good bastard! I hope you're happy now."

Bill had so many questions. "Why didn't Shirley let me know she hadn't drowned? I'm sure she wouldn't have gone along with your sadistic plot to make me suffer."

"Well, for one thing, big shot, she didn't remember anything following the sailboat accident—she had amnesia. She didn't know what day it was or what year it was. Her mother and I took care of her with the help and counseling with mental health professionals while you were sailing around the tropics without a care in the world."

"What about her mother? I'm sure she would have told me of Shirley's survival. Did you threaten her?" Bill balled his hands into fists.

"I never threatened that woman. I just didn't tell her where you were, or how to contact you."

"Well, Richard, I thank you for going above and beyond in your effort to help Shirley. I'm sorry it had to end this way for you," Bill said in a dead calm voice. "Would you like some time alone with Shirley before I go in? All I ask is that you control yourself. These people did all they could to save her."

Richard bolted for the door. "May you burn in hell, you scum!" He slammed the door behind him. Remaining in his chair, Bill reached into his pocket for his cell phone and placed a call to Mike.

***

It was the middle of the night when Molly received Bill's call. He was just about to leave a voice mail when she answered. "Hi, Molly, it's me. Sorry to call you this late, but I wanted to tell you I'm at the airport in Vieques, trying to get a lift into town, but it might take a while. Could you meet me on shore?"

Molly was stunned to hear Bill's voice. "Sure, I'll be there." She hoped to hear more but was afraid to ask.

"Thanks." Bill hung up.

Molly got dressed. Not wanting to pace the decks again, she made herself a pot of coffee and filled up two large Tervis tumblers. Placing lids on them, she carried the drinks to the dinghy. The beach was such a short distance away, and there was no rush, so she decided to row the boat to shore. Remaining seated in the dinghy, she drank her coffee, wondering and worried, thinking countless thoughts dooming her place in Bill's life.

The dark moonless night reflected her mood, and finally she left the dinghy. Walking along the sandy beach, she settled down on the sand, which still held the warmth of the day's sunshine. Sitting close to the shore she allowed the water to lap at her feet. At first it tickled her toes, which made her smile. Wiggling her feet she felt many small smooth clam shells buried in the wet sand, and she began pushing them around with her toes.

The sweet smell of the night-blooming jasmine normally would lift her spirts, but it's fragrance only seemed to smother her. Soon the light from the dawning sun reflected on the waves rolling in from the dark ocean. The birds began their morning serenades, but Molly remained restless.

The noise of a car engine stopping on the street startled her from her thoughts of intolerable troubles. When she heard the slamming of the car door she ran toward the boardwalk to see Bill stepping onto the sand. He smiled as he approached her. Reaching Molly, he took her in his arms and kissed her.

"Thanks for being here for me." He paused with a sigh.. "Shirley didn't make it."

"I'm sorry, Bill."

Holding Molly in his arms, he breathed in the scent of her hair and her skin. The curls of her red hair bounced around her face. He tilted her head upward so he could look into her eyes. "It's been a long two years of heartache and guilt, but now it's over. It's time for me to move on."

Molly was content to stay in his embrace, and her body relaxed.

"You are the most amazing woman I've ever met. You are my little turtle dove. Would you like to join me while we plan a new life together?"

Molly's eyes sparkled with joy as her fingers caressed his neck. "You remembered about the turtle dove! Bill, you're the best! And so dear! Yes, more than anything else, I'd love to share your world. Like true sailors we'll plot a new course together."

"One more thing; I have to go north for a while; I need to pay my respects to Shirley's mom, and I would like you to join me."

"Oh, Bill, do you think that will be okay?"

"Yes. I need you there, because after the funeral I want you to take me to Fall River and introduce me to your father. I have an important question to ask him."

Arm in arm, Bill and Molly turned toward the rising sun as it revealed a bright new day.

THE END

"Life is short and we never have too much time for gladdening the hearts of those who are traveling the journey with us. Therefore, be swift to love, make haste to be kind."

Henri Frederic Amiel

Great White Shark Facts*

- Ocean's most feared predator
- Can grow to over 21 feet
- Can weigh over 2500 pounds
- Feed mainly on large sea mammals,
- such as seals, sea lions and dead whales
- Have a bite force of 4,000 pounds
- Live mostly in waters between 54 and 75 degrees
- Are protected from harvest by federal laws

*Source: International Shark Attack File
University of Florida Museum of Natural History

Post-Traumatic Stress Disorder (PTSD) Facts**

- PTSD, is an anxiety disorder that can occur after someone experiences a traumatic event that caused intense fear, helplessness or horror.

- PTSD can result from personally experiencing traumas or from witnessing or learning of violent or tragic events.

- While it is common to experience a brief state of anxiety or depression after such occurrences, people with PTSD continually re-experience the traumatic event; avoid individuals, thoughts or situations associated with the event; and have symptoms of excessive emotions.

- People with this disorder have these symptoms for longer than one month and cannot function as well as they did before the traumatic event.

- PTSD symptoms usually appear within three months of the traumatic experience: however, they sometimes occur years later.

- One of the most important factors to prevent PTSD is having social support either at home or through work.

- Having effective coping strategies also may lessen the impact of experiencing traumatic events.

- People with PTSD often have recollections, nightmares or hallucinations of stressful events.

- Symptoms may include difficulty falling or staying asleep, irritability, jumpiness or difficulty with concentration.

- Sufferers also sometimes abuse drugs or alcohol.

- PTSD can be treated with psychotherapy and/or medication.

**Source: urnotalone support/ptsd.html./

SUSANN ELIZABETH RICHARDS is a Registered Nurse with a Master's Degree from Barry University in Miami, Florida. She has published articles in the Journal for Healthcare Quality.

Susann and her husband have sailed extensively throughout Long Island Sound, down the east coast of the United States, spending time on the Chesapeake Bay, then to Florida and the Bahama Islands, where they visited the Abaco's, Grand Bahama Island, and Bimini. They have also sailed throughout the American and British Virgin Islands. Susann is a certified Scuba diver.

She lives in Sebastian, Florida with her husband Dan and three Persian cats.

Made in the USA
Columbia, SC
26 May 2019